Under

"Echlin's music
Echlin is a wonderful story

Winnipeg Free Press

"Echlin has created two women who
practically explode off the page with their desire,
talent, and brilliance. They are both incredibly
flawed, making all the wrong choices, falling for
difficult men, and raising kids on messy kitchen floors—
and yet, like most women, they find a way to make life
work through the chaos. The result is a book that
has the rhythm, cadence, and sexuality
of a piano tune played in a little theatre on
the wrong side of a big town."

Heather O'Neill, author of
Lullabies for Little Criminals

"Nothing short of a masterpiece."

Quill & Quire

Praise for *Under the Visible Life*

"Kim Echlin's novel takes us into a poetic and musical world of two women mesmerized by their love for jazz and art. As readers, we dive into two cultures so distant from afar and yet so close from within. An absolute must-read."

—Monia Mazigh, author of *Hope and Despair: My Struggle to Free My Husband, Maher Arar*

"[Echlin] delivers a clinic on how to conjure emotions readers didn't even know they had. Not since *The Diviners* has a Canadian novel explored the complex, messy, and sacrificial nature of creative self-actualization with such skill … Readers will revel in every charged scene, every breathtaking reversal, every hard-earned moment of wisdom that this devastating novel delivers … This book is nothing short of a masterpiece."

—*Quill & Quire* (starred review)

"[Echlin's] talent is on full display in this lyrical, exciting story … [her] excellent novel introduces two complex women who sometimes succeed and sometimes suffer, and whose stories are moving from start to finish."

—*Publishers Weekly* (starred review)

Praise for *The Disappeared*

"Echlin's masterful novel of meetings, partings and cross-cultural love ... Precise, expressive ... A powerfully vivid narrative ... Luminous ... A complex expression of annihilating loss and eternal love that is best experienced, in a sense, like the final act of a tragic play: as something inevitable and beyond the calculations of reason."
　　　　　　　　　　　　　　　　　　—*The Globe and Mail*

"An elegiac, beautifully told memory-tale of obsessive love ... On one level, the novel is a young Canadian woman's bildungs-roman; on another, a profoundly moving account of the geno-cidal horrors of the Cambodian killing fields and its terrible aftermath. Written in elegant, spare prose, *The Disappeared* confronts one of the most painful conflicts of our time: the collision between our private, personal desires and the brutal, dehumanizing facts of modern history."
　　　　　　　　　　　—2009 Scotiabank Giller Prize Jury

"Electrifying ... The voice is singular and arresting ... This is a very sensual book, written in an aroused but taut and plain prose ... Echlin's heroine is a risk-taker; so, on the literary level, is Echlin ... Through [her] technical and stylistic virtuosity, allied with elliptical narrative brilliance, Echlin raises Anne's climactic ritual action to a level of tragic sublimity."
　　　　　　　　　　　　　　　　　　　—*The Guardian*

PENGUIN

UNDER THE VISIBLE LIFE

Award-winning author KIM ECHLIN lives in Toronto. She is the author of *Elephant Winter, Dagmar's Daughter,* and *Inanna: A New English Version.* Her third novel, *The Disappeared,* was nominated for the Scotiabank Giller Prize and won the Barnes & Noble Discover Great New Writers Award for Fiction.

ALSO BY KIM ECHLIN

The Disappeared

Dagmar's Daughter

Elephant Winter

Inanna: A New English Version

Elizabeth Smart:
A Fugue Essay on Women and Creativity

Under
the
Visible
Life

Kim Echlin

PENGUIN
an imprint of Penguin Canada Books Inc., a Penguin Random House Company

Published by the Penguin Group
Penguin Canada Books Inc., 320 Front Street West, Suite 1400, Toronto, Ontario M5V 3B6, Canada

Penguin Group (USA) LLC, 375 Hudson Street, New York, New York 10014, U.S.A.

Penguin Group (UK), 80 Strand, London WC2R 0RL, England
Penguin Ireland, 25 St. Stephen's Green, Dublin 2, Ireland (a division of Penguin Books Ltd)
Penguin Group (Australia), 707 Collins Street, Melbourne, Victoria 3008, Australia
(a division of Pearson Australia Group Pty Ltd)
Penguin Books India Pvt Ltd, 11 Community Centre, Panchsheel Park,
New Delhi – 110 017, India
Penguin Group (NZ), 67 Apollo Drive, Rosedale, Auckland 0632, New Zealand
(a division of Pearson New Zealand Ltd)
Penguin Books (South Africa) (Pty) Ltd, 24 Sturdee Avenue, Rosebank,
Johannesburg 2196, South Africa

Penguin Books Ltd, Registered Offices: 80 Strand, London WC2R 0RL, England

First published in Hamish Hamilton hardcover by Penguin Canada Books Inc., 2015
Published in this edition, 2016

1 2 3 4 5 6 7 8 9 10 (RRD)

Copyright © Kim Echlin, 2015

LIBRARY AND ARCHIVES CANADA CATALOGUING IN PUBLICATION

Echlin, Kim, 1955–, author
Under the visible life / Kim Echlin.

Originally published by Hamish Hamilton, 2015.
ISBN 978-0-14-317833-0 (paperback)

I. Title.

PS8559.C45U53 2016   C813'.54   C2015-904751-X

eBook ISBN 978-0-14-319442-2

Visit the Penguin Canada website at **www.penguin.ca**

Special and corporate bulk purchase rates available; please see
www.penguin.ca/corporatesales or call 1-800-810-3104.

For those who cannot name themselves

I start in the middle of a sentence
and move in both directions
at once.

–JOHN COLTRANE

Under
the
Visible
Life

I

No Memory Is One's Own Alone

MAHSA

What she is I am. My mother ran away with my father from Lashkar Gah when she was eighteen and gave birth to me in Karachi, the pearl of the Arabian Sea. She liked to make us laugh with her Pashto-Urdu-American jokes and her proverbs and idioms in English. Her name was Breshna Najibullah. She had bright grey eyes that were interested in everything, especially in me and my father. She wore her long hair loose and she had a half-moon scar on her chin from a fall as a child. It looked like a little second smile. She moved with great energy, and gracefully.

My father was an American water engineer who came to Afghanistan to work on the dam projects and he liked home movies and playing piano. His name was John Weaver. He bought our piano from Hayden's and he used to say with a shrug, I only play party music but your mother likes it. He filled up our living room with "Blueberry Hill" and "Be-Bop-A-Lula." When I was three, I have been told, I began to copy him, picking out tunes. He showed me how to find the chords on the bottom and after that it was easy. I made up my own songs and I liked to do this and spent a lot of time at it. I do not remember ever not being able to play.

From the beginning my parents were teetering on their own brink. I did not have them for long. They were murdered when I was thirteen.

Their favourite place to go dancing was the Beach Luxury Hotel and my father's eyes were always on my mother. He was handsome in an American way, with his shaved-smooth face and his hair short and parted to one side. There was a little stoop in his shoulders that was from tallness not humility, and he was enthusiastic to see or try anything new. He liked to wear a narrow tie, unusual in the heat of Karachi. I sometimes tied one of his ties around my own neck so that I could pretend to be him.

The timbre of his voice was gentle as if he were leaving lots of room for me to think, which he was. He spoke slowly but not stiffly and he pronounced his consonants clearly which he said was useful to people who did not know English. He said, When I try to understand other languages it helps if people speak slowly.

My mother laughed and said, John, you only know how to speak American. It won't matter how slowly a person speaks.

He said, That's nonsense, I speak English and I know how to say thank you in Urdu and Pashto and Goan, listen, *shukriya*-verra-much-indeed venerable wife-ji.

There's no such thing as Goan, she said.

Then he sang the Falcons song "You're So Fine" and took her in his arms to dance. He stopped singing and put his face in her hair and he kissed her neck and they stopped dancing for a moment and he said, That's Goan.

They did not mind me seeing how much they loved each other and they liked to tell over and over the story of how they met in western Afghanistan on the Helmand River that rises from the Hindu Kush. My mother's eyes were soft and bright like winter mountain stars when she said, He asked me to dance in Pashto. He said if I was married his grave would be his wedding bed. Your father was full of hullabaloo.

I repeated, Hullabaloo, because I liked the rolling sound of it.

She looked at him to see if he was delighting in us.

She may mean baloney, said my American father to the ceiling fan as if there was no one else in the room.

It did not matter if we said hullabaloo or baloney, it was love that he was full of. He said, I could no more not love your mother than stop locusts.

I called my mother Mor, which is Pashto, and I called my father Abbu, which is Urdu, and when I wanted to tease them I called them Ma and Pa which I learned in an American book. Abbu laughed when he heard that and said it made me sound like a hillbilly, but Mor and I did not know what that was.

My name is Mahsa which means like the moon, and my family name was Weaver-Najibullah which Abbu said was a mouthful but Mor said, She will need both our names one day. The girls at my school had all kinds of names, Moslem and Christian and Hindu, but mine was the longest. My father mostly called me Porcupine because when I was a baby my mother sang, Do you know what the porcupine sang to her baby? O my child of velvet.

Abbu used to tell me, You have my big hands and your mother's beautiful eyes and you will someday be as graceful as she is and touch a man's heart and I hope he will be a good man.

Like you, I thought.

He said, Where your Mor comes from, women are protected from lions and the likes of me. But I saw something in her eyes so I took a leap, and I sent her love notes and I asked, Are you promised to anyone? Are you married?

The bird sees the grain not the snare. My parents were in love and they did not wait.

In Lashkar Gah my father wrote a report that the underground water from the karezes was too salty for vineyards and orchards, that the soil was good only for pea shrubs and poppies. No one wanted to hear this. Abbu had already been accused of being a communist in America. Now he was criticizing the American projects and he was speaking to a Pashto girl and the Pashto men were outraged. John Weaver, the honest water engineer, was offending everyone.

He said, Porcupine, sometimes the truth gets you into trouble.

He hid Mor in the back of an American supplies truck as far as the border and paid a guide to help them cross into Pakistan on foot. Mor was pregnant. They slipped into Karachi, the Bride of Cities. In those days it was a green place where men washed the streets at night and people took trams from the Empress Market to Keamari. Mor was eighteen and Abbu was five years older and they liked to talk with the musicians in the clubs where Abbu played for fun. He took home movies of Mor sitting with them, holding me in an Afghan-style baby sling. She is smiling and young and prettier than European girls. Abbu used to joke, I was always afraid your Mor would run away with a real musician.

In Karachi they had gone to the only person they knew, Mor's grey-eyed uncle, Barak Dilawar. He was the first man in our family to learn to read and to leave Afghanistan. In Karachi he met a Pathan wrestler who told him that he could get a job at the Beach Luxury Hotel which employed Bengali cooks and Sindhis and Punjabis, local Urdu speakers and Baloch people. The man told him, Mr. Avari is looking for all good workers. Come.

Uncle was impressed by the graceful and spacious buildings and the long dormitories on each side for the hotel workers, where troops had lived during the war. He had never imagined living in such opulence. With his reading and his wrestling strength he was hired and he rose quickly to become the night manager at the front desk of the Beach Luxury Hotel.

According to our tradition, Uncle had to offer them

nanawatai, or sanctuary, until they got on their feet. Abbu and Mor stayed with him only until I was born and then we got our own home in a part of Karachi called Saddar Town near St. Joseph's Convent School, which I attended. I learned to read left to right and right to left, in English and Arabic, and I could decipher Nastaliq. I took in languages easily like Mor did and Abbu said, You have ambidextrous eyes that go back and forth like a carpet weaver's shuttle. Abbu taught at the university and Mor with her polyglot tongue got office work at the Pakistan International Airlines and wore a uniform designed by Pierre Cardin.

Abbu was proud of her and said, That's jim-dandy. PIA is the first airline to fly the Super Constellation and to show in-flight movies. Then he winked in his American way and said, Maybe your Mor could get us some tickets. Would it not be good to watch movies in the sky?

But I liked going to movies with them on the ground, at the Paradise and the Nishat. After we saw *To Kill a Mockingbird*, Abbu said to Mor, See, America ain't so great, and we corrected his grammar though he did it on purpose.

Mor liked *Barsaat Ki Raat* with qawwali music about the policeman's daughter falling in love with a poet who sings, In all my life I'll never forget that rainy night, for I met a lovely girl that rainy night.

I saw *Casablanca* so many times with Abbu that we memorized the words. Abbu played the piano and pretended to be Sam, and I always said to him, Here's lookin' at ya, kid.

I began to have my own tastes too. I liked dancing the twist with my friends and I liked Chubby Checker, and I especially liked Sam Cooke singing "Twistin' the Night Away." When I practised in my room Abbu came in and smiled in a way Mor called fond and said, You're turning American.

Mor and I spoke Pashto. I remember sitting in a big chair looking at our chinar tree, listening to her tell the love stories of Layla and Majnun, of Antara and Abla. When I was afraid of anything Mor said, No matter what anyone says, you think, Though I am but a straw, I am as good as you. And she reminded me over and over, Never forget that your grandmother knew only Pashto, and only to speak it. Can you imagine what it is to not read?

I did not care. I did not care in four languages. Mor said the same thing every day.

Thirteen years after Mor and Abbu arrived in Karachi, I was in bed, listening to Mor weeping and pleading with Abbu. She said, We have lived here long enough. My father is dead and there is no one to stop my brothers. Let us go now to America.

Stop them from what? I wondered.

Abbu said, We never bothered them.

She said, John, the sun cannot be hidden behind two fingers.

But we are far away.

Far away from what? I wondered. I heard him move close to her. I imagined his arms around her.

She said, You do not know my brothers.

Then someone closed a door and I could not hear so I fell asleep.

We are going to go on a trip to America, said Mor to me in the morning. Will it not be good to see where your father comes from? Perhaps we will finally find out what is a hillbilly.

I did not want to leave my school and my friends and my only home but I also imagined flying in an airplane and seeing for the first time American teenagers dancing the twist. And maybe getting some red lipstick.

Two weeks later Mor's half-brothers appeared in Karachi. One went to the university, shot Abbu, and left him on the steps to bleed to death. The other went to the PIA offices. There were two shots. One in Mor's chest. One in her head. My uncles were not arrested, only questioned and released to disappear back to Afghanistan. This is the unsayableness of my life.

We have a proverb: Me against my brothers; me and my brothers against my cousins; me and my brothers and my cousins against the world.

Family can kill family to make things right.

Why was I not killed? The murder of my parents began my unrootedness. I had no home to return to. I could not fathom how my own family could kill my beloved Abbu and Mor.

The day before he was shot, Abbu had taken me to Clifton Road to a little shop where anyone could make a record for ten rupees. I played a tune I made up and then I played "Autumn

Leaves" for the other side and they pressed it into a little 45 record which had in the centre a yellow disc called a spider that popped in and out. The woman printing the label asked what was the title of my tune. I had not thought of a name so I said, That is called "Abbu's Song," and his face flushed and he put his long arm around my shoulders and said, Thank you, Porcupine. That is the best gift I ever received. In this way I learned how important my music could be. I do not know what happened to that record. It is lost to me, just as the Karachi I grew up in disappeared.

KATHERINE

They took me away from Ma. I was three months old and she was in the Belmont reformatory because she got put away for living with my Chinese father, Henry Lau, in a garage on Barton Street in Hamilton, Ontario. The year was 1940. They said she was incorrigible. A woman could get arrested for not using the Ladies and Escorts door at a tavern, much less sleeping with a Chinese migrant worker. *Ching chong Chinaman sittin' on a fence, tryin' ta make a dollar out of fifteen cents.*

Ma said, Henry had already left for work the morning they came for me. I heard a knock and men shouting, We know you're in there, and when I opened the door I saw two policemen standing behind my father. He was drunk and his jaw was clenching the way it did before he took a swipe at me. I wondered why he'd bother coming all the way from Toronto. He left my mother and me when I was thirteen years old and he had been living with another woman.

He was acting all affronted and saying, Yellow kisses. Who do you think you are?

The police drove me back to Toronto. I sat in the backseat and there was a mesh metal screen between us. I felt like I was already in prison and I knew I was in real trouble. They took me to a basement cell in the courthouse. A girl social worker came and interviewed me and asked me why I would run off with a Chinese and how far did I go in school and how old was I, and was I pregnant.

I was eighteen and I had only been with Henry, but I was worried about getting him in trouble for me being a minor so I pretended not to know who the father was.

Ma lit a cigarette and said, The social worker asked for the fellows' names so I had to say I never knew their names and then the social worker looked disgusted and asked, How many? Three sounded more believable than two so I said, Only three.

I was terrified in the cell and I kept thinking my mother would come and get me out to spite my father but she did not come. She was always busy running the rooming house and she was afraid of my father and I suppose she did not like me living with Henry either. When I was a kid and we saw Chinese men carrying laundry past our house on Parliament Street, she used to tease me that they would steal me and put me in one of their bags. It was illegal for them to employ a white woman, and they weren't allowed to bring their wives here. It was a miserable life and I felt sorry for them. When I left for Hamilton with Henry, Ma said, You've always had a brass neck.

In the morning they took me upstairs into a courtroom that was the fanciest place I had ever been. Behind the judge's head was a carved wooden picture of two women holding hands. The judge looked down on me from his big wooden chair and I recognized the younger police officer who arrested me and he seemed embarrassed to see me again. I mouthed Hello to him but he pretended not to notice. He told the judge I was wearing pyjamas at the time of the arrest.

Everyone wears pyjamas. Why would he have to say that?

The judge asked if I was pregnant and how far gone, and I said we were saving up for the marriage licence which was true. Then the judge said, Jenny Goodnow, your father is acting in your best interests.

Ma bounced her foot when she told this part of the story, and fiddled with the enamel flip-top lid on her little Ronson pocket lighter making the flame shoot up and down. She said, That was supposed to be my best interests? To be put away by a judge and my own father because I was pregnant? Because my boyfriend was Chinese? That is supposed to be fair? I came out of the court and the matron said, She got eighteen months. Get her ready for Black Maria.

It sounded like spiders. It sounded like something Catholic.

What's Black Maria?

The court van, she said. They should let you girls get on with things. Why you go with foreigners is a mystery to me.

Ma's best friend at Belmont was a girl called Violet. She

was sixteen, and she already had a baby and she was pregnant again. Violet used to get the other girls to give her and Ma their supper milk because she said pregnant girls needed it. After she had her baby Violet was transferred to the Hospital for the Insane in Cobourg. The judge said immorality was a symptom of insanity even though her doctor said Violet was not insane. They took both her children away for good and gave her shock treatments. Ma said, They might as well have killed her.

I was born in the Toronto General Hospital. They kept me away from Ma but she was screaming she wouldn't give me up. Finally a nice nurse, not a mean one, brought me to her and showed her how to put my lips to her nipple. Ma said the best part was she finally got to look at me and she could see Henry's almond-shaped black-brown eyes.

Your eyes always remind me of secrets, she said. Then she added, Good ones.

After three months at Belmont, they took me away from her again and put me in a children's home for nine months and when I turned a year old they put me with a foster mother because I was not trying to walk or talk. What's the point of talking if no one is listening? The Children's Aid worker was still trying to get Ma to give me up. She said, Most girls who aren't married give up their babies. Yours'll be better off.

Ma said, I'm not giving her up. I'm going to marry the father and move back to Hamilton.

He doesn't seem to be very interested.

How could he be? He doesn't know yet.

So the first thing she did when she got out of Belmont was take the bus to Hamilton and find Henry Lau who did not know where she had been for eighteen months. They got married on January 26, 1942, at the city hall in Hamilton. There is a single black-and-white photograph taken on their wedding day that she kept in a children's workbook where she practised writing Chinese characters. Henry Lau is wearing a fedora tilted low over one eye. I used to stare at it trying to get an idea of who my father was. Ma always found him handsome but I thought, Why are his eyes averted? Ma said, The photographer was in a rush.

Ma is wearing a dress nipped in at the waist, the same dress she wore the night she met him. Even after a baby she was skinny. The dress looks white in the photo but she told me it was light blue. Something old, something new, something borrowed, something blue, and a silver sixpence in my shoe.

Your father liked that rhyme, she said. She showed me how to write some characters—加拿大 for Jia-na-da, and 爱 for love. She knew the numbers up to twenty. She used to say, Can you imagine? You need three thousand characters to read a newspaper. The wedding photo was taken somewhere near Barton Street. There are steel mills behind, probably the old Dominion Foundries. Wispy snow blows around their ankles on the sidewalk like pretty little snake-ghosts. Ma's face is not open like I imagined the face of a happy bride should be. She is turned from the camera, toward him, and her lips are not loose and smiling but tight.

Why aren't you holding hands?

Wasn't he good looking? she asked. He lined the walls of our place with brown parcel paper to make it cozier. It was like living inside a present. He was the first person I ever saw cook garlic. He used to tape newspaper on the walls around the stove to catch any splatter, and he always kept his shirt tucked in, even at home. The night before I got arrested I lit candles at dinner and he said it made him think of temples and spirits. I was going to tell him about being pregnant that night but I held back because I thought I'd buy something for a baby and leave it around and see if he guessed. I wanted to have some fun with it.

She handed the photo to me and said, Us holding hands was not acceptable in those days. A lot of things were not acceptable then. I used to walk so my shoulder touched his through our coats.

Ma got a job in the coffee shop at the Royal Connaught Hotel on the corner of King and John in Hamilton. She rented our basement apartment in a little clapboard house in a respectable neighbourhood on Mountain Brow from old Mrs. Rose and her grown-up daughter Lily whose young husband was killed in the war. Their shoes click-clicked above us every night and Ma used to make fun of them but we always had Sunday lunch together upstairs in their dining room. Lily called us the four dames and she taught me to play hearts. Ma was afraid Mrs. Rose would not rent to Henry, so she said he wasn't around right now. During the war people did not ask too many questions. Better to marry and divorce. She had to beg a credit union to give her a bank account where she could cash her paycheques. Most banks wanted a husband or a father to sign for a girl's account.

Ma said, I was frantic when I first got out. I had no money and I needed to find work and a place to live and a way to take care of a baby. They did everything they could to make me give you up but I fought tooth and nail for you.

She was long limbed and she painted her fingernails and toenails and lips all the same shade of red. She was so thin her own mother used to say, You look like a washboard. She smoked more than she ate and her cigarette butts were always smeared with red lipstick. I'm built lanky too. In anything scoop-necked you can see the bones on my chest and around my shoulders. I gave up trying to look sexy because you need flesh for that. My skin's not as white as hers. Ma always said burnished and she meant it kindly. On her day off she put cotton balls between her toes and she twisted her hair into big spiky rollers. She smelled of stale smoke and Nivea cream. She tied a scarf printed with little Scottie dogs over her hair when she was setting it, and she balanced her burning cigarette on an ashtray shaped like a music note and she waved her fingers in the air to dry her polish quicker while her toes set. I got my height from her. Her hair was chestnut and she said it thinned out when she got pregnant but I think it probably thinned out when she was in the reformatory because they kept the girls hungry. The visiting doctors did experimental treatments on them for venereal disease and if any girl complained about waiting in line half-naked, or squirmed during the internal cauterizing, the matrons made her sit in a closet. Ma got locked in a closet for a full day because they forgot she was in there. I think that would thin out your hair. My hair is poker straight and black. When I was sixteen I permed it out big and wild and I've always kept it that way. Some people think it makes me look half black or something. I have large hands and large feet that go with my tallness and Ma said those hands must come from her mother's side of the family who, way back, were big-boned Irish potato farmers.

Before I was two, my father left a folded piece of paper with neat printing for Ma at the hotel:

Dear Jenny,

Life here too hard, I must go back. I never forget you.

Your husband, Henry

The people who condemned Ma lived scot-free—her father, the social worker, the police officer, the judge. But Ma got herself a respectable job in a good hotel, her own apartment and a bank account. We had one of the first televisions on the street. She always talked about being independent, as if it were some kind of specialized state not available to most women.

Our neighbour Nan took care of me when I was a baby and Ma worked double shifts on weekends to pay her. Nan used to say, What's one more? I don't have any other way to get my own money, and she helped us a lot. I think she secretly envied Ma working. Her job was taking care of me and three sons, Mac, Eddie and Little Johnny, and her husband who was Big Johnny and worked shifts in the mills rolling steel. They had tin foil on the bedroom window so Johnny could sleep in the daytime and us kids had to keep quiet. Nan was the family Ma and I did not have. Little Johnny was a few years older than I was but I always seemed to be organizing him and Ma laughed and said, Just like a girl, trying to run things.

Nan said, You're lucky you got a girl.

One time they were drinking instant coffee at Nan's Arborite table when I heard Ma say, Getting married didn't work for me. The deck's stacked against a married woman.

It's not that bad, Jenny.

I was hanging back by the counter and they hadn't shooed me away so I asked, Hey, Nan, how'd you meet Big Johnny?

They both looked around because they hadn't noticed me I guess. Nan laughed and said, I grew up beside Johnny.

Nan, will you do my Tarot?

Not for you yet, she said. You're too young. I'll do your ma's if she wants.

I liked watching it and I hoped the High Priestess would come up because I liked the blue gown and the crescent moon at her feet.

As she was laying out the cards I said, I hope you get the Priestess.

Nan said in her low, mysterious voice that she always used for Tarot, You can't control fate.

Ma said, Get money for me. I want to start my own shop.

I wanted admission to their grown-up women life. I played with the boys but they did not talk much. I hung around and listened because I never knew things about Ma like she wanted money and a shop. I thought she liked our life. Why didn't she tell me what she wanted?

Ma's solution about a lot of things was to lock up her heart and keep her real self hidden. How many women have done that to protect their children? To make their own lives possible?

Nan started turning over the cards and I said, Find out when my father's coming back.

I saw the look between them and I felt the moment ruined and I did not know why because we had been having fun. Ma said in her firm voice, He's working in China, Katie. Don't you worry, he'll be back.

After that Nan rushed and turned a few cards and saw lots of money in Ma's future and then she said, Do me a favour, Katie, and go see what Little Johnny's doing.

There is a tone in women's voices that stops their children pursuing. I was secure with Ma and Nan and I accepted their silences and diversions as the way things had to be. I liked living on Mountain Brow and I was good at school and I liked going to the big library with the wide stone steps downtown and meeting Ma at the Connaught and taking the bus home with her. When she tucked me in at night she said, *Sometimes in the winter and sometimes in the fall, I sleep between the sheets with nothing on at all.* I liked our cozy apartment and our Sunday lunches and card games with the dames upstairs and playing on the street with the boys all through the long springs and summers and autumns of my growing-up years, free to do what I wanted, free to stay outside until the street lights came on.

MAHSA

Sister Devan called me out of class. Aunt threw a burqa over me before they rushed me into a car. Outside the sun was hot and bright and two little girls with yellow and blue ribbons in their hair walked hand in hand. Aunt's words were crashing through me: Your parents are dead.

They hid me for seven days in someone else's apartment in an alcove where a maid usually slept until they knew that my Afghan uncles were gone. Aunt came each evening to visit. There was darkness and not sleeping. There was a jagged crack in the plaster near the window ledge. The glass pane was covered with a heavy blind. There was one coil in the narrow, mildew-smelling mattress that was different from the others and poked into my side until I organized my body around it. The sheets were coarse, not soft as on my bed at home. Aunt did not smell warm like Mor, and her feelings were thin as if they had been squeezed through cheesecloth.

Where are their bodies?

She said, They are gone.

Where?

Gora Qabaristan.

I want to see.

Mahsa, the graves are not marked.

But isn't that the Christian cemetery?

Mahsa, we had to get them buried.

No prayers. No goodbye. Nothing. How could Mor be buried there? Where would I live now? Who would love me?

Uncle came to my little room on the seventh night and Aunt stood behind him in the doorway. He said to me, You will live with us now.

They had emptied my home and sold Abbu's piano. The end of my old life. The beginning of a new life, unyielding and severe. The sisters offered me a scholarship and Aunt persuaded Uncle to keep me in school, to learn some skills that might make me useful later. Aunt told me that I was lucky. Being lucky with Abbu was finding a coin on the street and making a wish. Being lucky is not your parents murdered when you are thirteen.

Grief is long. Vivid. Full of true and false memories, shreds like bits of lime inside a grater. Before my parents died, I roamed all over Saddar with my friends on our bikes and we played tennis and went to the Manhattan Soda Fountain for coloured iced milkshakes called Green Goddess and Hangman's Blood. At night with Abbu, I walked in Old Clifton and we heard the wandering Sindhi minstrels playing the *ektara* and sometimes we walked from Kharadar, the Salt

Gate, all the way to Mithadar, the Sweet Gate, where seawater mixed with fresh. Abbu liked to joke, Let's go to the Sweet Gate today, Porcupine, and I will buy you sweets.

Mor said, But that's not what Mithadar means, John.

Never mind, he said, putting his arms around her to say goodbye. Us Americans have got a nose for finding good things. I found you halfway around the world, didn't I? Isn't that right, Porcupine?

Abbu taught me a rocky-bluesy version of "Kansas City" which he always said was his song but when he sang it he changed the words to "Karachi baby" to make us laugh. To my mind, this was how life was supposed to be, growing up between two people who loved each other. The last Christmas my parents were alive they took me to the famous ball at the Beach Luxury, fairy lights strung through the verandas and patios. Talismen with Norman D'Souza was playing in the 007 Cabaret and that night Abbu sat in with them. He said Norman's voice was liquid soul. A Dutch band called Johnny Lion and the Jumping Jewels played down by the water. People danced and walked by the sea and the tide rose to flood the dark mangrove swamps. Everyone was dressed up, and Hindus and Moslems and Christians stayed awake all night listening to the music and eating fresh seafood and macaroon cake with almond icing.

An only child watches adults with great attention trying to get clues about what life will be like, and whether it will be less solitary, because there is no other child to share what life is right now. This absorbed watching disappears, but in the moment of growing it feels of great importance. That night Abbu traced his finger along Mor's blouse below her neck and said, Your collarbone is the place on earth I love most. He pulled me in and asked, Do you not think the collarbone is the loveliest shape? I asked Mor, Am I Moslem or Christian? I thought I was Moslem because Mor was and I always got a new gharara for Eid and at school the sisters sent me to study Islamiat to know the Holy Quran in Arabic. But our family spent more time with Parsis and Goans because Abbu loved their music and he was called an Englisher.

Mor said, Our family is both.

Abbu said, All religions say you must do unto others as you would have them do to you. This is what Mor and I think, Porcupine. Come play a duet with me, it's Christmas!

So we went to the piano and Abbu and I played "Deck the Halls." I did not know what *bausovolly* was but I thought it must be Christian.

KATHERINE

I decked the girl at school who called me chink and ripped my blouse. The principal pushed through the circle of kids around us chanting, Fight! Fight! and pulled me off her. Before he sent me home he said, Katie, you're fifteen. You're too old for that. Fighting is very unladylike.

He always liked Ma though she did not have a husband. He said Ma had exemplary community spirit because she volunteered in our school library every Monday afternoon on her day off.

I said, I'm not fifteen for another month. Those girls said I don't have a father.

Everyone has a father. Anyway, you can't fight. You get home, and I will call your mother.

I kept on my torn blouse to show Ma the wrong done to me. Hours later, I heard her open the door at the top of the stairs and she came in carrying a paper bag of groceries like she always did on Wednesdays. She was also lugging in two long-playing records, Frank Sinatra and Billie Holiday, and the new portable record player that we had been looking at in the Eaton's catalogue for months. It was a Bakelite RCA Victor three-speed. It was light grey with a lid on hinges and a little clip to hold the arm in place. I said, Ma, it's so expensive! She said in her light voice, What's the use of money if you don't spend it? You go get cleaned up. What's this about fighting?

Let's set up the record player.

We plugged it in and she let me choose the first record to play, and I put on Frank Sinatra, and I could tell she was pleased. We admired it for a long time and talked about the different speeds because the boys next door had 45s and we promised to clip down the arm so it would not slip and ruin the needle. We speculated on the possibility of a long enough extension cord to take it up the stairs and outside on the front porch. Its portability was intriguing. Then Ma went into the kitchen and she unpacked the milk and bread and said, So, I hear you were fighting because the girls said you don't have a father.

I said, They called me names.

She opened up a tin of Heinz Boston Baked Beans and put some Wonder Bread in the toaster. She dumped the beans into a saucepan and warmed them up on the stove. With her back to me she said, I know what they said. Listen, Katie, I loved your father and it never mattered to me where he was from. When I got pregnant with you I was not married. I was put in a reformatory. But there is nothing wrong with having a baby and don't ever let anyone tell you there is. They arrested me for *nothing*.

She turned around and looked at me and said, As soon as I was out, your father and I got married, but he had to go back to China. There wasn't enough work here. A lot of people wouldn't hire a Chinese. How's that for fair?

She put beans and toast on our plates and sat down with me. She said, You tell the girls at school to mind their own beeswax. You are better than any of them. Let's eat.

I was drawing on the table with my fingernail and I did not feel better than the other girls. I did not want to know that my mother was arrested, and that she got pregnant with me without being married. Even I knew that was shameful. I wondered for the first time what people thought about us. We lived in a basement and she was the only woman I knew who had to work full-time, except my teachers who did not count because they were all Miss.

I asked, How long were you in there?

Katie, it's water under the bridge. It was unfair. Let it go.

When I did not pick up my fork to eat she said, No matter what you think, you have a respectable home and that is more than what was done for me.

She was still wearing her heavy, white-polished waitress shoes and there were big dark smudges under her eyes. There was a cut-glass feeling in her voice and I thought she must have done something wrong and because of her I felt diminished. She'd spent all that money on the record player I'd been wanting but it was not a happy day. My ma had been arrested. That was not respectable.

The next day I said to Nan, I hate Ma.

Nan said, Don't you talk like that. She works hard for you. She's a waitress.

Katie, that's enough. What's got into you?

She never finished high school.

She didn't have the chance. I didn't either. You keep in school and do better.

Ma and Nan began to seem insignificant to me. Wasting their time drinking coffee. Sitting with cards and cigarettes. Most women were insignificant.

I dreaded the moment Ma woke up in the morning. I'd be reading and I'd hear the snap of a match, smell the whiff of a fresh day's smoke as she rolled over to suck on her first cigarette. I waited for her first cough, for her to call out, Katie, put the kettle on. I never wondered if there was any dread of the day for her.

Nan told Ma she wanted to take a job in a drugstore in the summer now that her boys were working and I was too old to watch. Ma said she couldn't leave me to my own devices and told me I'd be coming to the hotel with her. Every morning she sent me to Harold Kudlets' talent booking office on the eighth floor with a western sandwich and strong coffee. He booked musicians all over town, the Flamingo Lounge, the Golden Rail, the Armouries. I'd hand him the sandwich and he'd say, Thank you, Mrs. Goodnow, and I'd say, That's not me, that's my mother, which made him laugh. He let me read on his couch even when the musicians scraped and dragged themselves in. I liked their battered instrument cases and hats, their pants with black satin stripes, their narrow ties. They smelled of colognes and sweat and they always seemed smaller in person than on stage. Harold used to let me listen to their acts when Ma worked nights. I heard Tommy Dorsey and Duke Ellington and Jack Teagarden and Bobby Hackett. I liked a funny young guy called Ronnie Hawkins. He wore a snappy black suit and he did backflips on stage and a camel walk. A big bearded man called Garth played organ in his band which sounded good. Ronnie always had a sweet smile and patted the couch to come sit beside him but Harold looked up from his stacks of posters and contracts and said, She's tall for her age, Ronnie, you let her be.

Ronnie asked, Can you sing?

Harold stood up. Katie, go get me a cup of coffee, will you?

And out in the hall I heard Ronnie say, C'mon, colonel, I didn't mean nothing.

The group that made the biggest impression on me was a local singing family, the Washington Brothers. Their mother and father stood at the back listening. I used to wish I had parents who would watch me like that. It would be better than being alone with Ma and being half Chinese.

I stopped talking about my Chinese father and I invented a better story. I said, My great-grandfather was a Mohawk

Indian chief. They're from around here, you know. In my mind that sounded good. When I felt like it I would add with tragic eyes, My father disappeared in the war.

I got tired of Ma saying, Your father will come back someday. He had to make sure things were all right in China. I knew Henry Lau was never coming back for me.

That summer hanging around the hotel I taught myself to play piano. There was the big, beautiful grand in the ballroom that I was not allowed to touch. And another in Duke's Lounge. But in the basement was an old Heintzman, an upright grand with a sound board so dry no one could tune it for fear of the whole thing snapping. In the piano bench was a tattered yellow C.L. Hanon *The Virtuoso Pianist*. I could not read it but I liked the feeling I had when I stared at the staves covered in notes. Lines. Dots. Treble and bass clefs. Jimmy Alexander, the hotel maintenance man, saw me sitting there with the book of scales and he said, You read music? It was clear I didn't. He showed me middle C on the keys and where it was on the first line below the staff and how to count the letters up. A lot of people played by ear but I was lucky that he showed me how to read. I memorized the C on paper and the C on the piano. I could figure out where I wanted to go from there. It was like knowing where the mountain was, then looking for the footpath to the top. The notes seemed to pop off the page. I figured out the scales, and then the arpeggios. To this day, when I look at sheet music I feel excited. I like the look of my fingers going up and down the keyboard, up and down, up and down. Sometimes I played the scale one octave, eight notes, sometimes I did it the way the book said, two octaves, sixteen notes, but soon I was playing longer scales, four, five octaves. Sometimes I played the arpeggios two-handed. One afternoon Jimmy Alexander said from the doorway, You want some other music?

No thanks. I like what I'm doing.

He said, You're stubborn but you sure got a lot outta that middle C.

Yes, I did.

Ma and I had our favourite records. She liked Les Paul and Hank Williams. She liked big band music from the war and she had a record by the International Sweethearts of Rhythm. Someone gave her a Mary Lou Williams album that I liked. She liked Lil Hardin who wrote "Just for a Thrill" and died on stage while she was playing.

That would be a good way to go, said Ma and she held her hands up in the air and lay back as if she was dead.

The first day of my real life was when I heard "Dance of the Infidels." Jimmy lent me the album, *Bud Powell's Modernists*, and I listened to that piece over and over and over and Ma said she was going to have to buy Jimmy another record because I was wearing it out. It was the first time I heard of the Blue Note. Down fell the needle into the groove on the turning black record with its yellow label. I was bouncing with Bud, and bouncing out of the end of my childhood. Nothing else would matter again. No one ever said passion is a good thing but when it happens there is no escaping. I started transcribing Bud Powell. Note by note. It was the hardest thing I ever did. I got Harold to let me use a beat-up old record player sitting in his office. I set it up in the basement as close as I could to the piano. Stopped and started. Dropped that needle down over and over looking for the spot. Writing the note. Listening again. Running to the piano and playing it to see if I got it right. It took me the whole summer and it was a happy summer.

On Ma's breaks she brought down pie for me and sat smoking in the doorway, reading *Prevention* magazine, her bony legs crossed, her foot bouncing. I could tell she was impressed that I was teaching myself to play because she listened quietly. Upstairs, she talked all the time and put on a false brightness that amused the other waitresses and the cooks and customers, not me.

Why didn't the skeleton cross the road?

Because he had no guts.

Everyone in the hotel kitchen loved her jokes, the way she piled her hair up and laughed and ordered them around. But I knew the bus rides home when she was so weary she said, Not now, Katie, and then she would lean her head on the window and sleep.

MAHSA

Before Mor died I got little aching breasts and saw surprising hair. I disliked the string belt she gave me to hold my pads in place, and the flat cotton bra with narrow straps that snapped if you moved your arms too much. Mor tried to make me see advantages to growing up, said, Tonight Abbu and I want to take you for your first time to the Metropole to hear the Xavier Sisters. Would you like to try real stockings now? and I did, of course I did.

I layered on the belts, the first required to hold my pad, the second required to hold my stockings, six strings in all, and I wished it had not happened to me and I was achy and I called, Mor! I feel like a kite fight!

She called back, You will be fine.

I came out in my real silk stockings and my new dancing skirt and I felt a grudging pride at the hidden life beneath my clothes, and Abbu said, I cannot call you Porcupine anymore, Porcupine. You look so grown up.

The Hotel Metropole on Merewether Road filled a whole block, as if an elegant cruise ship with white walls and great rounded corners had run aground in Karachi. On the street level were Pan American's wide offices selling tickets to the world. Inside was the ballroom with crystal chandeliers sparkling over the polished dancing floor. Elegant waiters in black jackets served tall drinks with umbrellas and small tumblers with ice and tea in tiny china cups. Women wore silk and big clip-on earrings and perfume and men wore Western-style suits and shiny leather shoes and narrow ties and there were many languages in the room. My parents danced rocka-billy and it was the first time I heard Harlem doo-wopping and "You Belong to Me."

I needed people to mention them, I needed them to have existed.

When I saw your Mor, Abbu said from the foot of my bed at night, I knew I had found my home.

Mor laughed at him, sitting on my window ledge, and said, He told me that he was my cup of tea.

She looked at him past me on the bed as if I weren't there. She said, John, why did you come to Afghanistan?

He got up and did a little soft-shoe shuffle to show off to her. I came to find you, Breshna.

Then he said to me, Porcupine, never let anyone tell you that girls do not go to university. It is your ticket out.

And Mor said, My grandmother was illiterate.

They dissolved but Abbu reappeared at the window and

took my mother's hand the way they used to when they came home from the dance school at the Elphinstone ballroom. They demonstrated to me the foxtrot and also the Ramba Samba. I imagined little red foxes dancing and feather steps and telemarks and weaving. Always we were laughing about words.

Abbu used to say in Pashto to me in the morning when I did not want to get out of bed, *Aya ghwari chi ma sara gada wokri?* It means, Would you like to dance with me? Mor teased him, That is the most unuseful phrase in our whole language and that is the one you chose to learn, and Abbu answered, It was not useless with you, and I can write it too. Then, with the flourish of a boy showing off to please a girl, he wrote it in his childlike script to make us laugh.

I said to ghostly-Mor on the windowsill, Tell Abbu to take us to America.

But she shook her head and said, We are fine where your father is fine. If you do not appreciate the apple, you won't appreciate the orchard.

I closed my eyes to make them go away. I needed to sleep. I needed to study and please Uncle. I did not need to watch my dead parents dancing all night. I rolled over away from the window. I opened and closed my eyes again. I promised myself to try to talk to Aunt and to study harder. When Mor was still alive she said, On earth it is hard and heaven is far away.

Sometimes there are not enough words to explain things in English. In Pashto my father was *hamsaya* which means not from the tribe and in need of protection. In our way of speaking, a boy is called *neek sar*, good person, and a woman is *aajeza*, bad-luck person, and a girl can be used to pay off a murder or a man's gambling debt. Mor's brothers could not understand how a man could take someone's favourite daughter and then stay nearby, as if Pakistan were just another American frontier.

KATHERINE

Ma and I liked to listen to Oscar Brand's *Folksong Festival* on WNYC every Saturday night. I looked forward to staying up late with her and searching along the dial to tune in the radio show from far away in New York City. She'd make popcorn and we'd listen to Oscar strumming his guitar and I liked being part of the adult night world and feeling as if I were not stuck in some backwater steel town. Ma said every week, Oscar's from up here, you know. One night a woman with a low voice was singing prison songs from Texas and I was talking and Ma reached over and tapped my leg and said, Shh a minute. That's Odetta. I want to hear.

Odetta was telling Oscar that society's foot is on your throat and you can't get out from under that foot but when you reach a fork in the road you can lie down and die or you can insist upon your life. She said the people who made up the prison songs were the ones who reaffirmed themselves, they didn't just fall down. Then she said, I call these liberation songs. Oscar asked her to sing something else and she sang

"See See Rider" which I did not understand but Ma told me to be quiet and listen.

In those days guys needled girls, even Oscar, but he wasn't doing that to Odetta. There was something about her voice and the songs she chose that quieted him down. When the show was over Ma did not want to step out and look at the moon the way she sometimes did. She said, I can't take one more night, and she went to bed. I didn't pay much attention. I was used to her moods and I was absorbed in the things I liked. I'd learned there was nothing I could do about her problems.

I didn't think much about her lying around on Sunday, but Monday morning she didn't get up again and she said, I'm taking the day off.

I went to school and when I came home I was surprised to see her still in bed.

She said, Katie, I can't help this. She put on her old stained green robe and sat at the kitchen table and smoked. Day after day. Her eyes started to look like marbles in a dish. Lots of times she did not seem to know I was there. She had money hidden in a drawer and she sent me for cigarettes. I counted the money and tried to figure out how long it could last. I found the cheapest food in the corner store, macaroni and white bread. I called her boss and said she had the flu. Finally I went to Nan who was mixing up dried milk for her boys and she gave me a big jar of it and told me she'd come over and see Ma. I dreaded going back into our smoky hole and seeing her sunken, absent eyes. Nan came down, said, You go away now and let us chat a bit.

I sat outside the bedroom door but Nan turned on the radio and all I could hear was Ma crying and then I heard Nan say, Well, if he's married.

She came out and made some tea and said to me, Give it a few more days.

I got my period when Ma would not leave the basement, and there were no pads and I was too embarrassed to ask Nan. I stole a box from the drugstore because I was worried about money for food. I went to the Saturday morning ballet classes in our school gym and I told them they should hire me to play piano, I was cheap. That was my first job.

All of this is to say that because of Ma getting sick and having to count pennies and make sure she stubbed out her cigarettes before she fell asleep I grew up fast and I missed a lot of the self-consciousness that other girls had.

Ma was getting thinner and coughing all the time so Nan came again and said, Here's cab fare. Take her to the hospital.

I got her there and we sat with a lot of other beat-up-looking people. Ma was a cowering, skinny thing that smelled of stale smoke. They came to take her for an examination and she said to me, Don't let them put me away.

I sat alone and prayed which I wasn't used to doing so I said, Hello God, help her not get put away. I don't know what I'd do if I get left alone. Thank you. It's Katie.

A nurse came out and told me Ma was a little low and

could I handle helping her take some pills every morning. She told me Ma did not want to get committed.

Hun, that's a good sign.

A good sign?

Your mom's real scrappy, said the nurse. But she's gonna need your help. She handed me a little slip of paper with a public clinic phone number on it. Your mother told me you've got plenty of family and friends around to help, she said, but I don't see anyone.

I brought Ma home on the bus and I borrowed some more money from Nan to buy the pills and she said, I'll come back later tonight. Mac is bringing a girl to meet us and I have to get dinner ready for them.

I thought those boys were lucky to bring friends home and to have a mother who made dinner for them. I wished Nan would invite me.

Ma did start to pick up a bit. I telephoned Harold at the Connaught because I could not pretend anymore that she had the flu and I told him the truth and he said, Jeez Louise, Mrs. Goodnow. That's tough. You tell her she's got a job when she's ready.

He was good for his word and worked it out with her boss. When she got herself back to work, Ma said to me at our kitchen table, Katie, I'm sorry you had to go through that. Don't do what I did.

What did you do?

I told you already.

Got pregnant with me.

I was trying to dream up a future that was not a woman lying smoking in a dark basement. Learning music was easier than fixing my mother's life. I wasn't going to be like her. I was going to write my own music and say, Take me as I am.

That ballet job got things kick-started. After I discovered I could make money playing piano there was no turning back. By sixteen I was playing blue murder. I found an old bandino hat with a floppy brim and I attached a black net veil to the front of it that covered my face to the bottom of my nose. I had seen *Love Me or Leave Me* that year, and I got some ideas from Doris Day, but I was more James Dean. At the Sally Ann I found a pair of pointy black high-heeled shoes and a black cocktail dress with a full skirt and cap sleeves. All dressed up like that I thought I looked twenty-five, my eyes behind the net, my painted lips below. I teased up my hair and outlined my almond eyes with kohl. I fixed my second-hand clothes to fit like they were made for me, and I was learning to play standards as if they were my own too. I snuck out regularly to see bands. Mo Billson's band came to town often and I went to listen to them every chance I could and then I started dreaming of playing with them. It was crazy that a gangly sixteen-year-old girl thought she could play with a jazz band from south of the border.

Then, that amazing first night. Wednesday, February 15, 1956.

I, Katherine Goodnow, stepped out, all dolled up in my black cocktail dress, a big hat and shoes with heels. I took the bus downtown, walked into the Alexandra on James Street South, and when Mo's band took a break I stepped up on stage, sat down at the piano, leaned in and began to play covers people knew, "The Things We Did Last Summer" and "Autumn Leaves," and when I felt them digging it I played a bit of Bud.

No one stopped me.

A girl needs to figure out what she wants to do and have some nerve. That's what happened to me that night. Ma always said, I'd rather try than stay dry. When she was not angry and felt generous she'd say, Katie, I'm rooting for you.

The band came back to the stage, kicked a chair to get my attention, but I already knew they were there. I knew everything. I was taking it all in. Mo said, We got no piano player. You can stay if you can keep up but we got no money.

That was the door cracking open. I played with them every time they came to town. I wasn't legal yet so I had to figure out how to be invisible in plain sight and I got Mo to pay me. I found a wider hat. If a cop came in I let my hair fall forward. In those days guys called out things like, You look good in that dress, you'd look better out of it. One time some smart aleck called, Hey, what's with the chick? She looks about twelve years old.

Billson's band had toured the South and played every dive in all the industrial towns along the border. They knew about hotels that paid them to play but would not let them sleep, and had restaurants where they would not be served a cup of coffee and they could not use the restrooms. They had already heard every heckle in the book. Mo liked me. I had a powerful sense of rhythm and I knew my chords and I learned fast as the devil. He said I had uncanny abilities. I was most myself on stage.

What chick? said Mo to the heckler with his smiling charm. I jus' see a piano player.

We hit the first note of the last set. I played so hard he'd stop thinking about me as a girl and as soon as we were finished I got outta there. I played with Mo off and on for four years every time they came to town. Mo changed the band all the time which made it interesting for me. I guess he didn't pay very well but that didn't bother me either. Sometimes there was a new drummer, sometimes a new bass. Near the end of my high school, a tall, sexy sax player who called himself T Minor joined Mo's band. The night we met he said to me, I'm from Roanoke, Virginia. We call it the Big Lick. All the guys in the band laughed but I was in the habit of not paying attention to how men talked. I just wanted to play. Still, I felt something unfamiliar. T had a way of teasing with his eyes and an intimate way of leaning one shoulder forward.

I went to school the minimum I could which no one bothered me about because I did well without trying hard. I went enough to write my exams. On the last day of school I

collected my report card and my graduation diploma and one
of the girls wrote in my yearbook:

For Katherine:
A girl who is different—style and dress
A girl who don't give a cent for men—
and for the boys still less!
See you in New York star-girl!

I showed my diploma to Ma and she said, I don't know
how you did it, all the skipping you did.

I was heading out to play for ballet classes and she said,
You're lucky, Katie, you've got a talent you can make money
with. How about I bake a cake tonight to celebrate? You're the
first girl in the family to graduate.

But I said, Ma, I've got a gig tonight.

MAHSA

The best thing Abbu ever brought home was a moving picture projector and an 8mm home movie camera and he made films about me and Mor and people in our neighbourhood. When he wanted to show his trip from America, he laid out a map of the world and we tied a thread to a little metal plane and I pulled it along over the map from Kansas to the ocean and then to Lashkar Gah while he shot the film. Then he stopped and tied the thread to a plastic camel and I pulled that from Afghanistan to Karachi to show where he and Mor came from. I asked, Did you really ride a camel all the way here? He laughed and said, No, but it will look better for our movie. I watched him put the film together in different orders with a metal film splicer and some glue. Sometimes I helped him make titles. We drew *A day at the beach* in the sand and he asked me to write it in Urdu too, and then we filmed the waves erasing them. He filmed Mor walking into the ocean with me eating Kwality ice cream. Sometimes he filmed the bands and dancing in the clubs where he went with Mor at night. Projected up on the bedsheet I saw the shadowy life of adults, dancing and laughing together. They looked like children playing but dressed up in ties and high heels. Abbu used to watch the images, especially of the bands, and say, This scene needs music, then he would jump up and go over to the piano. Sometimes Mor and I watched his movies by ourselves when Abbu was working late at the university. She liked to see the pictures he made of me as a baby. She looked young. I asked her if we had pictures of Lashkar Gah and she said, Abbu did not have the camera then, and it would be difficult to take pictures there. You will be free like me. Our people say, Know the mother, know the daughter. She said this seriously and then she laughed and played the movie of Abbu holding me as a baby. She said, I filmed that one.

I did want to be like her.

After they were murdered and I had to live with Aunt and Uncle, for a long time I came home from school and stayed in my room alone. I set up the projector to watch the movies by myself. I could see us all together happy, soundlessly waving and smiling and laughing and talking to the camera. A couple of times Uncle found me doing this and told me to put it away and study.

Most of the time he left me alone. In bed I lay in the dark and went through my catalogue of everything I could think about Abbu and Mor to help me remember: the way her bottom teeth crossed a little and the length of her painted fingernails and the scar on her left hand and how serious she could be when she was trying to teach me something and how we would end up laughing anyway, and Abbu saying the summer was so hot it hurt even to move his eyes and going with him on the clattering tram to Paradise Point, or fishing at Cape Monze and sitting between him and Mor in a horse carriage to Clifton Beach.

I could not sleep well and when I was awake I felt not awake but grieving. One dawn after a restless night when I heard the morning *Bismillahir rahmanir rahim* I decided to feign illness again that day to stay in bed and not go to school. I wanted my parents so badly that I got up and I threaded a film into Abbu's film projector and started to watch. The images were faint on the wall. I liked listening to the soothing ticka ticka of the machine. Suddenly my door was thrown open and Uncle walked in.

It is morning and you do this, he said. What about school? He tore the film off the projector and picked up the others and dumped them out of their tin cases into my waste paper basket. Then he pulled a matchbook from his pocket, lit it and threw it in. I screamed and tried to reach in and pull out the unravelled films but he pulled me away and pushed me onto the bed and stood listening to the films cracking and melting and I heard Aunt outside my door not doing anything to help me and I was crying and the burning film smelled acrid like rotting radish, and when it was all a ruined mess I had lost my Abbu and Mor all over again. Uncle turned to me and said, Get ready for school.

*

The sisters at St. Joseph's asked me to play piano for our school operetta, "Little Gypsy Gay." I told them we did not have a piano at home to practise on anymore. Sister Devan said, You can practise here, and I will contact your aunt and see what else we can do.

Aunt persuaded Uncle to allow her to take me on Saturday mornings to the 007 Club in the Beach Luxury to practise piano while he played field hockey at a maidan in the suburb of Cincinnati-town. I loved those Saturdays away from school and their apartment. Aunt dropped me at the door and disappeared until noon and I could do whatever I liked. For a long time I played only music that Abbu had taught me.

KATHERINE

T Minor stood apart and aloof when he played. His sidemen listened hard to him because they could never predict where he was going. I liked to watch his eyelids begin to droop, looking for a place he had not been before. He was a man on a rock face getting pulled toward terrifying eddies. A beat away from oblivion, heading into the night's brutality, the night's new thing. He bent the sound of his soprano sax around dark corners and did jigs in louvred light and after a long, long time resurfaced. He drank blood from the underworld, listened to grieving-for-life ghosts before turning to go home on a sax odyssey where he played for nymphs and daughters of man-eaters, and a long-waiting son. T played desire drawn out to breathlessness, holding, holding, balancing along the wire's edge, until his eyes opened again and he breathed and brought the notes back to the beginning. I saw him look over at me, checking me out, and I was concentrating like crazy to keep up, and feeling what it felt like to be checked out by him on stage. Even when we were in front of an audience, I always

51

felt as if we were alone together. The first time he tried to kiss me, quick, after a show, I told him my mother was waiting for me, but he did not believe me and he did not relent. He put his arms around me and he whispered in his low voice, Tell a real woman-lie, girl, tell your mama you were out dancing with your friends. Night after night he was talking with me and taking a kiss and touching my hand but always I felt him most intense when we were on stage.

One night I went alone to the Downstairs Club on McNab. Peter Appleyard was playing and I wanted to hear him, but mostly I wanted the people who came to listen to him to hear me. I put on my hat, walked down the marble stairs, slid through the club entrance that was wallpapered with Folkways album covers. I did not pay admission to the guy at the desk. I'm playing, I said. He looked confused but waved me past the seedy red leather walls behind him into the club. There was a broken cigarette machine on one side and a tiny plywood stage with a beat-up piano. The ceiling was a maze of black painted pipes. No one was playing and I did my usual trick, walked onto the stage, sat down at the piano and started to play. The tables had red-checked tablecloths and I do not know how many people were in there, maybe thirty.

That night I misjudged. The audience came for Appleyard. The manager did not like a girl invading his stage, even a lousy piece of plywood. They were serving Coke and vanilla but people had smoked and drunk and shot up before they arrived to settle in on those noisy wooden chairs. A guy who was wasted shouted into the tiny room, Take your clothes off, sweetheart.

I played harder. Did not hide. Wished I could. You need a burning desire. It takes guts. And then I saw T in the doorway and he walked right over and stood in front of the heckler. When I was done T clapped, all alone, until a few people joined him, and the manager came out to tell me to get off the stage and T said, Let's go, and I said, I'm not running away. I'm staying.

So we sat down and listened to the set and I was thinking like crazy because I knew if I did not want to go with T I should get out of there before the set was over. He intended to stand up and walk out with me. He intended that it was going to be *T 'n me* that night. It was the end of seduction and I had to decide. One way or another. I let him walk out with me. I did not say, Drop me at the bus stop. We drove to a motel at Cootes Paradise. Maybe this was something he did regularly because he already had a key balanced out of sight above the door jamb and all we had to do was park the band's big Chevrolet in front of door No. 9 and walk into that little room. I guess he did not know how old I was. I did not know how old he was and I did not care. I guess it played on his mind that I was half white. I did not care about that either because I was not born in the southern states of America where men got lynched for doing what he was going to do with me that night. It was a sweet night, and I think T was surprised it was my first time. I woke him up at dawn to try it again and the second time it was very good and I understood why the world needs the word *quenchless*. He held my head against his shoulder and I was tracing my fingers over his beautiful skin, and I loved the little moons on my fingernails against his sax-playing fingers. He said, My granddaddy used to call my grandma his best girl. Would you be my best girl?

So this was what Ma had been warning me against all these years. This sacred thing. This beautiful thing. Ma always said, Once it starts, a girl gets lost to herself. It would have been more helpful to give me some ideas about birth control but she did not. She was right. From the first time with T Minor I knew that I liked this kind of being lost. I liked the feeling of this cheap motel with the smoky paisley curtains.

Can I be your best girl piano player too?

That's how I got my husband and my first steady band.

MAHSA

I know the shared silences of those who deceive together. When Aunt came back to pick me up at the Beach Luxury on Saturday mornings, she looked happier and flushed but we never spoke of where she went and I never mentioned her absences. I think Aunt loved me very much for keeping her secret but I did not love her. She was a rag in a dry sink. She was Uncle's cousin and she had been promised to him at birth. Her lips were thin from being held tight and she was sixteen years younger than he was and she never looked him in the eye. She had known Mor in Lashkar Gah. She told me stories about family picnics at the great ruins of the Ghaznavid mansions. Mor's brothers were jealous that their father spent money for her to go to school. The men were jealous too of Uncle for moving away, and after the Americans came to build the dams everything changed and many of the herdsmen were made to give up their herds to make room for the dam projects. The men who were resistant got their herds shot down in a single afternoon of carnage, rolling eyes and panicked squealing and blood and wasted meat and hides. Uncle was one of the first to leave and Aunt told me this with pride as if his accomplishments were hers because she had none of her own. He came back to marry her and she had been frightened to leave everyone she knew to live in a foreign city.

She said, He learned to read and he worked in the hotel and then he began his carpet-selling business and now he has another business partner and is exporting to America.

I asked, Why did Mor's brothers kill her?

Aunt put her finger to her lips and whispered though the only person at home was their servant, Minoo, an illiterate girl who was frightened of Uncle. Aunt said, Your Mor's mother was her father's favourite wife. The other wives did not accept her and made things difficult for her. She herself was young and she could not control your mother who was pretty. Especially after Breshna went to school she became headstrong.

And should be killed?

No, but a girl should not run away with a stranger.

She loved Abbu.

She was not married and she was pregnant.

This is my family's memory. No memory is one's own alone. I liked Mor's and Abbu's stories of falling in love better than Aunt's story of transgression. Mor used to say, However tall the mountain, you will find a way to the top.

Aunt said, Your father did not understand our ways.

I always felt rage when she said things against Abbu. I loved him and he knew everything and he always made Mor and me laugh.

I said to Aunt, I am not going to be like you and do nothing all day. I want to be a musician.

My childhood began to grow distant, as if I were on a boat moving away from shore, and my parents stopped visiting me in bed. I was weary of grief, and one Saturday morning at the Beach Luxury when I was playing all alone in the 007 Club, a boy came in and startled me and asked, Do you know any jazz?

His eyes were shining black opals, warm and amused and interested. The club was always empty except for a waiter sleeping on a couch. I did not speak but played a childish version of "Autumn Leaves" and when it was clear that he was listening and staying, then I played for him "Kansas City" which I had made a good arrangement for. I looked at the clock and saw that Aunt would be still with her lover. The boy took a chair from the stacks by the wall and sat boldly near the piano and said, I like how you play. What is that last song?

It was the first time I had ever been alone with a man who was not Abbu or Uncle. I had talked to boys in the marching band from St. Patrick's with my school friends, and we sometimes met them at the Manhattan Soda Fountain but this was different and I liked the feeling.

Little Willie Littlefield plays that song. My father taught it to me.

He asked, What is your name? and I told him.

My name is Kamal Jamal, he said. I've never seen you here before.

Then you have not come on Saturday morning because I always practise here on Saturday morning. My uncle is the night manager. Do you know the American Ahmad Jamal? He is one of my favourite piano players.

I do not know him but I will look for his records. Is your uncle here now?

I felt confused at his teasing tone and I answered seriously, No, he is the *night* manager. Why are you here?

I study at the university and there will be a conference here and I am making arrangements. You play very well. Do you know any show tunes?

I did not know what a show tune was but I thought perhaps it meant something from the movies and I played for him "As Time Goes By" and I hoped that was right. I felt as if my toe were dipping into a stream and I did not know yet if I would jump in or sit on the shore. When I finished he said, Play it again, Sam. For old times' sake.

I said, I don't know what you mean, Miss Ilsa.

Then he tipped back on his chair and said, Why did you come here?

I came for the waters.

But this is a dry and mountainous place.

I was misinformed.

He laughed and I looked at the clock because I felt heat

gathering in the room and thought it must be getting close to noon. I said, I have to go.

Let me play for you too. I play very badly and I only know one song.

He banged notes, but I knew the melody from a popular Indian movie. I danced a little while he played, shoulders bouncing slowly at first, the way I practised with the girls at school. I turned my head with pursed lips, hands pointed in toward the ears, flirting hips. He was a noisy player and made the room feel like a party. People rarely came in when I practised but I saw some kitchen staff peek around the door, smiling, and I stopped dancing. I thought, Aunt will soon be here.

Kamal said, Mahsa, you dance well too.

All week I thought about him especially alone in my bed. The idea of him was new air that I suddenly needed, having never needed it before. I imagined that I was sitting in the trolley on the way to school and he sat across the aisle and talked with me, and I imagined that he appeared at my bedroom window and passed me a poem or a love message. When the real boy reappeared at the Beach Luxury the next Saturday before Zuhr prayers, he was a little taller and his shoulders wider and his eyes were more beautiful than I remembered.

I knew he was there as soon as he came into the room but I kept playing as if I had not noticed him. The chairs and tables were stacked against the walls, the floors swept and wiped down after Friday night. Without pausing I changed keys and played "All the Things You Are" because I had worked out an arrangement that I liked and I wanted him to hear it. I glanced over and tried to look surprised that he was there and our eyes met and I had dressed for him and I had painted my nails pink which Uncle did not like, and I wore lipstick. When I finished he came closer and said, That was beautiful.

How was your conference?

I am still preparing it. I will have to come often here.

I lifted my hands from the keys and turned to him but I did not know what to say.

He asked, Why do you play all alone on Saturday mornings?

There is no piano at home. I am practising.

Who are your parents?

They died. My father was John Weaver and he too taught at a university, not yours but NED.

When I said my father's name which was still painful inside me I watched to see if he had heard about what happened, but his eyes revealed nothing.

He asked, How old are you?

I am sixteen and soon I will write my exams. How old are you?

Nineteen.

I thought, Impossibly older.

He said, I study English. I want to teach. My father wanted

me to be an engineer but I want to start schools all across the country.

I said, If you like literature so much, do you know the poetry of Aa'isha?

Why should I say yes to a dog when I am deaf to lions?

There was something that had become strutting about him so I asked, Do you know who wrote, I am a lioness and I will never be a man's woman?

He shook his head but still smiled and answered in a mild voice, You tell me.

I did not yet know that a man showing off means he likes you. I also was showing off and I recited a raga pahadi, *I have not a moment of peace without you, not a moment of peace without you, my beloved, without you, my heart misses you, my heart misses you, there is no peace without you, my beloved.*

I had not thought about what the words meant until I was already saying them and when I finished I was embarrassed so I said, My mother taught me that when I was still small, I think it is religious, but my parents were not religious.

Kamal was smiling in a way that was protecting and teasing, as if he were indulging a younger sister. It made me annoyed but he said, Your mother was very wise to give her beautiful daughter such poetry.

Then I saw Aunt and I got up quickly and said, I have to go. I ran out to the front desk to her and she asked, Who was that?

I answered, No one.

KATHERINE

T 'n me. Ba bap dap, touch god's cheek. I am always going to be in the last place you look, babe, T said. Depths so deep. No light left. Sheets of sound. We could not settle until we found each other before the end of the night. He had played rhythm-and-blues bands, sax players honking and shrieking on their horns, overblowing, distorting. T loved to play Hawkins' "Body and Soul" and I loved to hear it and to see the curve of his spine and how he posed like a man. Nights of chicory coffee and any bar with music and cheap beer were ours and we talked about playing and ourselves and we saw no peril anywhere.

Sometimes when we played we caught the same feeling we had when we were having sex and after we would check in with each other, ask, Did you touch god's cheek?

Yes. You?

I showed T my Hanon and he started practising arpeggios across the octave key which he had never thought about and for a while he played over and over Hanon No. 46

which is a workout in trills. We were listening to Vi Redd's "Bird Call" and "Lady Soul" and of course we were always listening to Coltrane who was beginning to play around with Indian sounds. When you are young you want to get on with your life. There was an unease in T that I did not pursue. He said a woman changed the feeling of a band, and he said he did not like the sound of a woman's voice so he was glad I did not sing. One night he handed me, as a joke, a pair of pink frilly gloves with the fingers cut out. I ignored it because most men more or less acted like that in those days, and women skittered across the surface of this humour that we had no name for. I wanted to play. I was unwavering about what I was doing and I was scared I would not get there.

Our stories were slow-absorbing into each other. I told T about my Chinese father. He told me his father was murdered young. He wanted to know why Ma let me run around and I said, She can't stop me. We're more like roommates now, which was not true but I liked the sound of it.

Where's the rest of your family? What happened to your father?

They say he was tied to a railway track.

I did not know how to understand what he was saying to me. I asked, Why?

That's what they did, babe.

But what happened?

After that I left home.

I did not know how to ask why because he was saying it as if I should know. I said to him, Where was your mother?

When my daddy got killed things fell apart. They took us kids away. They said she couldn't take care of us.

Even though we were lying naked in bed together, close as two people could be, there were things that we could not explain or understand and were not capable of talking about. I knew the tone in a voice that meant no more questions.

So what about your mother?

Babe, she broke down when they took us kids away. They put her in an asylum.

I wrote and gave my arrangements to Mo and he tried some of them out. T resisted playing what I wrote but I ignored that too. I was not drawn to thinking about his irritation and I was not going to slow myself down with anyone's idea of me, even his. I had self-belief, so strong that I knew I would die if I did not do what I was supposed to do. I ignored T's moods when I got offered a gig without him. I knew how to reach over and stroke his thigh. I knew how to say, Oh you sounded so good last night. Put him in the centre again. Make him want to make love which he always did. It was our favourite thing. Our bodies always wanted each other. I knew how to keep my own struggle burning away in the corner. When you're young you do it all smooth as butter.

Of course I got pregnant and I thought I had to marry T, and anyway, I wanted to. It was 1960 and I was not going to give my baby up and I had no idea about abortions. It seemed everyone was pregnant and hiding it in those days. Girls were travelling across the country, having their babies, giving them up, coming home again, pretending nothing happened, the Baby Scoop Era they called it. The magazines said we were *outcasts and moral lawbreakers*. Ma was right. Before I got pregnant I thought of myself as a teenager and a good piano player and a good student. After I got pregnant, I was unwed. No one ever called T unwed.

We were stepping off the stand after a show at the Alexandra. The crowd dug us and we were going to get something to eat, then go over to the Cootes Paradise Motel. I said to T, I'm pregnant. I think we should get married.

He was unhooking his sax. His fingers stopped a moment and then he took it off and held it in his right hand and I stepped under his left arm to feel his hand around my shoulders which was where I liked to be. I said, I been thinking it over. It's not the end of the world.

But we got no place to live.

Well, I guess we better fix that.

He pulled me in close to him and his sax clip was pressing against my skin and he kissed me and Mo said, You two lovebirds coming?

T let his arm drop to take my hand, still holding his sax in the other, and he looked into my eyes deep like he was looking for something he lost in a moving river and he asked, You sure?

I answered, I'm sure.

And then T said, Hey, Mo, we want you to be the first to know. Katie and me are gettin' married.

Mo shook his head and said, I shoulda known better than let a chick in the band.

But I knew he liked me and especially he liked how I played and he was joking and I said back, Don't you worry. I'm gonna keep playing.

We never thought anything through. It was night-star good when I think back, loving him like that. I had no money and no help in a world hostile to what I was doing. But that meant I didn't need anyone's approval either. I was opening up and swallowing life like a Leviathan and having a baby was part of it. I never imagined I wouldn't. But I was not marrying the boy next door and I banged against new ideas, mixed marriage and miscegenation and illegitimate and bastard. I sometimes had the impression that I was waking into a bad dream, not out of one. There were places I could not go with T. I started to pay attention to the news because I had a stake in it. On television, Ma and I watched four students in Greensboro, North Carolina, who asked for coffee and doughnuts at a whites-only Woolworth's lunch counter. All day they wouldn't move. The next day more students came. The sit-ins spread to other towns as if those four young men had been a bit of tinder in dry grass. We saw women wearing dirndl skirts and clean white blouses with faces hatred-twisted shouting outside the stores because they did not want to sit beside a few students. Ma said, Look at that, Katie. That's what your baby's got in store. There are things you can do.

But North Carolina felt far away and foreign and I was thinking about me and making love and playing gigs. One young man who got pulled off the chrome-and-leatherette stool and beat up by police with clubs said, If it's possible to know what it means to have your soul cleaned—I felt pretty clean at that moment.

Did T feel he had a clean soul? My neighbours with their orderly lives on Mountain Brow shook their heads when they talked about the protests south of the border and said, Things are different up here. Ma said, Things aren't so different, I'm just saying. I never wanted to be like Ma, but somehow I had become an engine barrelling down the same track and I wasn't going to hide myself away in a basement the way she did.

Ma said, Well, at least we don't have separate schools for white kids here.

If we did, where would I have gone?

Oh, she said, you would have passed. I would have made sure of that. I never let anyone stop you from doing anything.

T 'n me's ceremony happened at five o'clock in the afternoon at city hall. Our band was booked to play Diamond Jim's later and I wore my black cocktail dress and my hat with the net veil from the Sally Ann. I was already standing in front of the justice of the peace when I thought, Maybe I should have told Ma, but I didn't want to hear any more of her opinions. I was doing exactly what I wanted to do and I was doing it the way I wanted to, and it felt right and exciting. We got married, played our show, and we tore it up that night. After the show we went to the White Grill at two in the morning for omelettes and home fries and ketchup. Mo brought bottles of champagne and the manager served it in coffee mugs. My wedding feast. Perfect, in my mind.

His real name was Theodore Lincoln Jones, best soprano sax player on the southern Ontario–upper New York State border. Our first morning married we were lying in bed at the motel, and I asked, When did you leave home?

Babe, I ran away from the foster people when I was fifteen and I never went back.

Where did you go?

Around.

But where did you live?

Friends. You know.

No one came after you?

T pulled himself up and lit a cigarette, said, I got arrested for theft. They put me in juvenile for a couple of years.

I thought, I am married to this man now.

There was an edge of something challenging in his voice. He said, I met a cat inside who asked me, Who taught you to hate yourself?

He rolled over and slipped his arm under my shoulders. He said, To have once been a criminal is no disgrace. To remain a criminal is the disgrace. Malcolm X said that. Him and playing sax saved me. After I got out I waited tables and then I started getting some gigs that paid. Going to prison was my education.

I asked, Where'd you get your first sax?

That's what I stole.

So you're T X?

He laughed and said, You're a smartass.

Then he stubbed out his cigarette and we turned to each other and slipped down on the bed again.

Inside him was a blade of rage, alive as spring grass, spit-shined and hidden. There were bound-up feelings like switchblades ready to snap open. He had dark, shining skies for eyes, and hands big as puddles and legs like iron and, oh, I loved to look at him standing sideways with his sax. His arms were open to me in room No. 9 at the Cootes Paradise Motel and it set the path of my life. T 'n me. I was having our baby and I wasn't going to have an only, like I was. I wanted another, real quick, so they could take care of each other. I had no idea.

MAHSA

It was easy to keep Kamal a secret from Uncle. I met him at
different places along the trolley routes, walked the beaches,
went to Zelin's Coffee House, the Paradise movie theatre.
There was war with India. Ceasefire. Strife stirring in East
Pakistan. I studied for my exams. Kamal had a small battery-
run cassette player that we took to the beach to listen to
music. He would finish his studies at the university at the
same time I was finishing at St. Joseph's and he said that
perhaps he would continue to study and teach there, that
he wanted to make schools for every child in Pakistan, and
I said I wanted to study at the university too but he could
not be my teacher and he laughed at this and said, You will
always be my teacher, which pleased me. Uncle would not
approve of me being with a young man, and on my surfaces
I was an obedient orphaned schoolgirl but with Kamal I was
becoming someone with opinions and I had my own tastes
in music and reading and he listened almost as Abbu used
to listen. He had an idea for marriage that I did not want,

70

but this we did not worry about. Everything we shared, and in this way, for three years, we grew up gently, and passionately, together.

One day, Kamal invited me to the house of a friend but there was no friend. He prepared some tea and we sat at the table together, pretending we were waiting. Then Kamal said, He is not coming. He reached across and touched my hand. I waited for him to lead me where I wanted to go and that day I said, Yes, now.

He said tenderly, It feels a bit strange, like I am kissing a friend.

I am your friend.

And then our lips searched for each other in a different way. We were young and strong and we gave and took generously, standing up and lying down. After that first time, we were always looking for a friend's house and sometimes I came the first moment he touched me. I was afraid of getting pregnant and I think he said not to worry.

When we parted, the pressure of his touch on my skin lingered. His young man's love was demanding, devouring, irresistible. He was coiled and raw, and I did everything with Kamal and we learned everything from each other. My body was without reluctance. Men had different chances than girls. He had joined the National Students Federation and he described to me the struggle for democracy. At home with Aunt, I heard about Ayub Khan toppled because of student groups like Kamal's. I wanted to be part of this outside world too but I felt young and I did not know how to fit into that part of his life.

I said to him, The girl students in your group must be interesting.

He said, They are. And then he added, But I love you.

He wanted to protect me and perhaps was afraid of my uncle. I did not want to be protected. I wanted to do things I had not yet figured out, and I feared how much I loved him and how completely I could lose myself. In this way the ease of our first years together began to give way.

One day we walked up the rough path to the ramshackle shrine of Shah Ghazi Mazar. We slipped off our shoes and I pulled my scarf over my hair and we walked past the rakhwallah who looked after the place. A small, wiry man near the tomb gave us roses for offerings. After pausing beside the marble tomb, we passed to a smaller second building and from the west windows we looked over the sea and watched the turbulent waves that come with the monsoons. We heard the muezzin's call to prayer, *Allahu Akbar*, God is Great, woven into the cries of gulls, a man's voice chanting into time and human distraction, *Hayya alas Salah*, hurry to prayer. These sounds of searching and the sea I had heard all my life, and I felt what is divine in the ordinary because I was listening now with the man I loved. Below us on the beach, faqirs rested companionably near fires, close to a small circle of European tourists who had wandered over from Hawkes Bay, storm-coming waves grey and black on the silver sand.

Richmond Hill Public Library
.   Check OUT Receipt

User ID: 22971004066599

Item ID: 32972001298795
Title: The homecoming : a
novel
Date due: July 3, 2019 11:
59 PM

Item ID: 32971016230538
Title: Under the visible life
Date due: July 3, 2019 11:
59 PM

Total checkouts for session:
2
Total checkouts:2

Richmond Hill Public Library
Proudly Enriching your
Connections, Choices and
Community.

That Saturday, Uncle returned to the hotel early from his field hockey and he saw Kamal walking with me back into the lobby.

At home Uncle shouted at Aunt, Where were you? You do not watch her well enough! To me he said, That boy should not be around. He is not suitable. Do not pursue it.

Aunt was upset. She too needed her Saturdays. She said to me, Be more discreet. Uncle has other ideas for you. About family. About business. He will not approve your choice. He is already making plans for you to study abroad.

I did not want to go abroad. I wanted to go to university here and to live in the dormitories. I wanted to keep studying and seeing Kamal and I did not think far ahead at all. I did not imagine myself as someone who would marry and live behind walls. Women who married got murdered by their families.

I met Kamal on the trolley the next day after school and we rode to the end of the line and back twice. He was like a madman and he said, We must leave. Your uncle will never let us be together. Please, Mahsa. I know how these things are.

I wanted to mend the torn veil. I felt we could protect our love from the world.

Kamal said, I cannot hide how I feel about you. Love is like the sun and penetrates the clouds.

Passing outside was one of the hippie buses that took the Westerners to sightsee around the city. It was painted with red and yellow hearts and words in English: *Enjoy the Love.* I saw the Western girls with their boyfriends travelling without parents or relatives, wearing jeans and their hair loose and headbands around their foreheads and sandals and bare shoulders. They looked so free.

Where would we go? What about university? Always Abbu said that I must study. I had believed I could do what I wanted if no one saw. I had believed I could love Kamal if no one knew. I believed in a hidden life for women.

Now that I had been caught with him, the danger for me was great. The trolley clattered along the tracks and I watched a camel carrying heavy furniture and I did not tell Kamal that things were much worse than he imagined, that Uncle seeing us together was a small thing, that I was pregnant and I had decided to take care of it alone.

KATHERINE

Our band played the roadhouses and lounges and clubs along the highway from London to Toronto. I'd never had motel rooms and meals out. I'd never been away from Ma or lived with people who only thought about music and sex. We performed up and down Yonge Street and at George's Jazz Room and the Colonial and the Penny Farthing in Yorkville and the El Mocambo and the Bourbon Street Jazz Club. We played six nights a week. Mo was a hard-working band leader. Any night we finished early we went to see other musicians, and I heard Oscar Peterson and my old friend Ronnie who had a little place above the Coq d'Or they called the Hawk's Nest. I liked pumping it out and I learned how to get the audience to come along with me. Mo said, You gettin' it, Katie girl, and T sometimes walked right over on stage beside me, my strings and hammers talking and seducing and joking with his breath and reed. T 'n me were hot together, sax and piano, in and out of each other's heads, and the more pregnant I got, the sexier things were on stage. I was unusual. You hardly used to see a pregnant woman on the street.

We got recorded live one night at George's by the national radio who were recording Nimmons 'N' Nine. The sound guy said to Mo, I'm gonna record your band, and he wrote down our names and when I listened to the show later the announcer said, Katherine Goodnow is new on the scene and she seems to be playing for two. She's got a sound people are going to be listening for. She's an original.

I wondered if Ma heard it and hoped she didn't because she would not have liked that crack about me being pregnant.

After the shows I went back to wherever we were staying and when T came in later we made love, quieter now. One early dawn I said, T, I think we need to make some adjustments. But he kissed me and started all over again and when the rising sun turned the cheap motel curtains dirty pink, he said, No adjustments necessary, babe, you are perfect.

Phones were expensive so Ma and I used to write postcards and she'd mail them to the clubs. She sent me a surprising one after Christmas. The front was a picture of a floral clock in Niagara Falls and on the back she wrote, Guess who's got a date for New Year's Eve? I bought silver slingbacks. Happy New Year!

I wrote back on a picture of a Mountie, Who's taking you?

Her reply was on a chipmunk in a forest. You won't remember. A fellow called Sean. I knew him in high school.

Of course I remembered him. He was the only man

who ever told me she was great. I saw him around at the Connaught. Then she got rid of him and never mentioned his name again. He seemed to be back.

After New Year's when we played George's I wrote on a card with a picture of the Royal York, the tallest building in Toronto, How'd it go? Happy New Year to you too!

She wrote back on a picture of the Stelco steel mills, Not my type. When are you coming home for the baby?

I had this half-baked worry that something might happen to me like happened to Ma. I heard the Children's Aid Society could ask questions about whether a woman smoked or drank or went to the movies. I figured playing in clubs with a band of Negro men might not be on the social workers' to-do lists. I was married but I thought I better get under the radar because in those days pregnant women weren't allowed to be teachers or to work anywhere. I didn't know what we were allowed to do and I didn't know how to find out and I wasn't going to be called unsuitable to keep my baby.

More students were getting arrested for sit-ins and sneaking into segregated theatres and Martin Luther King said that it might take more jail to arouse the dozing conscience of the nation. In Hamilton things felt different but Ma said in a bitter and hurt way, Just scratch and you will see what is under the surface anywhere. Hipsters were playing music and reading poetry describing America as an empire, a hellhole, a freedom-place, a prison. I was fascinated by student non-violence and speeches about supporting any friend and opposing any foe and letting the oppressed go free and paying the price and bearing burdens. The rhythms appealed to me but T wasn't very interested. He said, I don't know, KK. I got a Moslem name so I could travel as a white guy.

Then he showed me his American cabaret card with his other name, Talib Salaam, because he had converted to Islam, like Rudy Powell and Idrees Sulieman. A lot of jazz musicians were doing the Islam thing in those days because the law said if they were Moslems they were not Negroes anymore—and they could go into restaurants and bring out sandwiches and coffee.

I said, I didn't know. You never showed me. What's Talib Salaam mean?

T laughed and said, Lots of things you don't know, babe. Talib's for T and Salaam just means peace. When I saw guys blacker than the inside of a chimney with White on their cards because they converted, I did it too so I could not be a nigger anymore.

Where?

Prison. Cats in prison talked about Allah and all that. Katie, you talk about non-violence but you don't know.

T 'n me made a silent commotion inside people who passed us on the street when we walked together holding hands and it bothered T but I always felt right. People could look at me however the hell they wanted. I was used to being different with Ma. Sometimes he would drop my hand if he thought someone was staring and I would take it again. I said, We're better than them.

Babe, I been in places where there's effigies of niggers hanging from church steeples as a warning. Last time I played the South, there was a manager who wouldn't let me in. He said, This is a white dance, and I said, My name is on the marquee out here. He sent me round to the back door and I did the gig and I walked the bar, but I got a fever on stage, ran out to throw up. I came back in, finished and left. I did not stay to pick up my money. I could not look out one more time on those faces dancing to my music.

Like mine?

Babe, you don't stick a knife in a man's back nine inches and pull it out six inches and say you're making progress.

What about our baby?

Well, that's your fault. You got me all excited.

So we laughed it away and we could be sexy as hell up on the stand but not walk down the street. T 'n me preferred the night. In Hamilton clubs, Negroes and Mohawks and Chinese and whites were mixing it up.

I asked him, When am I going to meet your momma?

Ain't gonna happen, babe, we can't go to the Big Lick together and she don't travel.

There was a bottomless pain in T that he did not want to touch so I did not touch it either. I did not realize that things can suddenly whip up from underneath and claw at you like a nervous cat. I just kept going.

MAHSA

The Sweeper worked at the Holy Family Hospital on Aga Khan III Road where there has always been a good maternity ward. She stole a speculum and dilators and a curette for the little business that she ran with her midwife friend. A dishwasher at the Beach Luxury told me about her. The first time I went alone and I was afraid to knock on the unmarked door in the mohalla. But a bigger fear gave me courage and when the door cracked open I said, I heard you help girls who are pregnant, and the Sweeper moved back to let me pass inside. I was wearing my school uniform. Two women asked things like how long I had known and my age and I showed them my money which was not enough. I said, I will get more, and the midwife said, You should not wait too long. Come back in four days. The Sweeper would not tell me her name and she called the midwife Rabia.

Are you sure it will work?

I'm sure.

I told the girls at school I was collecting money for an Aga

Khan children's charity. That's how I paid for my abortion. The third day of my fundraising, one of the sisters brought me to her office. I was afraid she was going to take the money away from me and I hid it in my underwear. But she gave me a cup of tea, told me how proud the school was that I had taken the initiative to work for a charity though I was a girl who had suffered a great deal. She congratulated me on my exams.

In went the speculum, twist twist opening twist twist and the Sweeper was holding a light for Rabia whose hair was completely covered and the lines of her face looked angular and harsh. She pushed in the dilators and stretched me until I felt open like the mouth of a river. The Sweeper gave me a rag to bite on and hissed in my ear, *Chup raho*. Don't get us in trouble.

It was the beginning of many forced silences. I bit down on the rag that tasted of cotton and soap. I squeezed the Sweeper's hand, and when I could bear no more Rabia finally said, *Ahcha*, and I lifted my head to see, but the Sweeper said, Oh no, do not look, some girls faint, lie down.

But I did see the basin of blood, flesh, end-of-the-world mess.

Rabia said again, *Ahcha*, and removed the dilators and loosened the blades and slid the speculum out of me and packed between my legs with old cloth and said, You did well. Now. You will stay here for two hours. Do you see my fingers? Place your fingers from both hands like this and massage here, over your uterus. This will help it to contract and it will stop the bleeding and the cramps.

I had never heard a woman name these things. Now that she was not inside me anymore her lined face seemed not as cruel as I had thought, and her eyes were kindly. The Sweeper said I must go back in a taxi and she would call one they knew and that I should have brought someone to help me.

The pain between a girl's legs is hers alone. I did not tell Kamal about my abortion because I was angry that I suffered and he did not. I thought, Why does he get away with no worries and I have been worrying every month and now we were unlucky and I have all this danger and trouble alone. I thought, I want to love him and I do not want to marry him. Why was this so? We could not be unlucky again. I wanted to study and to be free. I lived in this jumble of unclear thought. I was invisible at home, a girl whose parents were dishonourable. Outside there were growing demonstrations and rumours of war in Bengal and Uncle was nervous. Two weeks after my abortion, he called me to the sitting room. When Uncle and Aunt wanted to talk to me together, in the same room, it was always unpleasant for me. Uncle said that things were unstable in Afghanistan, that he had heard again from the family there.

Aunt said that Uncle wanted me to go abroad to Canada now, that they were worried about me.

They were secretive and they organized things and told me nothing as if I were only a lapis amulet to be kept or traded for luck. The consulate was in the hotel and it was easy for Uncle to do everything without telling me.

I said, I do not want to study in Canada. I want to study here. Why did you not tell me?

I went to Sister Devan. She said, I knew your mother and father, Mahsa, and they loved you and wanted you to be educated. Do not forget this no matter what happens later.

She had helped Uncle make my application to go abroad. Why was everyone's idea more important than mine?

Aunt said, We did not want to tell you and upset you, and Uncle said, You will do as we say. All is arranged.

I'm not going, I said. I want to stay here.

I started to cry and Uncle stood and came to me and lifted my chin roughly with his hand which stopped me crying immediately. He said, You are ungrateful. Most girls would consider themselves lucky to have a chance to study abroad. Go now and get ready.

He pressed his thick finger hard into the soft space at the back of the jaw, near my throat, and lifted it until I could feel it stop my breath.

When he left the room I said to Aunt, I don't want to go.

Each time Uncle forced me to do something, her eyes fell flat until he was out of the room. Then she would try to comfort me. I felt in her a satisfaction that I too had to suffer his brutality. It was easier that I wear the same bit and halter. But she had also watched, famished, as I went to school and she sometimes tried to read my books.

What did you hear from Mor's brothers?

They are jealous men, she said. They know you are of marriageable age and they know that Uncle has money.

I learned how divisions and rivalries were continuous in our family. Aunt often spoke of them while leafing through her fashion magazines. She did not look at me, as if this made her telling less dangerous. She had told me about the time of Queen Soraya who took off the veil. She would turn another page and say, Sometimes the change appears only on the surface. I shrugged. Mor never wore even a scarf.

Mahsa, Uncle's mind has been made up for a long time.

She continued in a voice that was not whispering but private, This is a chance for you. I never had a chance to do what you are going to do. The nuns helped find a scholarship for you, Mahsa, that is why Uncle agrees and now also he thinks there may be opportunity in business over there. Go. Things will be free there.

But why did you not tell me?

Uncle said no.

I had no choice. I hated Aunt for her weakness but she had given me an idea about being free in a faraway place.

When I told Kamal, he got up roughly, knocking over the chair in Zelin's, and everyone looked at us and he threw some rupees on the table and said to me, Let's go outside.

I want to finish my tea.

So he set his chair upright and sat down again, a bit ashamed and the colour softened in his face and he leaned across the small table toward me and said, Say no to your uncle. Tell him no.

Always I had loved to meet with Kamal wherever he suggested and to share the books he read and to listen to his music and always I had felt less free than he was. An unfamiliar part of me was slowly admitting that I wanted to go, that I did not want to live with Uncle any longer. I too could go into the world, and never had I imagined that I could do it alone. I thought, Perhaps I am like Abbu. He went across the ocean in the opposite direction. Would I look as strange there as the foreigners looked here on hippie buses? But my father was American. Aunt had one picture of McGill on a pamphlet, stone buildings and a stone entranceway and a large grassy area in front of the main buildings. Aunt also had a pamphlet about the city and together we looked at pictures of Saint Joseph's Oratory and Marie-Reine-du-Monde cathedral by the train station with carvings of holy men across the top and a mountain in the middle of the city with a tall cross lit up at night and people with white teeth wearing fur hats and mittens and ice skates. I said, Does not everyone look happy in Montreal? And Aunt said, Well, maybe they are.

Are there any people from Karachi there?

I do not know. My friend said someone was trying to build a mosque.

Maybe I will be Christian over there then.

Aunt said, Do not talk like that in front of Uncle.

My father was Christian and I have both their names. I will not be Najibullah over there, I will be Weaver. Mor always said that one day I would need both their names.

Your papers that Uncle sent say Najibullah.

Kamal found a friend's place the afternoon before I left and our lovemaking, the first since my abortion, was slow and silent and tender. That day his eyes were saying, Do not go, this cannot be right, and when we rested after, he was sad instead of raging and he said, We will never find this again.

I could find no words to comfort him and I was going away so we made love again and with my body I could say the true thing, that I loved him. I did not know how to say the complicated thing which was that I did not know who I was and I now had a chance to see and I wanted that too and would he keep loving me and would he wait for me? These are all simple words, short words, but I did not know how to say them to him.

In that sweet moment when I still had my lover, my music, my books, my own city, I was already turning toward things exciting and unknown. I discovered that I was not objecting to this adventure imposed on me. My body was trying to say everything to him, that I loved him, and that I was frightened to leave him. What was I releasing myself from? My Karachi uncle. My Afghan uncles. From worrying about getting pregnant. From dead Mor and Abbu.

Kamal said, I will always love you.

Always we undressed each other and then, after we made love, we quickly pulled on our clothes to leave and go back into the streets of Karachi. That day we lingered and I did not want to leave and it began as a game because I did not want to get out of bed. He teased me and said, Come, my friend will be back and your uncle will be waiting.

He began to dress me in bed, laughing, slipping on my panties first, then my skirt.

I said, My turn. And I found his boxers and trousers and helped him put them on.

He put on my bra and my blouse and buttoned each button slowly, kissing each glimpse of skin before he covered it, and my wrists and forearms and the lovely place inside the elbow, and then he combed my hair, touched my ears with his lips and when he was finished I put aside his T-shirt to keep for myself and I began to slowly put on his shirt and button it from top to bottom moving my lips from his throat toward his navel and I felt him aroused and we made love again, not removing our shirts this time, quickly, like taking a drink of water, coming quickly, and then we dressed ourselves, but with no kisses, and he held me close to him and through his clothes I felt his warmth and he said, Now you are dressed to go away from me. This is a mistake. I should lock you naked in a room. Mahsa, do not forget me.

What at first we are unable to read we must endure later on. That night I looked out the window at the fleet-beauty of moonflowers in their pots and then I lay in bed, falling asleep, my body sated from Kamal, my mind agitated with the thought of flying alone for the first time in an airplane and arriving in a faraway place and not knowing where I would sleep or how I would find things or how would I be in Canada with English and French, with people who did not know me and from this half sleep I sat straight up in bed and thought with panic, I forgot to say goodbye to Abbu.

And then I awoke fully and remembered he was dead.

KATHERINE

When I was big, I sat at the piano before they turned on the stage lights and waited in the dark. People noticed me less. I played and ate and slept like a hibernating bear. I loved the road. I wanted a never-ending tour. But two weeks before the baby was due, Ma called and said, What are you thinking? and she got me worried and I figured I'd better start to get organized. I said to Mo, I gotta take a break from the band. I'm going back to Hamilton to get an apartment and have the baby.

He took a roll of bills out of his pocket and gave me some and said, I thought you were gonna have it right up there on stage.

I asked, Was it you who called Ma?

He answered, Why would I do that?

I could earn more playing piano in a night than Ma made in two days on her feet wiping counters and she was furious. She had kept a roof over my head and made me guilty enough to stay in school and graduate. It was more than anyone did for her. Now, with all this advantage, I was throwing whatever-it-was away. I had gone and got knocked up by a Negro, and worse, I was walking around like a cock in a henhouse.

Ma said to me, You should get that look off your face. I had it too.

Ma, I found an apartment down from the Connaught. Come see after work.

What are you going to name it?

Dexter.

I knew enough not to get going with her. I put out her cup of Maxwell House Instant, her ashtray, her sweetener and whitener. She was taking in my life with jealous fury but she also wanted to be proud of me and to take some credit. *Her* father got her arrested.

Where's Dexter come from?

It's a name we like.

One of their names?

I'm not talking about it.

I am not calling any grandchild of mine Dexter.

C'mon, Ma. Her eyes were convex mirrors and I looked tiny in them. I asked, How did you think up my name?

She put out her cigarette and lit another. I started to flip through the *Ladies' Home Journal*, looking for my favourite column, "Can This Marriage Be Saved?" *Her turn, His turn, The Counselor's turn.*

Then Ma coughed and said, I never named you Katherine. My mother wrote that on your birth certificate at the hospital.

I set down the magazine and picked up a sugar cube and sucked on it.

She said, They thought you shouldn't have a foreign name so they did it without asking me. I named you Ming. Henry liked it. It means precious. I looked it up in a book at the library. By the time I got out of Belmont and got you back, Katie was the only name you knew. You cried all the time for the foster-woman. You sat on the floor with your back to me and you would not answer to Ming. I gave in. I shouldn't have. I should have kept calling you Ming. It's a pretty name.

A dark pinhole opened in the centre of me as if Ma had taken a photograph I did not want. I was not going to let her pain be mine. I was never going to let people walk on me like that. I was going to do better. Keep my baby. Protect it. But she had named me. A name my father liked.

She bounced her foot, said sharp-edged, You should reconsider. Dexter sounds like a kitchen appliance. I'll call him Sammy.

I could see she was going to claim the baby. I wanted T to claim it. And I was hiding from social workers because I was afraid that they would claim it.

Dexter did not come fast. I got on the bus to the Henderson after my water broke and signed myself in and my labour lasted fourteen hours. A nurse told me to stop hollering and they gave me an injection and tied me down. They called it twilight sleep. I didn't know what was happening to me. When I woke up I had marks on my wrists from struggling.

Dexter had marks on his little head from the forceps. My baby and I had given each other new lives and we both got beat up doing it. By the time I woke up, Ma had come and gone back to work, but T was there, grinning, and though I remembered nothing, I felt happy and groggy and relieved.

He got me up and we went along the hall and looked at Dexter with all the other babies in cots through the glass windows. A nurse behind us said, They're kids themselves, and her friend answered, Well, it'll be a long row to hoe being mixed like that.

No one was going to talk that way around my baby and I turned, but T pulled me in tight, said in a low voice, Don't mind them, babe. We're beyond colour.

I loved him so much.

I was startled by the pain of the milk coming in and startled at the relief as the baby sucked and I was glad to have T's arms around me holding our baby, like we were stacking dolls. That first time nursing Dexter, staring into his inquiring eyes, that moment, right then, was precious.

T went back on the road. I was lonely and I missed the band but I was fascinated with Dexter and what had happened to me and I set up my days to keep things interesting. I took him down the street to the Connaught every morning to see Ma, to see Harold and his musicians, to the park, to the big library. Lots of times Ma came after work and said, Get out for an hour. Go do your shopping. I know what it's like.

The nights were longest and that was when I sat by the window looking over the cenotaph and said to myself, You have to make the best of the cards you get.

I started writing down my tunes. When Dexter cried I could squeeze in a few more notes, put it down and pick it up again. When T came home, it always felt like a celebration and I pulled him to me, smelling of cigarettes and beer and his sax. I loved falling asleep together, T 'n me and Dex. Sometimes T took a little suck and a nibble from my breasts. You leave that for your baby, I said, and found better things for him. All that sticky, birthy, sexy stuff was messy, and I said to T, I'm so happy I feel like I should pay you, and he answered, If you gave me a penny, I'd owe you the change.

I did everything at once, ran over the notes for "Money Jungle" in my head, changed Dex, planned our dinner. I held him and wrote and I looked deep into his eyes and sang and made his lips mirror mine and still I was thinking of my next note. I said to T, Let's have another quick so Dex won't be alone, and T who never could be bothered with birth control said, Suits me. Not quite a year later, I had King Jimmie. Then, when I was twenty-two, I had Bea, my daughter, and that was the end of it.

Ma said, Don't have any more babies, Katie. I know a woman doctor down by the train station. She's eighty-four years old. She'll give you the pill.

I'd heard about that but I thought it was illegal and I asked Ma how she knew about her.

I went to her too.

Why?

Guess.

That gave me something to think about.

Dr. Elizabeth Bagshaw had short curly white hair and a wide mouth that was mostly closed and serious and when her lips opened into a smile, there were dimples in her cheeks. From behind her frameless glasses her eyes looked right into you and a deep crease between her eyebrows up from her right eye deepened when she was listening to your heart. She was a no-nonsense kind of person. She asked, How can I help you today?

I said, I have three children and I don't want any more.

She said, That seems reasonable.

I heard birth control is illegal.

She smiled and said, People say Planned Parenthood is for heretics and devils. She paused and said, I'm a devil. I will give you a prescription for the pill. Take one a day and don't forget. It's for regulating your periods. There, that made it legal. Come back and see me in a year, or if you have any problems. What do you do, by the way?

Mop up most of the time but I'm a jazz musician.

Where do you play?

With three it's hard to get out much.

Well, find a babysitter and get out and play.

I have one. I trade piano lessons for her kids because I don't have a cent to pay her.

Well, I'll be watching for you. I like music.

I told T I wanted to come back and play with the band. He said, Katie, we already got a piano player, and you got three babies.

When I went back to Bagshaw the following year for more pills she asked me how the music was going and I told her about T and the band.

She said, Well, you know, when I went to register for medical school the men told me to go stand in the line for nurses but I didn't budge. Start your own band.

II

The Visible Life

MAHSA

No one knew my name. It did not feel good but it felt compelling. I walked into my small single room in the Royal Victoria College, partway up the mountain with a great cross at the top. Our dead are in us but in Montreal I could forget mine for a while. I thought, I can do anything.

I fell asleep and I woke up in the dark, still in my clothes from the plane, sticky, a stain on my blouse where I had spilled a glass of juice. I liked flying alone and I had asked my seatmate why we were bouncing in the air and he said, Clouds probably, and this was a new way of thinking about clouds. Here the world smelled foreign, and I took Kamal's T-shirt out of my suitcase and sniffed it and put it back and closed the case to safeguard its scent of salt and sea and his skin, the smell of us together. I was famished. I was a child of hotels so I walked down to Sherbrooke and west to the Ritz-Carlton and into the lounge. No one came. Where were the servants? Sleeping in some corner? Then I thought, Mahsa, you sound like Uncle.

I walked over to the desk. Excuse me, I'd like to order something to eat.

A young woman said, I'm sorry, the kitchen is closed.

How dare they? I was a guest. At the Beach Luxury someone would be woken. And I started to cry.

She asked, What's wrong?

I'm sorry. It is my first night here and I have come from Pakistan and I am going to McGill and I don't know where to go.

She picked up the phone and spoke in French and said to me, They're bringing some tea and bread. I go to McGill too. My name is Monique.

In this way I met my best friend in Montreal and began the marvellous first days of my student life. I bought jeans like the other girls, wore my hair loose, watched students dancing the Popcorn like James Brown and learned to dance rock and roll with boys, not only girls as I did at home. Uncle had chosen for me studies in English and math but I wanted to study music.

Monique said, *Change.*

But what if Uncle finds out?

It will be too late. *De toute façon*, it is your life.

This idea felt strange but I dropped all my courses except one English because I liked the teacher, a writer called Professor MacLennan, and I started music and practised piano in the small rooms of the music building with its mad, shaitanic din and its enormous statue of Queen Victoria out front. I did things because I wanted to and because there was no one to stop me. I watched a human dissection in the medical school. The big toe of the cadaver made a deep impression on me. From it hung the naked and nameless corpse's number. I went with Monique to a bar on Crescent Street that had Allen Jones furniture shaped like buttocks and breasts which imprinted on my mind like the cadaver's big toe.

I walked on the mountain and watched wild squirrels running on streets and saw trees coloured orange and red and gold-brown like Mor's old veranda chair. I learned the names of streets and buildings, so many royals and saints.

There was no Aunt telling me not to make a noise as I crossed a room, and there were no nuns teaching us to listen. In Montreal, girls sat cross-legged on the floor in their jeans, put their heels up on desks, let their breasts show through their T-shirts. They snuck boys into our residence and everyone saw and did not see and there was no real danger. They kissed on the street. What if I had met Kamal here?

On Friday afternoons, I followed my English teacher to his office after class and we talked about books and I watched the light disappear outside and snow crystals sparkle like Shigar Valley topaz in the darkness. He was kindly and tall and courtly and he made me think of Abbu if he had grown old with his easy smile and his interest in me. He had written many books but the one I liked best was called *Two Solitudes* and it was about love and loyalty and families in trouble. He drank from a little silver flask and he said to me, You're welcome to borrow my books if you like.

I sat across the desk from him and said, You are my best teacher.

Well, he said. Thank you.

I knew that his wife had died and I knew that he had loved her deeply because he wrote about her, and when I read the essay I felt the way I used to feel when I watched Abbu and Mor dancing. I wanted to tell him that but he was a great writer and I did not know how to say it. I wanted to say something that would interest him.

I said, My country has many solitudes too.

He nodded and took another drink and said, Perhaps you will one day write about that.

I was pleased but I shook my head and said, Oh, no. I want to play music.

That is what you will do, then. Time for me to go home.

I walked to the Ritz to meet Monique when she got off her shift. She studied theatre and I went to plays and dances with her and she did not know my parents were murdered and she did not treat me carefully but with the liveliness of real friendship.

I told her about the great poet Khadija whose brothers wanted to stop her from falling in love. She wrote her lover's name in her poetry—*Abu Marwan, I cannot stop flying out of myself to reach you*—and when her brothers read his name they killed him. But after he was dead she kept writing his name.

Monique said, Lovers always die—Romeo and Juliet, Tristan and Isolde—*c'est comme ça.*

But women here are free, I said.

Tu penses! My mother barely spoke English and had seven of us and scrubbed and went to church. My father drank. The women in my neighbourhood took pills and played cards and read *romans d'amour* and passed their rage down to me. Is this better than your lover Abu *quoi?*

I laughed, said, Same donkey, different saddle.

Kamal wrote, I do not want to tell you about my life in the military. After I am finished I will work on building schools.

He missed me, wanted me, loved me.

When I saw his handwriting, I felt my blood throb the way it used to when I first saw him each time we met. I wrote back, described some of the new things I had seen, but I did not say much for fear that it would somehow get back to Uncle.

I studied Bach and jazz composition and outside of class I was listening to the Vedic drone in Coltrane's "India," to Ravi Shankar and the Beatles. I heard George Harrison and his harmoniums and I was thinking about sacred qawwali. My new friends in Montreal took up swarmandal and sitar and tambura. Girls here played men's instruments and nothing happened to them. People said things like the ragas could make rain and cure the ill and I thought that this was blasphemy but the world did not end.

George Harrison sang in great innocence, *Do all without doing*. I bought a harmonium and took it to my theory teacher and I said, You play piano and I will play this with you, and he said, It is like an accordion, which I found funny. I said, I want to learn to notate this, and he said, Cool.

I was shocking myself. These were my first moments of musical daringness. I had stepped off a cliff and I was flying, not falling, and the valley below was green for anyone, even me. I was often alone and the air felt empty in Montreal. There were church bells on Sunday mornings but there were no male voices chanting *Allahu Akbar* reminding us to pray five times a day, even if we did not pray. To not be lonely I went often to the listening library, and the librarian, Anika, used to come and talk with me. She asked me lots of questions about music from home. I listened to odd rhythms and tala, to Irish slip jigs in 9/8 and to the Mahavishnu Orchestra and John McLaughlin riffing on his two-necked guitar with Jean-Luc Ponty. Of course I listened to Santana. Everyone everywhere loved Santana, especially in Karachi.

I listened to the CBC recordings in the library to know who was playing here and I heard Nimmons 'N' Nine and Mo Billson's band with a pianist called Katherine Goodnow. Her rhythm was perfect. I played it for Anika who had never heard of her and went to her card catalogue and pulled out little wooden drawers, flipping through white typed cards with numbers and finally came back and said, I can't find any other recordings of her. The bandleader is still around. And the sax player, Theodore Jones.

Most frightening was my first piano tutorial. Never had I had any real lessons, only Abbu and my own ears. At my first lesson I played note for note something I heard on a Shankar recording. My professor had a beautiful half-French, half-English name, Jean St. John. He wore jeans and a tight T-shirt and a brown corduroy shirt open over it and brown leather sandals and his feet were not clean. His dark hair was shaggy over his collar and touched the top of his metal-framed glasses. He paced when he entered a room, looking for the place he would be, like a dog circling before it lies down, and he picked up the wooden chair and straddled it, resting his arms and chest on the straight back. He chain-smoked Camel cigarettes. He was known in the faculty as a genius double bass player who tuned his bass in fifths to get to the purest sounds, so low most people could not hear them. I play for the underworld, he liked to say, I have sympathy for the devil. A few of the students told me I was lucky to have him in my first year. A girl who was not chosen to study with him said to another girl so I could hear, Foreign students are taking over, it shouldn't be allowed. I was nervous playing for Jean St. John and my fingers shook, the first time this ever happened to me. He listened for a few moments and then he swung off his chair as if he were getting out of a saddle and he dropped his cigarette on the floor, stepped on it and walked to the door. He said, Play with your eyes closed. Play backwards. I don't care how the hell you do it, but make it yours. Use your own ideas. See you next week.

I sat for a moment, then got up and looked out the window and I thought, What am I doing here? Uncle did not want me to study music. My professor walked out on me. I was startled by such rudeness as if someone had slammed a door, but in fact, he had opened one. I looked around the room, still and tiny and quiet, and I put my hands back on the keys to try again. What were my own ideas? I had no idea what my ideas were.

Later I told Monique, At home we have to repeat, to learn the tradition.

She laughed, Here everyone wants to be original. Don't worry about it. Listen, come on Friday night and play standards at the hotel and make some money. You can play however you like. It's only for drunks.

I arrived at the Ritz and sat down at the Steinway near the curved staircase. This hotel piano felt familiar, like at the Beach Luxury, except fancier. I started to play and I loved the sound of overtones I had not heard before and Monique slipped out from behind the desk and put a dish with a five-dollar bill on the piano and some men listened and put a few more bills in it. The manager watched them order drinks and he came over to the piano and said, Mademoiselle, if you want to come back next Friday you can play again and keep the tips.

I showed Monique all the money I made and she said, You have to give it back. The men were friends of mine, actors, so the manager would let you stay. Don't you have something more dramatic to wear?

I showed her a gold sari that revealed my midriff and I wore my hair loose. She said, Yes, yes, try that, and the next week I walked through the lounge and sat down and people who were not Monique's friends were staring. I myself slipped five dollars in the bowl and soon someone put some money in, a quarter, the first money I ever earned playing piano. A man who was drunk with his arm over a woman's bare shoulders asked me to play "All the Things You Are" which I knew, but when other people began to ask for tunes I did not know I had to ask them to hum and I would follow and chord. Someone said, Give her a break. They don't have this music in India. Someone else asked, Are you Indian? I said, I'm from Pakistan. I will play you something from there. The little group of men around the piano were laughing and drinking and Monique got off her shift and said, I should be your manager.

I thought, I have to get a cheat book. There are too many Western songs.

Uncle would have been enraged and I was shocking myself and I liked my own daringness. I learned to fend off lonely men. One night a drunk guy leaning on the piano said, Wanna meet later, wanna show me what's under the dress, and I played softer and I looked up sweetly and said, Fuck off, *mon ami*, and kept playing. I must have sounded funny because a few men around laughed and he was startled and moved away. At the end of the evening I counted lots of money in my tip bowl and when I was leaving one of the waiters who was also a student said, Watch out for Mahsa, she might call you *mon ami*! I liked this new feeling of answering to no one. I was as happy as the goat who escapes the wolf.

KATHERINE

Five in the morning. Baby Bea was calling, and those two little sweet-faced boys were one on each side of me and damn damn damn Jimmie peed again that pee-stale smell on me and I was still tired. I climbed over Dexter and walked down the hall and picked up Baby Bea and she was already rolled over, holding the edge of her crib and her diaper was heavy. I unpinned it right there and dropped it on the floor and wiped her, chanted low and soft and slow so she would not wake up too much, Hey Sweet Pea, look at you, look at me, tempus fugue-it, baby, fiddly doo diddly dee, and pressed my lips into her soft skin. Let's get you clean, and I picked up a warm white cloth and already she felt better, and I took her into the big bed with me and the boys, and I prayed please to the mother's sleep-god for one more hour.

Damn. T had promised he'd come home last night. I had a cup of powdered milk left and a box of cereal and some potatoes and that was it. The baby years were tough, no money and all that desire, my babies for milk and me for his mouth on mine. There was one pretty night when he came in and gently nudged the little boys over and set Baby Bea on a pillow and slid in beside me whisper-cursing too many bodies in our bed, making me laugh, and we made love and did not wake anybody up oh that was a beautiful dawn his eyes dark stars above me.

I could not fall back asleep and the more I woke up, the more angry I was that he hadn't come home again. I tucked them all in and got up and put T's clothes in a brown paper bag and then I went outside to sit on the steps, to watch the dawn and think about the clubs and I wondered if I could ask Ma to bring me some powdered milk and about how I used to come home about this same time of morning and sleep. And I thought about grown-up perfume and after-shave and T 'n me playing together and all the things I was discovering when I was on the road with him and why was he still out there and I was here? We used to go so deep that people held their breath, listening, because when you go far away like that there might be a train wreck and this is what it feels like the split second before it happens, cars jamming and jack-knifing into the air and the music gets risky and beautiful. I wanted that again.

But T was not coming home to fill me up or to leave money. He was going out to score. I was wondering how I could go on with the loud ticking of that man's time bomb inside me and how could I go on without it.

I did not mind anything he took except not what I needed to feed our babies. Then I saw him. Coming down the street in the grey dawn with the slow early-morning traffic and he was high.

I need money for milk, I said into the half-light.

That how you say hello? He reached down to take me in his arms the way he always did.

T, you can't do this. I gotta feed these kids.

Babe, I am out there working every night.

You're out there playing on my back, T, and not bringing anything home and they are your kids too.

Babe, I never asked for them.

The air went black-silent and a cold took hold and I pushed away his arms.

I have nothing to feed them, I told him. I cannot ask Ma again.

I'll get it.

I got nothing for today. I do everything for you to play. What do you do for me to play?

Then I said the thing neither of us had ever admitted, You're using our money to score.

Fuck, Katie.

I ran up the stairs and locked the door on him. He never carried a key and he started to pound and yell, You can't lock me out like that. Damn, Katie, you're hardass like a man!

The neighbours yelled, Shut up, and We're calling the cops, and T turned around and started down the stairs. He was always afraid of the police. I opened the window and yelled onto King Street, T!

He looked up and I threw the paper bag full of his clothes down onto the sidewalk.

The kids were awake and crying and I was saying, Don't worry, he'll be back, and they watched cartoons and I mixed up the last of the milk and stretched it with extra water and added some sugar cubes I'd swiped from the hotel and warmed it up.

That was the day I cleaned up our apartment.

We're going on an adventure, I said, and told the boys to get dressed while I dressed Bea and I took them on the bus up to Nan's house and asked her to keep them for me while I got myself a job.

It was a mistake to set up as old-fashioned married, him earning money and me doing everything else. T wanted to play and to have sex with me, in that order. I wanted my babies and sex with him and to play and to write all at the same time. I wanted to be recognized and get invited to play because I was good. I wanted to be more than a girl pianist. There is a too-narrow life that exists hidden under love and I escaped it because T pissed me off that dawn. I was no batter-my-heart type. I was not going to submit and be contained. I wanted to be unholdable. Women can get unsouled by marriage and I was not going to let that happen to me. Four years at home with the babies! I complained to Ma, and she answered, You can't break up a happy marriage.

I got a gig at the Baptist Church playing their services because I could take the kids with me. I played ballet classes and I picked up some students. I made enough for rent and food and got my life grooving again. Lots of days I was mad as hell about it. Ma gave me our old record player and I started listening again.

The first time I heard Coltrane's Quartet play "My Favourite Things," I was unpacking groceries and I was listening and listening and I had to listen more. McCoy Tyner was genius. Baby Bea was slowly taking the eggs out of a carton I'd left on the floor by the fridge and she was breaking them one by one. She was absorbed and worked with attention, feeling that sticky yolk, and I did not stop her so I could listen and listen and listen and not be interrupted, and when I am dying I will not think about the mess of a dozen broken eggs but how I heard Coltrane and Tyner talking to each other in "My Favourite Things." That sax sounded like a man getting up out of his chair to take a woman's hand to say, I wanna tell you something I don't have words for, da-daa-da-daa-daa, da-daa-da-daa-daa, then going deepdown inside, deedle-leedle-leedle-lee, those musicians' minds inside their instruments and the music catching at the passing phrase, each playing separate but together, tune inside rhythm, beat inside melody. I listened and listened and each man was absorbed in what he was finding to say, each hearing what the other three were doing and by some miracle—there is no other word—all playing together, though it makes no sense, how can two, three, four play solos together? That day I listened twenty times to "My Favourite Things" and when I felt quiet and whole and sated I lifted up the needle and put the record back in its sleeve and we were all fine. I told the boys to put on their coats and rubber boots and I mopped up the sticky mess of eggs and wiped off Bea in the kitchen sink and we went outside to walk along the mountain brow. The light was fine and the steel mills were majestic and the kids slipped their hands into mine. I was not lonely with Coltrane and Tyner inside me. I thought, This music is what marriage could be, playing solos at the same time and ending up together.

MAHSA

Over my desk I taped *Anxiety is the dizziness of freedom* when the kidnappings started but I was accustomed to city violence. Everyone here was shocked by tanks in the streets. Montreal felt more dangerous than Karachi. There were checkpoints on bridges and bombs in mailboxes. A cell of terrorists took credit for bombing the stock exchange. I hoped they would not close McGill because Jean had stayed through my entire last lesson. I had always played the raga scales by ear and now I could write them. Raga accidentals began to drop into my improvisations and in this I found a whisper that must have been my own voice because it was not in any tradition that I knew, and this pleased me. Uncle wrote that he was reading about the *libération de Québec* and said that Aunt asked if I was safe and she wanted me to know that in Karachi people were chanting *roti kapda aur makaan*—food, clothing, shelter—and the Peoples Party would not give up power. His letters irritated me and I wanted Aunt to write her own letters but writing was difficult for her and how would she get a stamp? Sometimes I saw other girls bent over letters from home, absorbed, smiling as if the person were there. I tossed Uncle's letters aside. Even his penmanship was harsh. Monique wanted me to go to the Université du Québec to protest but I wanted to practise. Never until now had I been able to practise as much as I wanted. On television I saw a reporter ask the prime minister to discuss the kidnapping and I was surprised that he was not pushed away by soldiers with guns. The prime minister asked the reporter, What would you do? I studied Coltrane's "My Favourite Things" and listened to McCoy Tyner's long solo over vamps on the two tonic chords, E minor and E major. I loved their rhythms. A man's strangled body was found in the trunk of a car. People criticized the police. How determined these Canadians were about their freedom. I played in my little practice room, running up the steps past the big statue of Queen Victoria, saying, Bonjour queen, locked myself in at least four hours a day. I was finding things inside my heart. There was the Bhola cyclone and on television, sad pictures of bodies in water and villages broken and long rows of people walking, looking and hoping for anywhere to go. I saw these things as if they were not my own people. I felt removed and I had been gone only a few months. The police found the terrorists in the north end of Montreal and they did not shoot them or put them in prison but flew them to Cuba as they had promised. At home they would have been killed.

I was absorbed in my music and I was observing from a different perspective the violence of the world.

Monique liked to lie on my bed, smoke dope and read me bits of de Beauvoir who she called Simone. We spoke French because I wanted to learn and she said, *Tant mieux, tu va en avoir besoin si tu reste ici.* She was directing *L'école des femmes* and writing her own feminist plays. She said, Listen to this: Simone says that a woman's *vital interests are divided.*

Her vital what?

Her interests. Simone says a woman is afraid of missing her destiny as a woman if she gives herself over entirely to things.

What destiny?

She must mean children. She never had any. She loved Jean-Paul and they both had lovers.

I think she is right.

You think so?

Well, do you think Jean-Paul would have changed the baby?

Merde, non!

Monique's latest boyfriend came in without a shirt and we laughed. Aunt would have envied my freedom. Uncle's peace of mind would have been destroyed. Boys in our rooms. Condoms and birth control pills in every girl's underwear drawer. Me playing in hotel lounges. I glimpsed a new possibility: I could fulfill my own needs. Outside marriage. Outside tradition. Alone, like the girls here.

Monique said, Let's move out, I found an apartment.

It was across campus, on the road up the mountain, an old high-ceilinged place with an iron staircase to the front door. I did not have much to move, the suitcase I arrived with, and when the residence reimbursed Uncle's money I had enough for almost two years' rent. We sat on the balcony, looking into the trees, eating cupcakes Monique brought from the Ritz, and I said, I don't know what will happen if Uncle finds out.

You worry too much. Want to see my grandmother's nightgowns? She gave them to me last year before she died.

Her bedroom was scattered with boxes and bags, and she pulled out a full-length salmon silk tulle and a shorter lacy silk black organza. She slipped the black one over her T-shirt and jeans and said, I wish I knew when she wore this. She told me she got pregnant the first time she had sex, when she was seventeen. These are not the nightgowns of a woman who had seven children. She wanted to take these gowns to the hospital when she was dying but *maman* would not let her. She gave them to me. She must have had affairs. I think she wanted me to know something.

I smoothed the silk, comparing it to Pakistani silk, and looked at the photograph of the tiny French-Canadian *mémère* on Monique's dresser, imagined her in such a negligee. Monique began to plan our housewarming party.

I wrote to Uncle that I would need to stay and study for the summer, and not to renew the residence because I would live with a girlfriend, and he imagined that I was moving in with her family and wrote back, Please thank your friend's father. I am beginning to think about your future.

During this anxious time I would awaken in the darkness thinking about home. When I was only half-awake, I sometimes saw Mor's smiling face, tender and concerned, and I missed her but I no longer needed her. This was the beginning of understanding how we mourn for those we love in different ways all through our lives.

The snow was silvery and at the end of the last class before holidays I followed Professor MacLennan to his office to sit in a wintry darkness that smelled like cinnamon, to give him the first paper I ever wrote that had my own opinion in it. We were to write about a Canadian story and I had chosen one called "Boys and Girls." I was worried and he asked, What is troubling about your idea?

I said to him, I wrote that the girl loved her father better than her mother even when he was skinning foxes and she called her mother an enemy even though she depended on her and this was like my aunt and I thought girls had separate solitudes. I said that I had never written my own ideas and they seemed dishevelled to me.

He nodded seriously but also smiled and said, Do not worry. You have put a great deal of thought into this. Do you have somewhere to go for the holiday?

I did not want to tell him that I was going alone to New York. I said, Back home there was a Christmas ball at the Beach Luxury Hotel and anyone could go, even non-Christians.

His face was tired and the skin on his hands was wrinkled under the light of the green lamp on his desk. He asked, Don't you have a young man waiting for you?

I would rather be here, sir.

Why?

The man I love is far away and my family does not want me to see him.

He looked out the window, slowly got up, pulled a copy of *Middlemarch* from his shelf, opened it to the last page and read, "For there is no creature whose inward being is so strong that it is not greatly determined by what lies outside it." Here take this, he said, a Christmas present.

I said, I think the nuns had his books at home. Thank you.

The writer is a woman, he said. She herself found love with a married man.

I flipped past the prelude and opened to the first chapter and read the beginning of the epigraph—*Since I can do no good*—and I became absorbed until he interrupted me and said, I am afraid I have an engagement this evening, Miss Weaver. Enjoy the book. Whatever god you pray to, pray that you do not miss love.

KATHERINE

Baby Bea was doing her little elbow crawl toward her brothers and Martin Luther King was speaking to people across America. *We cannot walk alone. And as we walk, we must make the pledge that we shall always march ahead.* He stood under the Lincoln Memorial, a carpet of a quarter million people unrolled at his feet and I wished I was there with my three kids instead of watching on television in a sweltering apartment. Mahalia Jackson and Marian Anderson and Joan Baez and Bob Dylan sang, and King's voice was like a bell over all those people, *We have also come to this hallowed spot to remind America of the fierce urgency of Now.* My boys were playing matchbox cars on the couch. I had run into Mo on King Street and he let it slip that T had other women and one was pregnant. I was having a hard time turning my back on the biggest, fattest love affair in the world and King was talking about urgency and whirlwinds and soul force and the people were listening together in an eerie silence. I was thinking about the way people looked at me and T and our kids on the street. I was thinking about King saying unearned suffering was redemptive, and I felt too scrappy to accept this idea. T's unearned suffering was not redemptive. Ma's unearned suffering was not redemptive. People learn to live with what they cannot change, or they die of it, but it is not redemptive. And I was watching and thinking about that speech and I heard Jimmie yell at me, Hey, Ma, look at Bea.

My baby girl was pulling herself up on the couch. Her toes were spreading to balance and her smile shifted to concentration and I was thrilled all over again to see my third baby working out how to take her first step and I wished I was watching it with T.

After the kids fell asleep that night, I sat by the window resting from their relentless love. That's the lonely time when you're on your own with children. I picked up Jimmie's peashooter and some dried peas and blew as hard as I could. The first time the pea rolled out the end and fell on the sidewalk. I kept blowing peas until I learned to puff my cheeks and put some lungs into it, to get some distance and loft. I aimed for the cenotaph, *Our Glorious Dead*. It was far and high and I had about no chance. I pushed my whole body out the window and thought, You better not fall out. Who'd take care of them then? I could see Diamond Jim's and the Palace Theatre and the Capitol. I could see Birks and the clock tower on the south side, and down the street, the Connaught.

One of my peas sailed all the way across. Ma was leaving

her night shift at the hotel and she waved up at me and called, Well you must be bored!

I went down to sit on the steps with her. She smoked and talked, said Bea's feet were like mine, and Jimmie was too busy, and Dexter was serious like a businessman and then she asked, How're the holy rollers?

She was lonely, like me. I said, They pay the rent. Ma, I'm bored playing churches and school gyms. I want to be on the jazz scene.

She looked across Gore Park, past Queen Victoria, said, Don't complain, Katie, you've had it all.

The Palace was emptying after the last show, *Lilies of the Field*, and a contented crowd moved out into the street under the lights of the marquee. Ma's words went in like a thin blade. I had a money-making talent, kids no one took away, a lover who was not in China. But I felt like a caged creature.

She said, Did you hear Ellen Fairclough's not running again?

Who's that?

She's only the first girl cabinet minister.

I said, Ma, the jazz scene is in New York. I have to get myself there.

She stubbed out her cigarette and said, You got three kids. You'll never do that now.

I put in six more years in Hamilton. When I could get a babysitter I took the bus into Toronto and walked to Yorkville and checked out the folk scene at the Riverboat and the Purple Onion and the Night Owl. The papers called the street a sore on the city and said that young people had lost touch with Christianity and all the meaningful values of life. Clayton Ruby and Paul Goodman set up a free legal clinic called the Village Bar to help the hippies have their sit-ins which Ma and I thought was funny. My old friend Ronnie was putting together bands and partying it up. The hippies made him honorary mayor and he said he didn't need honours, he needed lots of pussy. I asked him, What's with the go-go girls at the Mynah Bird? He said, There's something about girls in cages that men like. But he didn't have any work for me so I went down to George's Jazz Room and Doug Riley was playing organ and when he took a break, I got up and played, and later Doug jammed with me.

A guy in the audience said, I like your playing. Come to Rochester to the Rowntowner Motel next weekend. I'm helping Marian McPartland start a label. I'll introduce you.

I was thinking about my kids and how the hell did I expect to get myself down to Rochester, but I said I'd come. I had to run like crazy to make the last bus to Hamilton because in a few hours I'd be rushing out the door to play Sunday services for the Baptists. Dexter liked going. He liked being anywhere he could learn something and he had asked me how Thomas could put his fingers through a dead man's hands and he wanted to discuss god and why we should believe what we can't see. I told him there are lots of things he can't see that he should believe. I was thinking about that on the Greyhound bus and I was also thinking, If you don't get yourself to Rochester and meet people and get a break, you're going to be a nobody and feel bitter.

The next Saturday night, Ma couldn't babysit and I couldn't get anyone else either. I decided to put Dexter in charge, and I told him I'd be back about four in the morning and to stay in bed and keep the others in bed too. He was nine years old and I felt bad about it. It was the first time I ever left him.

I borrowed Harold's car, a big Studebaker, and I didn't have a driver's licence but I learned to drive with T in the band's car. The Rowntowner was in the Henrietta suburb along with automobile dealerships and shopping malls. I walked into the Monticello Room around eleven and everything was cooking. Marian McPartland was finishing her set with her trio, a drummer who had played with Thelonious Monk, Ben Riley and bassist Michael Moore. Marian had this accent that was half English and half jazz and when she said "cats" and "groove" she sounded like royalty. Her face was long and she had a strong nose and blond bangs and shy, assessing eyes and she could play anything. She was inventing rhythms and harmonies and that night Alec Wilder came in and tossed her a sheet of music with a piece he wrote for her, "Jazz Waltz for a Friend." She listened to me play and she liked my style.

She said, I left England with Jimmy and we entertained the troops during the war. When I left home, my mother said, You'll end up in a cold attic.

She laughed. Mother was right.

Jimmy drank a lot and Marian divorced him and things started to fall apart when her record label dropped her. Everyone was listening to rock and roll, and jazz was getting pushed aside and women in jazz were getting pushed further. Journalists wrote that women couldn't blow, beat and slap an instrument like a man, that jazz needed a strong, aggressive hand, not one that rocks the cradle. But Marian wasn't taking any of that. She had this repertoire inside her and she knew everyone. She did not care if you were a man or a woman or black or white or anything else. She only cared how you played.

She said, I am starting a new company and I'm going to call my label Halcyon. Those are the birds that calmed the seas to lay their eggs on floating nests. Isn't that beautiful? Sherman Fairchild offered me the money and a studio. He's got two gold Steinways.

I said, I want to record.

Marian said, Why not? Come to New York. When I get my label going, I can record you. Some women buy hats. I start record companies.

It was already three in the morning. I watched the sun rise on the drive home and I took the car back to the Connaught. Dexter's small face was in the window looking for me. I felt bad, he looked little and frightened. When I came in the door he asked solemnly, Did you get the gig? I told him I did and he said, That was my first time.

Your first time what?

Taking care of you.

I had to turn away, so he would not see my tear of exhaustion and love and the sorrow of eternally imperfect mothering.

First thing Monday morning I went over to the Connaught and found Harold.

He said, Hello, Mrs. Goodnow. You're up early.

I'm moving to New York, Harold. Time to clean the mirror. I want to get there soon.

Katie, I don't book jazz.

I'm not asking you to. I want a ride.

You leaving Jenny and your kids?

I'm taking my kids. Ma's got her own life.

I just lent you my car.

C'mon, Harold, two days, one down and one back. And a driver and a U-Haul.

He stood up and turned around pretending to move some paper but I knew he was thinking. When I felt him talking himself out of it I started in again.

Please, Harold, help me get there. Ronnie's got a million cars, borrow one of his. I'm gonna make a record. A producer promised me.

What ya wanna move there for? Go and do it and come back.

Who's gonna take care of my kids?

Got a contract?

You want to move in and take care of my kids?

Katie, what makes you think he'll even recognize you when you get there? He was probably trying to get in your pants.

The producer's a woman. Never mind, go to hell. I'll take them on the bus.

MAHSA

What were you doing in my closet?

Monique held out the boot from the back of my closet where I hid my money. She said, You need a bank account.

But why were you in there?

Looking for a pair of shoes to borrow. You can't leave your money like this. Someone like me could steal it and besides you could be getting interest.

What's interest?

She took my hand and pulled me out of the bedroom. Then she slipped on her jacket and still holding my boot, ran outside and said, Catch me! I chased her all the way to Sherbrooke and we were both laughing when she stopped at a corner with three banks and she asked, Which one?

The Royal Bank building had attractive lions standing on their hind legs carved into stone, so I pointed to that one and Monique said, Good choice. That's where I bank too. Then she ran inside and put my boot on the counter and said in

French, This girl wants to open a bank account. The teller said, She needs her father's signature.

She's from Pakistan and her father's dead. Her uncle pays everything. I want to talk to the manager.

The teller looked at me and said, Why don't you talk?

Monique said, Her French is bad. Then she dumped out my boot full of small bills and change in front of him and said, She needs a chequing account and she is going to be here for four years.

The manager came over because Monique was making a scene and said, If she wants an account her father must sign for her.

Monique said, Monsieur, she is from Pakistan and her father is dead. If you can't take her money we will take her boot to the bank across the street.

He placed his tongue between his teeth and squeezed down as if he were in pain, then he sighed dramatically and nodded to the teller.

I had never written a cheque. I began to giggle when they shook the toe of the boot to see if there were any more bills stuck inside and then they counted my money. Monique started to laugh too.

On the sidewalk I asked, Why did you do that?

It is the only way to get your own account. I had to do it too. Anyway, it's fun.

This way of thinking was new.

*

Rockhead's Paradise had the longest bar I had ever seen, with big chandeliers hanging from the ceiling that might have made it feel elegant except for the smells of stale cigarette smoke and spilled beer and the sweat of men and women. Uptown hotels were like Karachi, but this place belonged to the neighbourhood of Little Burgundy. It was at the corner of Montagne and Saint-Antoine, down by the railway station. I went because I heard Paul Bley was playing.

After the show I went up to him and asked, How do you get to play here?

He asked, You play?

Yes.

Let's hear.

So I sat down and played and I was used to clinking glasses and talking and I pumped it out. I had learned a few tricks like bending over the keyboard so my hair was falling forward and the skin on my back was revealed because Monique told me it looked very sexy. I was playing strong and I heard with relief the moment when the chatter dies down and the crowd is listening. Someone asked for "You Don't Know What Love Is" and I played it.

When I was finished, Paul Bley said, If you need bread you can get two gigs a night on this street. The Black Bottom bar is in a basement down the block. Across the road, there's Café St-Michel.

I'd read about Rockhead's, about all the greats who played

there, but I was twenty years out of date. The manager came out and asked Paul, Who's she?

I'm looking for work, I said.

He was a bulky, muscular man who could clear a room if he needed to. I felt like a paper doll beside him. I straightened my back and said, I play the Ritz.

He laughed and said, Well, la-di-dah, de Ritz. Anyway, I like your playing.

I felt something not quite safe in there, but I did not know what it was and I wanted to play. The neighbourhood around Rockhead's was tired. The bars along the street used to be classy, with jazz acts like Armstrong and Holiday. But that was a long time ago. I made good tips at Rockhead's. The men who went liked to watch a young woman in a sari with a bare midriff. I was exotic. I could not always understand the French of the girls who worked there but we were friendly with each other because we were all doing the same thing, earning money, serving men, matching ourselves to the night. I learned the dark rhythms of those places. Most men went there to drink and get some sex if they could. I was fair game and I had to learn to be aware of how men were watching. At the end of my first night, I picked up my tips and wrapped my coat around me and headed for the door but the bouncer grabbed my elbow. I jerked my arm away and banged his hand against the door jamb.

Doucement, I'm not doing anything, he said, rubbing his thumb. You're not walking home alone.

It's not far.

He stepped out the front door, whistled for a cab, said, Get in. *Écoute*.

And he paid the driver for me. I learned that the first hour I played was cab fare and when I complained about this Monique said, That's your overhead. You're a professional.

She thought it was funny and brave that I was working on Saint-Antoine. She said, Your French is getting better.

I said, My playing too. I can do an hour without repeating a song now.

When I got home, Monique was usually up with her actor friends. She'd call, Here's Mahsa, she knows every topless bar in Montreal, and I'd say, They're not topless, they're jazz bars. I didn't feel ashamed, I liked it. One dawn Monique was making crepes with gouda cheese and strawberry jam and everyone was talking about where they came from, what their parents did, Baie Comeau and the paper mills, the north end of Montreal and the rag trade, Sherbrooke and business.

What about you Mahsa. Where're you from?

Oh, you would not know Karachi, it is a port city.

That's near Afghanistan, *non*? What about your parents?

They died in a car accident. My father was a water engineer.

How could they understand? Everyone was a bit stoned or drunk. Afghanistan was the hippie trail. No one knew about East Pakistan or the people who would become the Mohajirs. They talked feminism and civil rights and Vietnam. Some had heard of Bhutto. Islam to them meant Muhammad Ali and Black Power and a clenched fist. They knew nothing of the tribes of my mother or honour or hospitality. I did not tell them my father was American. They sometimes talked about Quebecers and separatism and who was pure wool and who was not, as if they did not notice I was there. I did not think about being different most of the time because I did not care. These were my friends and we passed each other coffee and we talked and talked and they admired my music and I was making money playing and this was good enough for me. Always I had been different.

KATHERINE

Harold sent me a car and a U-Haul and his favourite roadie, soft-voiced Bill Carling. I loaded up my four mattresses and a kitchen table and five chairs and a box of crockery and four big boxes of our clothes and our television and record player. The heaviest box was the records. Jimmie was carrying his peashooter because Ma told him New York City was dangerous. Bill Carling did not grumble and he did not say, I'm not a moving man. He said, It's another gig, and that made me feel better and Baby Bea asked, Are we going on a gig? She and Jimmie were running back and forth helping like crazy, singing, *New York, New York* but Dexter was sullen. He did not want to leave his school where his favourite teacher told him he should be a lawyer. I told him we were going to be closer to Daddy and said he could study to be a lawyer in New York and asked didn't he like our great big red drop-top Cadillac?

Ma stopped by on the way home from work. She said to Dexter, You help your brother and sister, and to Jimmie, You behave, and to Bea, You stay nice. She did not say much to me but she handed me an envelope which I did not open. We chafed against each other and talked to each other every day and now I was going the hell away. I was getting free. I said, Bye, Ma, I'll bring the kids back in the summer to visit. Then I gave her a hug and said, I'm rooting for you.

I'm rooting for you too, Katie.

I was scared to death but it was too late now. We all climbed in and slid around on the white leather and I wondered how many rockabilly girl fans had put out to musicians in that backseat.

Wave goodbye to the steel mills, I said to the kids, as we headed for the Lewiston-Queenston Bridge, then through to Syracuse and into a Howard Johnson's with a red roof and a sign that said *28 Flavors*.

Bill said, Time to feed these kids, and I said, Bill, I packed lunch, I don't have money for restaurants, and he answered, Don't you worry, somebody left some money in this glovebox. I started to relax and feel like a celebrity driving around and having money to eat in restaurants, and I guess we were a bit of a picture, me with my black permed hair and my three brown-eyed kids and the old roadie. The kids ate hamburgers and I had my first fried clams, and then we all meditated a long time on the abundant flavours of ice cream and Dexter chose macaroon which Bill congratulated him on as adventurous, and Jimmie had frozen pudding and Bea took strawberry which the boys told her she could have at home but she said she wanted something she at least knew she liked.

As we stood watching them eat, Bill handed me a cigarette and lit it for me though I did not smoke and the last half of the trip, I was smoking Bill's cigarettes in the open car and we were singing and reading aloud the American signs and looking at American corner stores that sold liquor, passing through Mount Pocono and Stroudsburg and the Oranges and Jersey City and Hoboken and I was thinking, What am I doing? and How am I going to manage in New York City with three kids, am I crazy? I said to Bill, I've got a sick feeling in the pit of my stomach. What's New York like, anyway?

We stopped one more time and while the kids were in the bathroom Bill pulled out a joint and gave me some too. He said, Things go the way they are meant to. You'll be fine.

Next we were seeing the Empire State Building and the Woolworth Building and the Waldorf Astoria and I was feeling freer, lighter, happier than I had since Dexter was born. On the Brooklyn Bridge Bill asked, Where to, lady? How 'bout the Plaza? I hear there's good jazz there.

Bea shouted from the back, Eloise and Weenie!

Bill said, Well?

I said, I haven't got a clue.

About what?

About where next.

Bill paid a guy to watch the car and the U-Haul when he dropped us at the Y on Times Square and he said to me, The car's the only thing worth stealing.

I said, Can you stay with the kids in the morning while I go and find an apartment?

He shook his head and smiled the funny way he did when we were driving together and I knew he liked us. Lots of people liked me and my kids together, and I knew that he wanted to get back to Hamilton and I was taking advantage of his goodwill and whatever money Harold had paid him.

New York was a dump back then, bankrupt, prostitutes and sex parlours and peep-shows and porno theatres on Times Square. I said to the kids, Don't look. I wanted to live in the Village where the jazz clubs were and the rent was still cheap.

I found a two-bedroom in the building above the Surf Maid, across from the Village Vanguard. The neighbourhood was White Russian. I opened my wallet to count out first and last, and I took out the little scrap of paper from the nurse in Hamilton I had kept all those years. I dropped it down a New York drain. Wasn't going to need that anymore. We had enough money to keep us for three months.

The apartment was small and needed paint and a lot more, but I went back to the Y and got Bill and the U-Haul and the kids and we pushed open the door and I felt the kids' eyes searching the high-ceilinged, run-down place, asking themselves, Home? It was dingy and dirty but at least now I had a key that fit a lock in New York. Rent-controlled. Well, it was no worse here than in Hamilton. Part of me wanted to sit in the corner and cry but I had a long way to go before I could do that so I said, *Verrrrry eenteresting*, from Rowan and Martin's *Laugh-In*, which was a show Dexter liked.

I felt him hesitate, and I was crossing my fingers because the other two always followed him, and inside I was saying, C'mon, c'mon. Then finally he said, You bet your sweet bippy.

Jimmie said, Look that up in your Funk and Wagnalls.

To make the boys laugh, Bea said, One ringy-dingy, two ringy-dingies. Hello and a most gracious afternoon! We don't have to be fair, we're the phone company!

Bill laughed at them, said, Wish I could stay and help.

I said, Me too, this faucet needs a plumber, but he didn't know the song. Before you go, Bill, you gotta sit at our kitchen table with us.

So Bill sat on the fifth chair and I ran down to the deli that was run by a morose and kindly Russian named Igor, and I told him I'd see him often and I found out he liked jazz and he said, Welcome to the neighbourhood.

I took Ma's envelope out of my purse and opened it. She had put in a hundred dollars in American bills, without a note. It was a lot of money, enough for a couple of extra months, and I stuffed it back in. Igor watched with interest. I bought my first jar of New York Maxwell House instant coffee and my first carton of Farmland Dairies New York milk and I was happy to come home to my own apartment and I gave the kids Cocoa Puffs for their first New York dinner at our kitchen table, the best place to be a family around.

The second day, I signed up the kids at Public School

No. 41, at 116 West 11th, two streets over, and we practised walking back and forth until they knew the way. I gave them each a few dollars of Ma's American money. It was the first time Bea ever had her own and they examined the pictures of the American presidents and I said, They're not coloured like ours. You watch whether you've got a one or a twenty, and everyone found this interesting and we stopped at shops along the way to buy things and I introduced them to Igor and we talked to other shop and deli owners and I memorized names. We read a sign behind one cash: *Send a salami to your boy in the army.* I said to the kids, That's a New York rhyme. There were jokes about snow and I was trying to make a neighbourhood so we would not be alone.

On the third night after scrubbing that apartment top to bottom with new blue Ajax, trying to plug up cockroach holes, hanging some batik on the walls, making dinner and reading to Baby Bea, I said to Dexter, I have to find work. I'm going to be downstairs in the Surf Maid and I'm counting on you to take care of things here. You lock the doors and don't let anyone in.

Even Daddy?

Well he won't show up tonight. He doesn't know where we are yet. I'll tell him tomorrow.

Then I went downstairs to see Art Blakey's Jazz Messengers. My hands were all red from the scrubbing. Damn. No one was playing piano and I walked right up on stage and joined in. I did not need my bandino hat anymore.

I was plenty old at thirty. Blakey said, What do you think you're doing?

Well, I came to hear piano and there was no one playing so I thought I had better play some myself. I'm doing a recording with Marian McPartland's new record company.

I knew my chords. Art was known for hiring good musicians but he had never hired a woman.

We're here for ten nights, he said. I can't pay you because you're not in our contract. But I'll give you the tips.

A start. I was a jazzman. Not a single mother. Not a half-Chinese girl from Hamilton.

I asked one of the musicians on the side why they called him Bu, and the guy laughed, said, That's Buhaina, his Moslem name. All the cats knows that.

Marian McPartland was playing the Carlyle Hotel. I went and talked to her and she said she could not do anything right away but to come over and see her studio on 65th Street with the two gold Steinways.

Why did you bolt them together?

She said, I didn't, they came that way. Want to hear Halcyon's first recording?

It was Marian of course, with "Ambiance" and "Twilight World." After we listened she asked, Have you been up to the Cookery? Mary Lou Williams is playing.

Things were tight. I found thrown-out vegetables after the markets closed and made ratatouille. I stirred up tubs of polenta. I flavoured day-old bread with cinnamon. I told the kids that the favourite treat of a king is popcorn. I cobbled and juggled. I taught Dexter how to warm up spaghetti and Jimmie to make lunches and sweep. They did the laundry together at the launderette down the street on Saturday mornings and then they had a treat-lunch at the Hungarian, twenty-five-cent bowls of soup and Polish bread. Sometimes the owner, Tamás, felt flush and put a couple of schnitzels on their table too. I went to the Vanguard and dreamed about recording in that beautiful wood-lined triangular space. I went to the Columbia offices and tried to meet a record producer but the secretary said, Jazz? Why don't you leave your demo? I did not have a demo. In the evenings the kids sat around the kitchen table, did homework together, like I used to do with Ma, and they read to each other from their favourite *Book of Odd Events*.

What is the chance of getting injured from a falling frog? asked Jimmie.

None, said logical Dexter.

Wrong! said Jimmie with the authority of the printed word. This book says it is five percent.

They laughed because for-five-percent-sure somewhere frogs were falling from the sky injuring someone. Bea liked the picture of the man pulling a fire truck with his teeth. She tied a leash to a chair (she was always asking for a puppy) and tried to pull her brothers with her teeth. Every week they switched chores except Bea was still not allowed to use the stove though she did when she thought no one was looking.

Sundays we went to Central Park no matter the weather. Dexter wanted to know where the ducks went in the winter. I said they went south like Hamilton ducks. But King Jimmie said in his newly acquired New York accent, Don't worry, they go inna duck barn at the zoo. Ducks get treated pretty good in this town.

Getting enough money to keep us in food and clothes exhausted me. I couldn't get out as much as I needed to and there were nights when I felt like breaking all our dishes I was so frustrated. Those nights I'd get them to bed and lay out my staff paper and start writing again. I found a regular sitter for Sunday nights to have a night out myself and I always went to Paul Pines's Tin Palace on Bowery where I also wanted to play. I listened to Henry Threadgill and James Blood Ulmar, and sometimes I went across the street to the jams at Francis Hines's loft. Paul Pines lived in a tarpaper shack on top of a building on Second Avenue. He took me to see it and I looked inside, said, You are even poorer than I am.

I asked, Do you know anyone at the Vanguard?

Of course he did.

I want to record there.

MAHSA

The darkness of this northern place was lit on warm days with falling snow and on bitter days with rising columns of white exhaust that froze in the air. There were coloured lights wrapped around posts and buildings. I felt lonely watching the other students going home at Christmas after their first term away. Everywhere were decorations, red Santas and deer who pulled an imaginary sleigh. One with a bright red nose was beloved by the children. What a strange and frightening idea, a big fat man climbing into your house through the long, dirty chimney, but here the children liked it. People carried full, live trees into their houses. This I had read about with the nuns when we studied British writers. One evening after work Monique and I bought the tiniest tree we could find and we took it back to my room and leaned it against a wall and she pulled shining silver streamers she called tinsel from her pocket and decorated it and said, *Voila!* Your first Christmas tree! She gave me a red hat to wear and said, See if you can find a sari to match it when you play. People drink a lot at Christmas. You'll make lots of tips. Do you know any carols?

The shopping places and the churches were visited more than usual and people were having parties with cheeses and toasts and many sweets, like holidays everywhere.

I felt foreign and I remembered Abbu and the Beach Luxury at Christmas, and the music he taught me about kings and babies. I had especially liked one about a poor boy who was a drummer. I thought too of Mor and Eid in her village, holding her mother's hand and watching the blood of the dying goat on the ground and the new clothes she bought for me on the holiday. When she wanted to know why they made the sacrifice in front of everyone in the middle of the village, her mother squeezed her hand hard and said, Sh!

But why here?

Her mother whispered in Pashto, Be quiet! Your great-grandfather slew his newborn daughter on this spot because he did not want a female heir. This is why all ritual slaughter in the village is here.

I bought my bus ticket to New York City so I too had somewhere to go and because I had always wanted to hear American jazz.

I walked from Times Square to the Village Gate on Bleecker Street. Everyone performed there, Earl Hines and Nina Simone and Bill Evans. The place was empty but I went upstairs anyway. A man with a beard and glasses was talking to some people who were pushing tables around. He said, We're closed.

Are you Art D'Lugoff?

The same.

Could I play here?

He took a better look at me, my backpack. He gestured to the piano and I sat down, breathed, played. I started to pump it out. I had to get Art's attention.

How long you in town for?

A couple of weeks.

Got an agent?

I shrugged.

That was how I got my first gig in New York. He let me play warm-up for Larry Coryell for three nights. Later he told me he tried me because I surprised him. A lot of things happened in those days because of chance. People gave each other breaks. The atmosphere was very free. Everyone was playing each other's music and I did too. Abbu used to say, Porcupine, the best musicians always steal from people who play better.

I had asked him, Did you write "Kansas City"?

He said, I don't write. I got that song from Little Willie Littlefield. You could play it. That would be great, wouldn't it? A half-Afghan, half-American Karachi girl who likes jazz and *pahada* playing "Kansas City" like she owns it. Isn't that a world to live in, Porcupine? You play it.

*

The first set at the Gate I wore my sari like I did at Rockhead's but it felt wrong. Everyone was talking and clinking their glasses and I don't think one single person listened and I couldn't get their attention. Art came by at the end and said, Fantastic! Some lies are like ointment, meant for healing. I guess he'd seen lots of people bomb. I had to make myself stay. I went into the bathroom and changed into my jeans, listened to Coryell, and later I went downstairs to hear Art Blakey's Jazz Messengers.

That was the night I met Katherine.

She wore a black hat and she had huge hands like a man and she was tall. When she sat at the piano she looked like a question mark. She had a thing with the drums and perfect rhythm, and listening to her playing with the Messengers gave me ideas. I needed to stop hiding behind my gimmicky girl-from-Pakistan routine. I went up to her when the band took a break and I told her I liked her playing and that I was playing upstairs for a couple of nights.

I said, I heard a recording of you playing in the Mo Billson band.

Her serious eyes studied mine, absorbing. She said, Your eyes are grey.

I nodded.

She asked, How'd you get to play upstairs?

I asked Art if I could.

A tall man carrying a sax case came up to her and she said to me, See you, and left the club with him. I went back to my room at the Y alone and felt the city humming outside and I made up a new set list. Coryell's audience liked technical and complicated. I decided to play Mingus. Bud Powell. I lay in bed and wished I could fall into a dark crack. What if I was a zero in New York? What was I good for? Saint-Antoine joints. This was why men slouched around Times Square. They were so lonely they could die.

The next night I went back to the Gate and wore jeans and a coral camisole and my hair loose like Katherine and hoop earrings like hers that I bought on the street. I ramped it up and the chatter dropped away and people listened. Magic.

Art said, You got them tonight.

Sunday night I saw Katherine listening from the doorway. Near the end of my set, I stood up and said to the crowd, Can you believe it? Katherine Goodnow is here. Come up and play.

Everyone stopped talking and looked around, afraid to miss someone famous though they didn't know who she was. Katherine was a real performer. She blinked the surprise out of her eyes and she walked right up like a star. I slid over and she sat down on the bench beside me and I played "Autumn Leaves" and she spread her large hands over the keys and started to riff, and we were listening to each other like crazy and we played some Brubeck and we started cutting a little, showing off. We were bumping elbows, we needed two pianos, and the audience was into us.

Art said, They dug you two. Want to play next week?

Of course we did.

Katherine said to me, You got time for coffee?

I had time for everything. My bed in the Y was the last place I wanted to be.

The stars were faraway New York glitter that night, eighty-eight constellations, eighty-eight piano keys. We walked to the Surf Maid and listened for a while, and then she said, Let's go to my place. I got kids. Come upstairs.

Her apartment was all kitchen table. She threw her hat into the sink, slipped into the children's bedroom, came out, asked, Where're you from?

She made instant coffee with hot water from the tap and we talked about music and Hamilton and Montreal. It was her first few months in New York. She said, I play anywhere they pay me. Where did you hear Mo Billson's band?

At the library at McGill. You were playing with a sax. It was great.

I haven't thought about that for years.

I never heard the piece before. What's it called?

I wrote it. It's called "Tell a Woman-Lie." The sax is the father of my kids.

I told her I had a lover in Karachi. She said, Well, lovers aren't always around.

She put on Coltrane's "Crescent," very low, which I had never heard, and that was the night that I knew how I wanted to live. With musicians. I would write songs. I would stay up all night with strangers and listen to music and earn a living in music and I would be part of the unfurling beauty of the world. I looked through the window at the streaky black-blue of the Village and the flashing neon outside, my hands cupped around a stained mug full of instant coffee. It was three in the morning and Katherine said, I gotta get some sleep. You can stay here if you don't want to walk back to the Y.

She showed me her double bed behind a curtain in the living room. She said, Do you want a T-shirt to sleep in? and handed me one from a laundry basket in the corner of the room.

She said, Sometimes in the winter and sometimes in the fall, I slip between the sheets with nothing on at all.

I reached for the shirt and she said, My ma used to say that when I was putting on my pyjamas.

I brushed my teeth with my finger while she looked in again on her sleeping children and then got into bed beside me. She rolled over and said, We should play together again. Her breath lengthened and she was gone. That was how Katherine fell asleep. Like a penny in a fountain.

Those cold New York Christmas weeks. I wandered around the Village. I wandered uptown. I walked in Central Park. I went out every night to listen to music. Katherine asked, You got anywhere to go for Christmas? and invited me to join them. I bought a game called Monopoly because a store clerk told me children here liked it and I bought oranges and chocolate because there were pictures of these things in a Christmas basket in the subway, and when I arrived Katherine had decorated a tiny tree in their apartment and Jimmie knocked it over but it was small and I took down a picture and tied it to the nail. I helped her make dinner, a turkey with bread and butter and celery and an apple inside. Katherine said, This bird cost me a fortune, thank goodness you brought dessert. T came in and he filled the rooms and his children were happy he was there and they tussled about who was sitting next to him. He went to Katherine and stood behind her and put his arms around her and said, Merry Christmas, babe, and it reminded me of how Mor and Abbu sometimes were all alone in a room in which they were not alone at all. I watched the children watching and I knew their feeling too, and I said to them, Give me your hands, I will teach you a Karachi love dance, and we made a ring around Katherine and T and ran around them while I sang the Beatles song, *Love, love, love* and after dinner we played Monopoly and at the end of the evening everyone said it was lucky that I came for their first New York Christmas and I said I was lucky to be with them for my first Christmas ever. The next day, I got Art to give Katherine and me a gig for February. I asked him, Two pianos?

I can't get another piano up there.

I'll bring something.

Suit yourself.

Katherine said, Great. I need to get work as a sideman and make some money. I need to get Bea new ballet slippers, she's out of hers. How much is Art paying? You can stay here if you don't mind the floor.

She was doing it all.

Back in Montreal, Jean heard the new licks I'd learned from Katherine. He winked, said, Been playing Little Burgundy?

His hair was longer and he tied it back now at the bottom of his neck. He said, I've got a gig for us to play the Esquire Club on Monday nights.

I said, I can do that. I played the Village Gate in New York, and I have another gig there next month.

That stopped his ironic winking. He said, Come for coffee, I want to hear all about it.

I acquired one of the first Minimoog Ds because it was portable and I liked Sun Ra. Monique and I had parties, made cheap soups and saffron vegetable biryani. Jean always arrived with his double bass and stayed to the end and smoked and drank a lot and wanted me to play with him which was fine with me. One night an actor tried to stay. He said to me, I think I am falling in love. I said, You're drunk. Help me clean up.

I gave him a broom. I was picking up all the dishes and empty bottles and the place smelled of spilled beer and smoke and Jean was sitting in the kitchen with tea trying to stay awake. I told him to go home too, but he said, I'm not leaving you alone with that guy. By the time I finished the dishes the actor had wandered down the hall and passed out in my bed and I looked at him and thought, I can't move him, so I went back to sleep on the couch but Jean was sleeping there. I put a coat over him and he stirred and took my hand and said, Mahsa, come here. I said, Go back to sleep. You're my teacher. I figured he would not remember in the morning. He slept with a lot of students, but I was the one he played regular gigs with. Young men were drawn to me here and this was a novelty. Everyone was experimenting with each other and there was no one to stop me and it felt good to be desired. When boys flirted with me, I always thought about Kamal. I wished I could go to Karachi, stay for an hour or so, then come back. Monique was working at the Centaur Theatre. *Creeps* had opened and she was writing her own play called *Simone et Jean-Paul* for the Rideau Vert. It began with Simone de Beauvoir earning a second in her philosophy *agrégation* exam because the committee downstage secretly decided to give first prize to Sartre. They said a man needed it more for his career. Simone walked toward the audience and stage-whispered: Man is condemned to freedom and woman is condemned to be second. Marriage is a worn-out patriarchal oppression, a three-legged race.

I did not see any subtlety in Monique's writing but she said that it was not the time for subtlety. The women in the audience laughed and stomped. Monique said, Do the music for my next play, so I began to design stage music. I learned what the synthesizer could do and played and recited Arabic poetry at home for our parties while everyone smoked dope. Jean jumped up, said, Now I understand Persian, and danced with someone's scarf. He got a recording gig for us with Metamusic. He played double bass and produced. It was my first recording since Abbu's little 45. We started with me reciting from Ulayya bint al-Mahdi, whose brother forbade her to say the names of her slave-lovers in her songs.

وردّدْت الصبابةَ في فؤادي   كتمتُ اسم الحبيب عن العبارِ
لَعَلِّى باسم من أهوى أنادي   فوا شوقي إلى نادٍ خَلِيٍّ

I held back the name of my love, repeating it to myself.
I long for an empty space to call out the name of my love.

We ordered one hundred cassette tapes, gave them to friends, left them at record stores, sent them to radio stations. I mailed one to Katherine. She mailed back a new set list for the summer and said she was juggling too much, that I should recite poetry in New York too, signed off, *Peace, baby*. I played once a month with Katherine at the Village Gate and I slept on her floor. Jimmie started getting sent home from school and once she smashed a cup in the sink and sat down and cried at the kitchen table. I looked at her kids and they looked at me and finally Katherine said, Jimmie, what the hell are we going to do? He was too worried to say anything and then

Katherine popped her head up as if nothing had happened and said, Let's teach Mahsa to skate!

So we went to Central Park and rented ice skates at the Wollman Rink and I tried skating for the first time. Dexter and Bea held me up while I shuffled on those absurd little blades. I liked sledding better. Jimmie was sullen and sat on a bench. Katherine said, I don't know what gets into him. Ever since the move. I guess he thought T might live with us. I got to keep him out of bad stuff.

I let Jimmie play on my Minimoog and we jammed. He had a great sense of rhythm, like Katherine. I cut my hair myself and I got Jimmie to hold the mirror. I cut it like Mick Jagger but I left it long enough that I could wear it up when I wore my sari. Now I had two looks. Downstairs there had been a benefit for Timothy Leary and everyone came to the Village Gate and I was happy to be playing there. I loved those New York weekends and arriving at the Port Authority Bus Terminal and my first smell of bagel and exhaust. Katherine said, I'm going to get us a recording gig for two pianos. I'll send you the charts.

KATHERINE

Jimmie asked, Are there snake charmers?

Dexter kicked him, said, That's India.

Mahsa laughed, said, I have seen snake charmers on the beach at home. They keep them in big baskets.

I was coming in after playing the ballet classes and Dexter was helping Mahsa cook, rice and chicken with coriander that she grew at home and brought in her backpack.

Are they poisonous?

They're cobras, dummy.

Do they really hypnotize them?

Mahsa said, My uncle told me they sew the mouth almost shut to let only the tongue dart out. The venom comes from the jaws. People think they are dangerous but they are not.

Bea said, Sew their mouths?

Yes, it is very cruel.

We all felt satisfied with this behind-the-scenes information. I loved those years with Mahsa when she stayed with us on the weekends. Growing up, the kids on my street were boys and I had always played with men in bands. Then Mahsa came along and she had talent and liked my kids and she helped. She admired me. I could be myself with her. I never had a best friend that wasn't T until I found Mahsa.

We went with the kids to see George Harrison and Ravi Shankar at the Bangladesh concert in Madison Square Garden. When I took the kids home to Hamilton for a week Mahsa sat in for me with a trio. Don't you steal my gig, I said and she laughed. She studied on the kitchen table and I was curious about her books and she showed me what she was doing, music history and harmony and composition and I wished I had studied more too but she said, You could be teaching this, to make me feel good.

When the kids were asleep, we sat around and talked late at night.

Why didn't you stay with T?

It didn't work, with him on the road and me home. Once I threw his clothes out the window in a paper bag. He was mad as hell.

Do you miss him?

I see him enough. He's still the kids' father and I'm still in love with him. We're like loons that separate in the winter but come back every year to the same nesting lake. If the partner shows up, they get back together again. That's T 'n me, we travel alone. What about you?

I fell in love in Karachi but I was too young and I wanted to be free. What is a loon?

I loved those days and nights with Mahsa. She cooked. In every way.

But I wanted a recording gig. That was why I moved here. I was a pain. I kept leaving messages for Marian, acting like a kid. Can I play yet, can I play yet? Then one day she said, Listen, I have four musicians, Mary Osborne and Vi Redd and Lynn Milano and Dottie Dodgion. I've got the two gold pianos. Come to our rehearsal tomorrow and if it works, we record next week.

I placed the receiver back in the cradle and saw its plastic shine and the black numbers on white discs. I looked up and the room was brighter. I heard sirens down the avenue. Someone was hurt or dying inside one of those ambulances and I was getting a break. I was going to play with Mary Osborne, that gifted guitarist who moved to Bakersfield where her husband worked. I was going to play with saxophonist Vi Redd, who'd done ten weeks at Ronnie Scott's in London but hadn't played in public for a decade. I was going to play with Dottie Dodgion, legendary drummer. Jimmie's forgotten homework was scattered on the floor and he would be all right, and Bea needed a new leotard and I'd find a way to pay for one because I was getting a break. There was a package of pasta and half a box of cereal in the cupboards and four bananas and three apples and a bag of potatoes and onions but it was going to work out. I was getting a break. I looked out the window and New York was the best place in the world to be, right here, right now. My first recording. My turn. Dirty dishes. City-streak grime on the windows. Me too excited to breathe, and who could I tell?

T was in town, of course. Everyone was playing New York. He played the Studio Rivbea. I was jealous of that. He played Stanley's at 12th Street and the Annex. He was part of the loft scene and they were playing all night and smoking and shooting up and the music was very, very free. I heard lots about him. He was pushing it out and ESP records offered him a contract. There was another baby somewhere. One night I was playing the Surf Maid for a band whose pianist was in prison and I looked up and saw T standing shadowed in the doorway. I felt that same old flip inside and I thought, Damn!

I finished my set but when I looked out again he was gone. Sunday night he was at the Tin Palace. I listened and I saw him after and I said, Let's figure this out. The kids miss you.

He said, Figure out what?

So I stopped talking about what he was not going to talk about and took him home. I took him to bed and we made love. I missed him and I missed sex. We smoked cigarettes and fell asleep and an hour later at dawn the kids sensed him and woke up, jumped on him, Daddy's here! and everyone was laughing. They didn't want to go to school that day but he said, Ya gotta go, I'll walk with you and meet you after, and Jimmie stayed in school that day, and T came home to me and that felt right too.

We made love and slept and woke up in each other's

arms all morning. I loved the salt-and-smoke smell of him, the feel of his skin on mine, saw my burnish against his blue, thought, What the hell does it matter? And then I was thinking about our matter-of-fact Baby Bea at school. I told T that she spent too much time alone, and when I asked why she said, Jimmie and Dexter are lighter than I am, it's easier for them to get friends. My children often surprised me, but not so often sad-surprised me like that. It felt good to share it all with T.

I played hooky from whatever the hell I was supposed to be doing. I told him that I felt like the world was lost when he wasn't there, which was true in that moment but not in others, and he said, My world's here, babe, with you, which was also part-time true.

He went out and brought food home from a deli and he was not high when he got back. I thought, This is how it could be if I didn't have to do every damn thing myself.

I said, I saw you in the doorway at the Surf Maid.

He laughed and said, Babe, you never did miss a thing. He lit a cigarette and with one eyebrow cocked up high the way he knew made me laugh, said, A woman plays better when she's gettin' some. I was checking in to see how bad you needed me.

Well, from what I hear you're getting a lot.

He laughed again. Sometimes I play about what I don't got and want. It's always about you.

I've made love with T ten thousand times. That day was

one of the special times. I said, You're not one of those guys who rolls over and falls asleep.

He put his big hand on my thigh and I loved his eyes and he said, Babe, we never were like other people.

I said to him, Jimmie needs you. Stay for a while. I've got my first recording gig. The kids need you around.

But he left again the next night. There was a big hole in our crowded apartment and the kids missed him like crazy but I told them, Daddy's on the road. He'll come back, don't you worry. I told myself that our love was one-of-a-kind because it was. I had to think about my next dollar, my next gig, keeping the kids going. I had songs I was writing. I had unsayable things to say. Play. Tell the truth. Keep going.

T 'n me are room No. 9 and I like how I feel with him. I don't care if it is obsessive. When I get so old that I start forgetting, I want my love for him to be the last thing I remember, my sweet, good, complicated beginning and end.

So, I held on to that day in bed with T and I let him go. His love was somewhere out there for me. He could not stay and I was not going to be in his way and that was fine. Most of the time.

Only Mary Osborne looked funky, in wide pants with enormous pink roses on them. The others dressed in tailored slacks and flats. I walked right by them when they were standing outside the recording studio on the sidewalk. They wore their hair short and tidy and could have been any middle-aged housewives in town up for an afternoon of shopping.

Marian handed out our charts and I was aware of my wild permed hair and my black jeans and the white cotton shirt I wore everywhere because it worked for the clubs with big earrings but was suitable enough for my day jobs if I tied back my hair and took off the earrings. I never had time to go home and change. These women did nothing to make themselves look like personalities. But when they put lips to reeds and mouthpieces, fingers to strings, hands to drumsticks, they were some of the best musicians of their generation. I closed my eyes, and listened, and concentrated to keep up. I was feeling Dottie's drums pulling me into her groove and at the break I said, That was great. You had me in a sweat out there.

She laughed, said, I played so hard I'll have mops for hands.

I loved the feel of Dottie, smallish and round and cool on those drums behind me and that language coming out of her calm middle-aged-lady face. She said, It isn't how much power you have. It's where you put it.

They knew what it was to play punishing four, five hours every night in a different place on their tours, and it made them good and they knew it. They'd done a lot of it during the war. But things changed for them after V-day. The club owners did not apologize when the men came in and threw their music all over the floor and sat down in their chairs.

The club owners said, Shucks, ladies, the house band came back today. I told them they'd have a job when they got home.

We don't get notice?

I can't. The men wanna play.

What about our money?

Ah, c'mon, *you* understand. The boys are back from *war*.

There was resistance to them everywhere. People were trying to recover from the shock of terrible things. The women pitched in on that too, helped rebuild and move on. Maybe they should have stood their ground, but I knew why it happened.

Mary asked me, Where have you toured?

Only in Ontario. I loved it but I was pregnant and I had to stop.

They all laughed as if that were the funniest joke any woman in all time had ever told.

Marian went out to get us some food and one of them said, She still seeing Morello?

Nah. Now she's not with either of them. But she still sees a lot of Jimmy and she still talks with Joe on the phone for hours.

They looked at me and Dottie said, Marian's been in love with two men for a decade. Then she goes and divorces her husband and breaks off from her lover. How's that for love?

I said, Sounds like a song.

Everyone laughed. They were tight and professional and

I learned a lot during those sessions, following the groove, taking my turn when it came.

They went out for drinks before heading back to their homes in Rochester and California and Ohio. I replayed that recording session over and over in my head and practised their licks and thought about their stories of sidemen and husbands and lovers. I had asked at the table, What's the most important thing?

Marian said, Fanatical, unreasoning desire.

I said, I meant to get a gig.

She laughed and said, Oh well, being around. Knowing people. And once you get a gig, never miss it unless you're dead. The only time I ever missed one was for a man.

Dottie said, Morello.

No one was supposed to say her lover's name. Marian got annoyed and said, When I was with him I played freer, looser, more myself. I'm glad I broke the rule.

She turned to me and said with mock sternness, Never fall in love with two men. But if you do, you won't have been able to help it.

I wondered if Marian would bankroll a recording for me. I was ready. Here was this studio with two pianos waiting for Mahsa and me. Walking home I was thinking about those women who played so well and gossiped and got jealous and resisted what resisted them. Those women could really swing. And they had let me in.

I passed a market and someone had thrown out two quarts of bruised tomatoes and I picked them up. A cheese vendor closing down for the day called out, What you doin'?

I'm getting tomatoes for my kids' dinner. You know what, I just made my first recording.

What you play?

Piano.

Well good for you. Then he asked, What you cookin'?

Spaghetti bolognese.

Wait a minute.

He reached down and then he tossed a package to me and said, For your kids. You might need some parmesan.

A perfect day.

MAHSA

Crystal snowmelt flooded down the streets like a liquid chandelier, and I skipped class and walked up to the cross to look over the watery city, everything smelling of mist and earth. I had been away from Karachi for nearly two years and it was my second spring melt. I was planning to move to Katherine's in the Village for the summer, she had lots of gigs lined up. Jean offered me my first tutoring job. He said, I want you to teach here. Finish your degree and study some more. See if you can swing it.

We had regular gigs at the Esquire and we always played at home. Jean liked to smoke before we played, said he heard the low tones better when he did and he often asked me to go home with him but I always joked, You're still my teacher, and I have someone else.

He took my hand and said, I won't be your teacher forever. Dump the other guy.

Monique's boyfriend moved in with us and I asked her, Do you want me to move out?

166

She said, *Non, pas du tout*. I'd rather live with you. This way I get both.

I liked the strangeness of wild animals that were free among us in Montreal, squirrels and raccoons and on the mountain little otters and sometimes mink and once a deer that stopped traffic on the road. At home, no animal was free, but captured and used. Uncle had written that Aunt missed me and to come back to Karachi for July, I surely needed a break from my studies, and he enclosed my ticket.

Why not? I thought. For three weeks. I wanted to smell Karachi again, to walk on Seaview, to see the moonflowers under my old bedroom window. I was thinking about Kamal. I wrote to tell Katherine I was going, that I'd come to New York in August as soon as I got back. I found my old shalwar kameez in the bottom of my suitcase and bought presents for Aunt and Uncle and a small scarf for Minoo and I closed my suitcase all ready to go home. I kept thinking about seeing Kamal.

Katherine telephoned.

Mahsa, I've already got gigs in July for us. I've arranged for an album recording for us at Marian's. Two pianos. That's hard to get.

I know. But Katherine, I haven't been home for two years. Can't we do it in August?

Mahsa, you agreed. It is almost impossible to get two pianos recorded. I will have to do it alone. Don't you get that?

Uncle will be angry if I don't come. It is only for a few weeks. I can come straight to New York when I get back.

I was heedless. Katherine said, You're on the brink. Don't blow it.

But I said, You can get them to reschedule it to August.

I thought I had all the time in the world.

It began delicately. Sleeping in. Meals served. The unspoken luxury of life with servants. Aunt said she'd heard Kamal's father had sent him to work in Afghanistan. I wrote and did not hear back and I wondered if he was angry that I had written so little. The hottest time of the year was coming and my old school friends were married or abroad and I was annoyed that I had given in and come back. Martial law had been lifted in April and the Simla Agreement was coming. The streets were full of protests. Aunt seemed dwarfed to me, her heavy perfumes suffocating, and she would not look me in the eye.

On the third day, Uncle called me into the sitting room and I saw Aunt there too. No. Please no.

Uncle said, We are worried about you far away and alone. We think it is time to marry and we have found someone we think will please you. He is the son of my oldest friend.

My apartment with Monique. Rockhead's. My studies. The Surf Maid. The Greyhound bus. The mountain.

Aunt said, His father is expanding his business to Montreal. You will be able to continue your studies.

I do not want to marry.

Mahsa, we are only suggesting. Your uncles visited again. They think it dishonourable you alone in the West. Honour is like milk, which the lightest dust dirties. We are only your guardians. They have spoken of taking you back to the Helmand with them.

If I was in danger why did you bring me back? I will go back to Montreal tomorrow.

Mahsa, remember the angels, Yameen and Yasaar, who write down everything your right and left hand do? Things are known, Mahsa.

What things? My bank account? Little Burgundy? Kamal? What? What? *Shame on the two angels … It is better to live in hardship than end up as a whipping girl.*

Aunt said, Your mother would have wanted this.

I said, Mor married for love. She did what she wanted.

Uncle looked at me as if at a stranger. He got up heavily to leave and said, Know the mother, know the daughter. You have not asked one question about the young man.

I ran back to my room to get my passport, but Minoo had removed it while we talked.

The weeks that followed. Weeping. Wailing. Silence. Uncle's rage. Aunt's visits to my room and sighing and shouting and stomping out again. We were a bad Bollywood film. I had taken more freedoms than Uncle could have imagined.

Who do you think you are? he said and threatened to lock me up forever.

Mor always said about meeting Abbu, The first time our eyes met I felt strength and tenderness and love.

Why had I come back? How had I forgotten so quickly?

In the hottest days of July, Aunt had a heart attack and I still think it was angina. Uncle said to me at her hospital bed, You are stealing your aunt's life. You are humiliating me before my friends. We took you in.

Always I was to be a shamed orphan. I imagined Monique with her feet up on the balcony, smoking, talking to me. I imagined her saying, *Câlisse!* You pay your own bills. You get jobs in New York!

Uncle put a lock on the outside of my bedroom door and when I heard it click at night I felt a despair I had not felt since the servant's closet after Mor and Abbu were shot. His face was smooth marble. How long was he capable of keeping me?

The day after Aunt was released from hospital, Ali's family was invited. What a touching first meeting, the sick aunty-guardian cared for by her devoted orphan-niece. Aunt welcomed her guests from the divan while Minoo cooked and made tea and I served the traditional sweets, peeking to see what Ali looked like, complying, screaming inside, What am I doing? For a passport?

Ali was twenty-two years older than I was but vigorous and handsome, still young enough at forty-four. He was not some fat third cousin and he played squash and his skin was firm and his hair thinning a little at the crown. He was a British-trained lawyer. Now his parents wanted him to marry and to start another branch of TradeWorld in Canada. I looked at him, thought, You are my way back.

Was Katherine in Central Park with her children? Was Jean St. John madly playing the outdoor festivals? Had the mountain been littered with lovers after Saint-Jean-Baptiste Day? Who was Monique bringing home to our apartment? What play was she directing? Where was Katherine playing? What was I doing here? How could I get away?

Ali took me to his parents' club, the Muslim Gymkhana, a place I had never been. We sat across from each other at a small table and he asked, What do you do for fun in Montreal?

I thought, I play the bars on Saint-Antoine and take the bus to New York and fend off drunks in piano lounges.

I answered, Go for walks.

He said, Don't worry. I've been living in London for years. I know life is different there.

He was impatient as if talking to himself, and he said, I wanted to return to England. But the family wants Montreal, so I'm stuck with it. Then he looked up again, Is Canada all right? I heard quite boring.

He did not want this marriage either. He had been happy living abroad too. Was there a chance of anything? Why had he not married earlier? He said, Mahsa, my family says you are good with languages and that you have easily adapted and that you will be useful with our clients. I like you very much. Do you think we can find something together?

This measuring and questioning felt strange to me. Had I become Westernized? Kamal had loved me. Jean St. John reached for my hand with passion. I wanted to get out. I said, Yes, I think we can.

Mahsa, there is something I must tell you. We must begin our life together in honesty. I have had a girlfriend in London, a British woman. Neither of our families approve. They don't want her with me. My father threatened to cut me off. There has been a lot of tumult and I'm done with all of it.

He reached over, touched my elbow, our first touch, and he asked, Can you forgive me? We will find love together.

He did not ask me if I had a *past*.

I thought, I will make this work to get back to Montreal. I felt even a little softness toward him.

Ali must have taken my silence as acceptance because he withdrew his hand and called to sign the bill.

On our second date, Ali told me about a legal case in the north that he had returned from investigating for a magistrate who was a distant relative. Two brothers had stolen money from a cousin. One of their wives was accused of the theft, splashed with gasoline and set ablaze.

What do you mean, accused? I asked.

The family needed a scapegoat. She took the blame and they walked free.

But did you report it to the magistrate?

He was paid off, said Ali and shrugged. I was sent for appearances.

I would never forget that shrug.

At home Aunt told me that Ali's mother has visited to ask about my experience abroad. Aunt said, I told her you are good. Conceal your faults.

Tell her what you like, I said. I'm going back.

The tiresome three days of our wedding began two weeks later. The families wanted to do it before Ramadan in October, but I insisted on marrying immediately so I could go back to school. It was the single concession I won. The weather was unbearably hot. I shopped with my new sisters-in-law who were both married. We drank tea. Spoke of the latest Indian movies.

Why is your uncle letting you return before Ali?

School is starting, and it is taking some time for him to organize the business.

Now that you're married you won't have to go to school.

But I want to. I am teaching this fall.

Well, you won't have time for that once the babies arrive.

Babies?

They laughed and asked, Will you send us some jeans?

Monique sent a postcard of Montreal at night with the cross lit up at the top of the mountain. It looked exotic here. She wrote, *Félicitations!* Really? Jean-Claude moved out after you left. There's an empty apartment upstairs—I can take that one!

Uncle read it and said, Are you not living with her family?

I lied, said, She must be thinking of an apartment in the same building for Ali and me. It is a good idea, Uncle. The building is close to where Ali will have his office.

Aunt's *mehndi* ceremony for me was rushed and small, with my new sisters-in-law, Ammi-jaan, Ali's pinch-faced mother who adored her only son, and Aunt's neighbours. I was ashamed of this marriage. I wore green and the sisters and neighbour-women fed me sweets, according to the tradition, and hennaed my hands and feet. The women told funny stories about husbands and marriage and all that a woman must put up with. One neighbour whose husband hit her joked, Marriage is bliss and then becomes purgatory. But divorce is hell. Aunt stopped them and said, I'm bringing in the music.

The dholki group was the best part of the evening. The three musicians sang traditional women's songs about love and drummed and poked fun at the in-laws. I thought, If I get stuck here, I will run away with them. And I snuck out to Minoo in the kitchen and begged her to steal back my passport for me but she was terrified and covered her face with her hands.

On the day of my *nikah*, Uncle and Aunt organized a room in the Beach Luxury for the wedding, decorated with long tables for our feast. The maulvi presiding over the ceremony came to a side room, the money to pass hands was agreed on, and a great many rupees and American dollars came to Uncle from Ali's family. Though the *meher* is said to give a bride freedom in her marriage, I have never heard of a bride who got her money. Mine was used to start the business in Canada.

I was dressed by Ali's sisters in a purple gharara with elaborate red and green and yellow embroidery. A row of tiny roses along the edges of the scarf fell over my dress. The maulvi read the marriage sermon and the proposal and acceptance. I sat in the bride's room and Ali's father came to me from the men's sitting room and he read me the *nikah-naama* and I had to accept by saying *qabook kiya* and I stumbled on the words, said *kiya* twice, and Aunt looked stern and I could see Ali's youngest sister biting her cheeks to stop laughing.

I was caked with makeup and my hands and feet were hennaed and the embroidered dress was damp and heavy in the heat. They lowered the green shawl over us and put the *nikah*-mirror in Ali's hands. Alone together, under the stifling shawl we were to enact an old tradition in which I was to remove my veil and we were to see each other's faces in the mirror, as if for the first time. I jerked off my veil in the stifling heat. I wanted it all to be over. His eyes in the mirror were uncertain and eager to please but there was no desire. I took the mirror out of his hand and turned directly to him. His eyes did not say, You. I want You. I had seen love in a man's eyes. I knew what that looked like.

I took his dry hand which did not press mine and I whispered to him, Let's get out of here, and he looked much relieved. His London girlfriend and his mother and sisters had always made his arrangements. When the green shawl was lifted I would take care of him. Now he had a wife.

The *walima*-party after was easy and tedious, music, dancing, worn-out wedding jokes, girls stealing Ali's shoes and him paying to get them back, rose petals thrown, plenty of food, the pretending to be happy. Ali and I were sent away early while Uncle and his father continued to entertain the business guests. We spent our first night together in a room at the Beach Luxury. This was the beginning of my double life, pretending inexperience, pretending I would come to love him.

I did not want to be in the same room with Uncle and Aunt when I told them I would never ever return, that they should not have forced me. I wrote the letter from Montreal and I mailed it the first day I was back.

Aunt had the grace to write the single letter she ever sent me: Life is what you make it. Marriage takes many forms. The thought of you gives me hope.

Wistful words, sad fetteredness. The envelope was from the Beach Luxury Hotel and I wondered if she had found a way to continue her Saturday mornings without me.

KATHERINE

Marian hired Cecil Williams, a young double bassist, to play on my first album for Halcyon Records. For texture, she said. For rhythm. We're doing it at the Vanguard. He was just finishing a Juilliard scholarship, a decade younger and he played great ostinato. It was a revelation to play with a man who didn't resist, who assumed I knew where I was going. Our third day recording together we went deep, improvising, and he liked it. At the end he said, You're cool, cool Kat.

Mahsa finally came back from Pakistan, weeks late. She'd gotten the hell married over there. I told her to get to New York fast and we'd record a track for my album.

She said, I'm taking the morning bus. Did you record "Take Off Your Clothes" and "Tea for Me"?

She was right—those were the pieces I had chosen. She knew my music better than anyone.

She looked so beautiful the day she came into the Vanguard. She wore high leather boots and a cropped jacket and her hair was caught back in a huge tortoiseshell clip. She held open her arms and wrapped them around me and I bent over to hug her. I said, Mahsa, you look more French every time I see you. How's married life?

She laughed and said, He's not here yet. At least I made it back.

Before I could ask her what that was supposed to mean, she took off her jacket, said, Let's start. I'm going to play until my fingers bleed for your first album.

Don't out-cut me, I joked.

Oh, I will.

That recording of us playing "Two to Love" is one of my favourites. I've never heard any two pianists do it better than we did, and a lot have tried. We were like hands clasped in prayer.

At the end I said, Stay for a few days.

I've got to get back.

Why?

Well, Ali's coming.

Mahsa didn't want to talk about him and I wasn't very interested. She said something about her uncle putting it together. She was worried that she would lose her student visa now that she was married. But I was hurrying back to listen to my tapes.

T was supposed to play a piece I wrote for him called "Long Road." When he didn't show I said to Marian, I know he's playing at Francis Hines's tonight. Send someone up to record us live.

Marian said, This is a bad idea, but she did it anyway.

I showed up at the loft with the recording engineer and T was stoned and I said to the piano player, Excuse me, mind if I take a turn? The men fell back a bit because they felt a warring woman but T didn't budge. He saw me and smiled and his lips were pressed against the reed and he winked and I thought, You shit, you like a bit of battle, and we played together and it was sexy as hell. We went deep that night like we used to when we were on the road and everyone was digging us. The recording is rough. You can hear people moving around and voices and glasses. You can even hear a match striking just at the moment when the room fell silent and everyone started to listen. When Marian heard it she said, Recording's not perfect, but the playing is great. Want to put it in?

Yes, I want it in.

On the rest of the recording, there was just me and Cecil. I felt open. Raw. You can hear a bit of my caught breath at places and I decided to leave it. I liked the live feel. You're lucky to get one like that in a lifetime. Some people shy away from raw. I have made many, many recordings since that first one in the Vanguard and it is still my favourite.

I kept the first take of Mahsa's and my "Two to Love" and didn't change much. She was pumped to play that day and we sat down and played it right through. When we finished we sat back and just looked at each other.

Where did that come from?

I love to play with you.

I called the album *Katherine Goodnow: Precious*. I got them to shadow in the Chinese character for Ming behind the title.

The cover is a photo of me with my hair wild and my children posed as vagabonds out in an alley near our apartment. Bea pulled a stray dog into the picture. The kids liked being part of things. Marian wrote the liner notes and I wrote my thank-yous, including to Ma. I had worked my whole damned life to make that first recording.

I packed up two copies, one to take to Ma when we visited and one to mail to Mahsa. She phoned as soon as she got it, said, I've been listening to it for six hours. You sound so good.

We're both out in the world now, I said.

I should have stayed to do the whole album with you, she said.

We'll do one later, don't worry.

There were two reviews, one good and one that said there was a *feminine* tint to this jazz. I threw the paper on the floor and Dexter picked it up. Ma, you're out there now. You gotta learn to take it.

I have not been taking it all my life, Dex. I'm not starting now.

Some people want you to bleed for them. I wrote to the critic, When was the last time you said music had a masculine tint? Go make your own album if you don't like the sound of mine. I play my own vocabulary.

I liked moving into the smoke.

*

In Hamilton, I made Ma put on the album first thing. The same work-worn hands I had grown up watching on the edges of records now held mine. We listened together and Ma said, Katie, you did it.

I turned over the cover and showed her how I thanked her in print and then I said, Let's take the kids on the rail trail tomorrow.

It was a hike they liked from downtown up to the escarpment to see the falls. Bea said, I love being in the Canadian wilds. I wish I had a dog.

Ma said, You think Hamilton is the wilds? Baby-B, this is a steel town. Let's borrow the dog next door for you.

She was entertaining now that I had moved away. Her favourite things were telling stories and smoking and singing. I watched her with the kids and I thought, I'm going to write a piece called "Gold-Thread Slippers." We played cards and she sang the same songs she'd sung to me, the songs her mother sang with her, and she drummed on the old kitchen table:

What you gonna do when the bed breaks down?
Tried it on the sofa,
Tried it on the chair,
Tried it on the window,
Didn't get nowhere.
What you gonna do when the bed breaks down?

One night when Ma and I went for a walk she said, I've been working with some lawyers to get an apology from the government for putting me in Belmont.

What do you want to dig up all that for?

Katie, they didn't have the right to do what they did.

She tossed her cigarette and said, I'm going to get an apology. It's for you too. Whether you want it or not.

I wanted her to come back with us for a while but she was stubborn. Ma and I were changing and I knew she was lonely but I couldn't do anything about it and take care of the kids and keep playing. She'd kept the same job for thirty years and she was never going to leave and she was still looking for something but I did not know what it was. We were connected like the forked branches of a divining rod witching for underground streams.

MAHSA

Monique nailed tin cans and an old shoe to our apartment door. Her arms felt very good around me when I got back from New York and she asked, *Ma grande*, how could you get married and not invite me? I always wanted to go to a Moslem wedding!

What are these for?

She said, It's a joke. Fathers give the groom a shoe to seal the bargain and the groom taps his bride on the head with it to show who's boss. *C'est ridicule.* The cans ward off bad spirits. I should put some on my door. I have so many bad spirits I need the whole door to be tin. Claude moved out and I'm keeping the apartment and I'm opening a new play next week. You should do the music for the next one. Jean came last week looking for you. He wants us to have a party. I don't think he knows you're married. I didn't tell him. What is Ali like?

Nice, a solicitor.

C'est quoi ça? Un avocat? You sound like you're talking about someone's brother.

Never mind, I said. We have to get used to each other.

I went into my old bedroom and I found Kamal's letters in my bottom drawer. I gave them to her and said, Keep these for me.

She said, Mahsa, this is not right. You're not in love.

Monique was the single person who dared to say it.

I said, Love can grow. That is what we believe at home.

She tucked my package of letters into her purse and said, Love just is. No matter where you are.

Ali's first morning in Montreal, he rose and left me in bed. After a few moments, he put his head around the corner of the door frame, said, You haven't made tea yet?

The congenial first, best son thumped along the hall to the kitchen, banged pots, made tea. He set it on my bed table with a flourish, said, There you go! Then he went to read the papers in the front room.

The praiseworthiness of serving me. Was he trying to be kind? But there was no companionship in it. It was his mother's voice in his ear, You are better. It was a thoughtlessness about women and servants.

Once there were lazy Sundays with Monique and our friends, coming home at dawn from the clubs on Saint-Antoine, big pots of coffee, passing the newspapers, laughing and talking and filling each other's cups. Now I was alone. Because I was married.

Ali's face was handsome but I did not like it. When he was

asleep I examined the anxious crease between his eyebrows, and the thin lips under his moustache. His face was softer when he was asleep. When we made love I did not feel him exploring who I was but seeking his own pleasure. These were not things we were able to talk about. I looked on as if it were not me. But Ali was in my bed every single night and I felt unutterably trapped.

I had absorbed that a wife should want to please her husband. I gave in to Ali, thinking he would begin to give back. When I was not compliant, Ali resisted me. The beginning of a marriage is a kind of play-acting, becoming what you think a wife or a husband should be. We were preoccupied with setting up his family's business and bank accounts, renting offices, making government applications. I helped because I knew the city well and my French was now good. Ali's mother wrote to me that so far I was a pleasing wife though at times a bit stubborn and she meant this as praise. Ali was not curious about the university but I took him anyway. When we stopped below the enormous statue of Queen Victoria in front of the music building he said, There are too many queens in Canada. It was January and the cold bothered him. I showed him my practice studio. I told him I played the Ritz on Saturdays and I had a gig in New York at the end of the month. I said, When I graduate I will teach part-time and I will work downstairs in this building. Ali said nothing.

Our second Sunday in Montreal I asked him to have brunch at the Ritz while I was playing. We were walking along Sainte-Catherine together in the cold and I saw a French couple with their arms around each other and I slipped my arm around Ali's waist. He tried to put his arm around my shoulder but our hips hit and we felt awkward and fell apart. The hotel staff made a fuss over him and Monique brought him an *International Herald Tribune* and he started to read. I said, You should come to New York and meet Katherine.

He said, Perhaps.

I said, Well, I'm going to get ready to play now. See you after.

What?

I'm playing now.

What?

Ali.

You play here, for people?

Yes.

But it's a hotel.

I told you.

Why would you want to play here?

I make money. It's fun.

But we have lots of money. You are a student.

I like to perform. I like to have my own money.

What?

Ali, stop saying what.

You're not going to play in a hotel.

Ali, I already do.

I went to change. My sari was low-rise which exposed my midriff and I wore a sleeveless choli under a transparent chiffon shawl. It was a style meant for parties. But a sari is versatile so I pulled up the skirt and covered my head with the pallu for walking in. I could let it slip down later.

I did not need to worry. He was not there when I came out.

I was so angry that I played my gig and then I went to Monique's and did not go home until late.

Ali rolled over in bed when I got in and pulled off my nightgown. I did not resist. I felt something demanding and insecure in him. In the morning we did not say anything before he went to work. At dinner I said, Ali, we should talk.

What about?

About why you won't talk.

There's nothing to talk about.

Really?

Are you going to stop playing out?

Ali, I told you I played there. Did Uncle not tell you I used to play at the Beach Luxury?

Of course. But that is different. He worked there. I don't want you playing in hotels.

Why not?

It is demeaning.

Ali, you lived in London! Lots of women perform.

But when you do, it makes me feel that I am not a good husband. It is not respectful. He mockingly lifted his hands and waggled his fingers in a parody of playing piano and said,

She is too talented for merely being a good wife. She must flaunt herself.

Ali, this is who I am. I can work and be a good wife, as you do.

Now the charm of our Karachi outings was gone. Again that night I did not resist him. In the morning, we left the house at the same time. At dinner he talked about the new clients he had met and the differences between London and Montreal. London was better. He needed to work on his French. He came into the kitchen, put his arms around me from behind. I was washing the dishes at the sink, and he wanted to lead me to the bed. The dishes were not done, and I had a paper to write, but I complied, pretended I wanted to please him, made my pleasure mirror his, still hoped my feelings might change. There was no tenderness and no loving eyes. We were two strangers in a bed.

Uncle wrote, Ali complains that you are headstrong. Try to be a pleasing wife.

None of them knew about my life here before Ali and the thought of this filled me with secret pleasure.

I had become aware of my first pregnancy in Karachi slowly, with a sense of dread as I discovered the reason for the tenderness of my breasts. This time I recognized the feeling. I was not sure about having this baby. I wasn't finished school. How would I travel to New York? Monique had had an abortion here. She got hers in a hotel room. When I asked her why she did it, she joked, *Maman* would have had a fit, the church would have had a fit, all of Montreal would have had a fit, and anyway, I couldn't take care of a baby and do theatre.

I telephoned Katherine. She said, Oh hell, Mahsa. If you want kids, you might as well do it and get it done. That's why you got married, isn't it?

I was too ashamed to tell her I had been forced. But she gave me an idea. I did want a baby. Keep moving on. I could do it all, like she did.

When I told Ali I was pregnant he said, Let's celebrate! Where shall we go?

I said, Let's go to Old Montreal. Christine Charbonneau is singing.

I liked the crowded little *boîtes à chansons* tight against the cobblestones, dark and candlelit, chairs close together and lovers' hands on each other's legs under wooden tables.

I was thinking something memorable, said Ali, like Altitude 737.

I felt queasy looking down into the lights of the city from the top of Place Ville Marie. We sat across from each other, the edge of the linen tablecloth heavy against my thighs. I wondered if I would ever feel at ease with my husband. I took a clear consommé with a few croutons, and Ali looked impatient. In those days I still teased him and I said, Now that I'm having a baby, you'll stop complaining about me in your letters home.

But he volleyed back, I don't complain.

I was interested in my pregnancy. My body felt loose and sensual, and I wanted sex but Ali's interest stopped. He took his first trip to London and I knew when he came home that there was more than work in his London business. I did not mind very much. He felt remote to me, like an older brother, contented if he got his way. I teased him, Next time I will come with you to London, but he did not answer. He said, I heard you were playing at the Esquire Club.

Yes, with my teacher, Jean. I've always played there with him.

Ali said, My father warned me.

About what?

That you would be strong-willed, that I would have to work things out.

How, *mon cher*? Ali did not like me to speak any French with him, and especially not to drop in Urdu words. My friends here liked it but Ali said it made us seem foreign.

He said, My father told me to get you pregnant quickly. Then you'd settle down.

He had a way of leaving me stunned. I asked, Any other wisdom from your family?

He did not know that he was insulting me. He thought he was right. I reached for him that night but he turned away. A few days later I tried again and I understood with the feeling of the betrayed that our domestic life was only an accessory to him.

He said, Mahsa, I am working hard to get this business going. I need you to understand that.

So began our habit of silence. There is a Western fairy story about the woman who is made to live with a beast and after she learns to love him, he becomes a beautiful prince. But love cannot be forced. Love is not bound by wilfulness or old story.

KATHERINE

Close to the Doghouse Studios in Brooklyn is a holy doughnut shop where 10th dead-ends with 2nd. I often saw there an old couple staring in different directions. One time the old man got out of his chair to go to the restroom and I watched the old woman check him out. She saw me and came over and said, We've been together for sixty-one years. My father said it would never work.

Looks like it did.

Some days I should get a medal. He's got a bad knee right now.

She said this with the satisfaction of a loved woman, eyes bright, assuming intimacy with me for no other reason than that I was a woman. She had false teeth and spoke with a British accent. I gestured to her to sit with me but she shook her head, He'll be back soon and we're going.

Where are you from?

Here. Well, England first.

She had a rattle cough like Ma's. She said, I got married

and two weeks later I moved with him here. I've been the custodian at my kids' school for forty years. Now my grandkids are there. What do you do?

Musician. I'm working in the neighbourhood.

What kind of music?

Jazz.

I don't know much about that.

I feel like writing something for you.

She was pleased at this, but she was not surprised. Good, simple things had always happened to this woman. Through war and deaths and childhood illnesses she had stayed with the man who loved her. He gave her all he had, and she did not ask for more.

How'd you stay together?

This was something she had thought about. She smiled with those clean, perfect false teeth and said, My kids ask me that too. It's simple. We were always the most important thing in each other's lives.

Other people had glamorous jobs and travelled and spoke languages and owned things. She did not. But she had confidence in her marriage. Their love was ordinary and true and hers.

He limped up and put the arm that wasn't holding a cane around her shoulders and I watched how she leaned into him and fit there. His shoulders were straight and he had the large hands and the strong forearms of a working man. He reminded me of Nan's Big Johnny.

You ready? he asked. She nodded and their eyes met in a comfortable way. As they left, she put her arm around his waist and he dropped his hand down to squeeze her thin bum. She turned to see if I was watching and smiled at me like a girl, as if to say, See? Then she stepped away from under his arm and caught his hand in hers. She turned back and asked, What you going to call my song? I want to watch for it.

How about "New Thing" or "Long Love"?

I like the first one, she said.

Because she chose that one, I decided to write a tragedy.

MAHSA

What happened?

Jean St. John came into my practice room, smoking a cigarette, dragged over his chair, interrupted me.

What do you mean?

The playing. Ever since you got married, something is different. And by the way, you could have told me.

I recorded a cut on Katherine Goodnow's first album.

Bravo. But there is something else. I can feel it.

As well now as later.

I am pregnant.

Merde!

Jean, I am happy.

Great. *Félicitations.* When are you quitting?

I stood up.

He said, Sit down. Play "Thelonious."

Coltrane said when he played with Monk, he could feel like he'd stepped into an empty elevator shaft. To play Monk you have to stop thinking about anything but B-flat. So I did.

I stopped thinking about Jean and the baby and everything but the B-flat.

When I finished, Jean St. John dropped his cigarette butt on the floor, put it out with his boot, stood, said, Mahsa, you've got it. Don't waste it. People will tell you to quit. *As-tu le courage?*

Don't worry. If you deal in camels, you make a high door.

He laughed his delighted-at-me-laugh that I loved. He said, *Ma grande*, when's your next party with that women's-lib *comédienne* friend of yours? I want to do my scarf dance again.

When I confided in Ali that I was worried about how to finish school and teach after the baby he said, Don't complain. Each person thinks his own grave is too narrow. He became hovering and wanted me to stay home and he tried to insist that I drink whole milk morning and evening which I hated. To please him I brought home skimmed milk but still he persisted.

Ali, stop. I'll eat what I want.

Ammi thinks this is better for the baby.

I could hear his frustration, as Uncle was often frustrated by me. At first I had wanted to believe that it was a sign of his affection. But a wife is like a man's land.

Ammi-jaan wrote, Put your music studies on the back burner, enjoy your baby. Monique said, You didn't take birth control, you must want to be a mother.

Only Jean's words—You've got it—made me hopeful inside.

Our son was born on June 7, 1973. Asif. Mor used to whisper to Abbu, You are *janan asif*, which means beloved and pure, and my father used to answer, If you say so, but he liked it. Ali thought I meant the Arabic name that means forgiveness and he said, Yes, the prophet was most forgiving, Asif is a good name.

Ali left earlier and came home later and in the long and lonely and sleepless first months of nursing and walking with Asif, I wished for a woman to share my baby. I chanted my mother's verses to comfort my new son:

My baby's smell is all lavender.
Is every baby like mine,
or hasn't anyone given birth before me?

I telephoned Katherine and said, He's beautiful, but I'm going crazy alone so much.

She said, I used to sit by the window with a peashooter.

I don't feel like myself anymore.

You're not supposed to. Get out. There must be some other mothers. Better yet, get a babysitter.

You cannot clap with one hand. Ali softened toward me, delighted with his son. I spoke of going back to school but the months dissolved into a year and he brought home clients to entertain and we went to the new mosque on Laval Road in Ville Saint-Laurent. The community was small, two rows of men at prayers, and I watched Ali joining this new community. His contentment depended on my agreement to not be myself. Now I was to be a new mother and a hostess-wife, charming, invisible in plain sight.

My hidden life grew more complicated. Asif slept and I practised. I found a babysitter so I could play at clubs with Jean. When Asif was fourteen months old and I was already pregnant again, I told Jean I was having another and he said, *Es-tu folle?* Monique embraced me, said, A girl, make me a girl, you idiot, I do not know why you are doing this, but at least have a girl! And sure enough it was a daughter that I named Lailuma, and then there was all the baby-touching again, and sleepless nights and nursing and two children to hold and feed and bathe and care for. Monique visited my milky, sticky, dishevelled world, said, Can't you put them both in their cribs and come out for coffee with me? Then we'll go to a film. You need a break from this madness. I laughed and handed her Lailuma.

She said, I'm not having children. But I'll be an aunty to yours.

Katherine said, Girls are great. Bring her soon. We'll play.

I was fooling myself by appearances I myself was creating. Ali went to London for business and came back refreshed. He was habitually irritated at home, a strained man, caught between Western ways at work and resisting them with me and our children. I tried to be a djinn under the floorboards. But one day, annoyed, I said to him, You are probably still in love with your London girlfriend.

He said, I can't help it that you were too young to marry.

You were so intent on telling me you had lovers that you never asked me about mine.

My words smashed like a glass on the floor.

For the second time, he did not ask but he stored this against me. Our young marriage was full of silences. We fought and turned away and did not work things out and in this way we created a shallow life. I was nursing and looking after the babies and trying to play, and Ali was building his business and trying to shape the appearances of our family. He was not much interested in its real textures or in me. He began to talk about taking us back to Karachi to see his parents and I told him I would not go, that I did not want to see Uncle.

A few days later, Monique was playing with Asif, stacking a small pile of blocks for him to knock over. She wore her curly hair piled on top of her head and horn-rimmed glasses pushed up.

I sat facing her, cross-legged on the floor, nursing Lai, her flower mouth tugging hungrily, my milk like a drug to her. I said, Ali wants me to take them back to Pakistan for a visit. I can't go.

Why?

I'm afraid.

Of what?

I wanted to tell her about my parents but I could not. I said, My uncle forced me to marry. I do not want to see them.

Forced you?

I only got married so I could come back.

I did not want her to feel sorry for me but I did not trust her to understand. With shame, silence.

Monique made Asif's tower higher. His small hands tried to balance another block on top. I watched his tiny lips tighten in concentration. Then she said, Are you afraid they will force you to stay?

This time when Asif's tower fell he started to cry. Monique coaxed him to try again and I burped Lailuma and held her close and felt her tiny muscles widen and relax and her head drop in a smooth curve from her neck as she fell asleep. I tucked her into the couch, picked up Asif and with a light laugh said, Feeding time at the zoo. Come into the kitchen. Tell me about your new play.

Monique said, Leave him, Mahsa. You are not yourself anymore.

Where would I go?

I thought, How could I manage? What about the children?

But the next morning when I took them for a long walk, I passed by my old bank with the two standing lions. I rented a safe deposit box for my passport. Then I went to the university clinic, got myself the pill, paid cash for it, and hid the packages in a hollowed-out copy of Zola's *Nana* because Ali never read French novels.

I phoned Katherine to tell her I was so tired I was not

practising. She said, You'll start again. Don't worry. It's natural. I remember days when I did not have time to write even two notes. Keep going. If you get robbed of your dreams, you get robbed of life.

KATHERINE

T was jealous of my first recording. He'd recorded a lot as a sideman but he did not write. There is no mystery to writing. People write because they can't not write. Same with playing. T couldn't not play. But he was experimenting with macrobiotics and Scientology and the Free Life Communication project and psychedelics like a lot of the cats were. He moved west when things fell apart, when he got addicted to heroin. He said it felt like the sound of a rock dove cooing in a feathered nest. It was a hard time. When I saw him we made love as if it was a good thing because it was. But I was angry at him. He was mostly gone for years.

He said, Katie, I don' want the kids to see me like this but I want to see you.

See me, see your children.

Katie, don' be a hardass.

I mean it, T.

But I let him in and we were tender in bed. I said, You

gotta get straight, and then I tried to reach down to bring him closer but he started talking and I knew he had planned the things he wanted to say. His voice was soft and not remorseful. It was the voice of a man who is struggling hard to tell his thoughts.

He said, I have to leave. Things have to be the way they are. There are things I have to learn.

I know, T.

Every time I see you.

Me too.

You keep writing.

I want to be on the road like you. But somebody has to raise our kids.

He said, I get drawn into things. Some not so good things.

We set words aside for naked touch. I would have liked to be free enough to get drawn into things. He let me pull him up and we were inside each other. We were always inside each other one way or another.

Later, resting, I asked, How's your other family?

He grinned. You gonna throw my clothes out the window if I say anything?

Men like women in a rage over them.

He said, Babe, let's talk about us.

Next time I won't use a bag.

He pulled me closer. The kids needed him, that was one thing. And the other thing was that I never stopped feeling that damn little flip when I saw him, so I decided not to bury my love. If you cannot imagine being betrayed and still being in love, then you haven't been in love. I wanted to play, to write. I wanted my kids. I wanted him.

MAHSA

Katherine held tiny Lailuma close, cupped her large hand under her head like a cap and said, She's perfect.

I called Ali as soon as I arrived at her place, left a message, said, I'm in New York. Don't be angry. I had to go. I will be back in a week.

I felt like myself again and I decided not to worry about my problems while I was there.

We played the Surf Maid for three nights. I ran upstairs and nursed Lai between sets. Katherine said, You're playing better than before. Babies suit you.

It was good to not be alone. On our last day in the city, we went on an outing to Central Park and Katherine rented fishing rods and we kept the baby on the blanket between us while the kids went down to the lake. Everyone was lazy and satisfied in the warm afternoon sun, and Katherine and I talked about music and planned to go up to the Cookery and I nursed and changed Lai and she watched the light on the leaves with eyes that were grey like mine. I said to Katherine, Let's live like this all the time. She said, Yes, let's.

Suddenly Bea came running to us, Asif's gone. We can't find him.

I had been watching him on the shore. And then I was busy with Lai and talking with Katherine and my little boy disappeared.

I looked out and there was a hole in the world. The surface of the pond was flat. Was he underneath? Eyes open, dead, his small body sucked into the mud? Would police divers come and dredge the bottom and bring up the limp body of my little boy? Or had an evil person, not an ordinary person, snatched him and was already hiding him in a locked room in the horrible throbbing city behind us, dyeing his hair, renaming him, hurting him? Would he be found years from now and say to me in a flat, teenaged voice, Why did you not find me? What would I tell Ali? How could I go back to Montreal on the bus alone, with no Asif? It would be the unforgivable end of one life, the beginning of an unthinkable one. Katherine ran along the shore in one direction and I ran in the other. How long had it been? Three minutes? Ten?

And then the hole filled in. There he was. A quiet toddler near the water, bent over something on the shore, crouched under a little bush out of sight. Absorbed, touching pebbles, sand, shore-mud. Examining his world. His little lips were parted lightly as he breathed through his mouth in wonder and his eyebrows were lifted in curiosity. I ran to him and

I put my one free arm around him and pulled him close to me and the baby, and he looked up at me with startled eyes, his concentration harshly interrupted and he started to cry. I do not know why I did not squat down beside him and look with him and coax him away from the shore but I did not. I pulled him away as if my imagined dangers were more important than his contemplation of what was real. I called to the others and brought him back to Katherine.

She said, All children get lost sometimes. Bea used to hide under the clothes racks in the store and I'd have to look for her feet.

The kids told their getting-lost stories because now it was safe to be lost, because they had always been found by mothers who were determined to love them.

I got on the bus for Montreal reluctantly after our week away. I thought about staying. Katherine said, You could get some good teaching gigs here, you know. But I said, I still have to complete my degree. Anyway, he's their father.

Lailuma was fussy on the trip and Asif kept waking her and we were all exhausted by the time we got home. I put first Lailuma, then Asif to bed and went back to have tea with Ali. He had been affectionate with Asif and cold with me and when I came back to the kitchen he closed the door and said, Sit.

I hated it when he closed doors.

He said, Do you know how many people depend on me for their livelihoods? And you go running away to New York with our children without telling me so that I have more worry. Am I not enough for you? Is this life not enough for you? How do you think this looks?

It was a carefully practised little speech.

He said, What kind of mother?

He paced and spread his arms in the air. I had seen him make this impatient and demanding gesture with his employees. He said, You should be here with your son. Your behaviour is shameful. I have given you everything.

Ali, stop! I won't be treated this way.

He counted on his fingers, You have a son, a home, a good living from TradeWorld. Why can I not go to work without concern? I have done everything I was supposed to. What is this carelessness for me? My wife—broken word!—you are shaming us. Mahsa, I cannot succeed if I do not work the way I do.

Ali, before you came I made my own money. What I do does not get in the way of your work. Why should you have choice and I none?

If you had not married me, your uncle would have kept you back there, living in some Karachi-cloister, getting your nails done, having the massage-wallah. I give you everything. The children are mine.

He meant to shrink me. I said, I'm not stopping playing.

He flung his mug across the room, tea splattering, the cup breaking against the sink. The thick colour under his skin frightened me.

I pushed past him and ran out into the darkness. Was I so worthless? To ask for love from Ali was like asking a man without arms to hold me. Everyone affirmed that he was good, his mother, his employees, his customers. He was urbane and charming and a good manager. I walked through the darkness up the mountain. I could leave. But he would take Asif. I could try to hide, but if I lived in hiding, how could I survive? Why should I need to disappear? I walked past couples holding hands and men with their backs half turned from me. From the lookout I watched the river. Where would I go? To New York? Could I move in with Monique? How had this trap of a marriage happened?

Nothing new came from my flailing. The same thoughts circled inside, go or stay, leave the children or not. I was a woman who was shameful. Was Mor shameful? Was this who I was? When I got home Ali was still dressed, sitting under a single light in the living room. I thought, He looks old.

His face was flat and determined but I could see in his eyes a shine of fear. There was room for me still to resist. He said, Mahsa, why can you not understand? I work hard and I make a good living for us. I am respected. I want us to be a good family.

I said, I work hard too, Ali. I do everything for our children. My playing does not get in your way. We must try to compromise. I would never try to stop you from doing what you want to.

He slammed his hands on the arms of the chair, got up,

and without another word or touch we went to bed. I put my hand on his arm and he rolled away and our life together became that night more meagre.

In the morning I felt flattened in a dark oven pit in the ground, bread slapped against a hot wall. What would I do? What choice did I have if I wanted to keep the children? Make it work. I would force myself to be cheerful, like a poor relative in a rich man's house.

Fifteen years passed. I carved out what our family could be. I tutored students at McGill in the mornings and when Ali was in England I hired a babysitter. There was a new club called Biddle's that I liked to play at with Jean. I went to New York once a year. Ali always complained, Why are you so difficult? We loved staying at Katherine's, living crowded together in her small apartment. Asif learned to play chess with Dexter, Bea got Lailuma dancing. We took day trips up to the Cloisters to see the flat wide-eyed Madonnas and the *femmes couverts*, to walk through the wide breezeways and herb gardens. We walked to the Morgan Library and looked at the secret passageways and Mesopotamian writing and sculptures of the naked goddess with owl talons and eagle wings. Once, when I had a bit of extra money, we all went to the Plaza for tea which pleased Bea. Katherine and I watched our children growing up together and it was good to share them with each other. Only Jimmie was difficult. When Asif was older I let Jimmie take him out to second-hand record stores and gave them money to bring back something interesting. But I used to secretly hope that neither of my kids would get defiant like he was, and experiment with drugs like he did. Katherine was always worried about him and I tried to encourage her, said, He is tender and tough like you.

She answered, You don't know. Things sail into Jimmie out of nowhere and stick and sting and the more he flails the worse they hurt him. When I walk down the street with him, I try to imagine what he feels walking with me. Teenage boys are warriors without armour. They do not have yet what they need. People see us together and stare.

I had noticed this.

All my life, she said, I've ignored certain things. But I cannot ignore my children's pain.

Jimmie said to me about Katherine, She's only part white.

I told him, My father was American and my mother was Afghan. Everywhere is mixed. At school Lai and Asif are the only children with parents from Pakistan, but in their classes are children from Haiti and Senegal and they learn English and French.

But Jimmie was too caught up in his own turmoil to hear, and what seemed to be anger on his surfaces I recognized as the rawness of loss, of a boy desiring what he could not have.

Each summer Ammi-jaan and Daadi came for two months. This was a burden and the time I dreaded most in the year. They did not like to hear me play in the living room so

I set up a small keyboard with a headset in our bedroom. Ammi-jaan had a wrinkle between her eyebrows like Ali's, but on a woman's face it made her look perpetually angry, even when she was not. Her talk was critical under a guise of helping, my seekh kebab could have been more moist with slower cooking, Lailuma's skirt was too short, would I not like to take them all shopping? She said, Is Asif not handsome like his father? Is he not brilliant with his French? Lailuma's grades were always better but I did not contradict her and took the children on long walks up the mountain where Ammi-jaan could not walk. In all the years I did not go back to Pakistan because I could not bear it. I sent Aunt a letter at Eid and when she wanted Western magazines and vitamins I mailed them to her with photos of the children. I received a letter from Kamal who had moved to Australia. It felt shocking to see his handwriting and as I opened it, blood pounded in my ears as if he himself were in the room.

Dear Mahsa,

I have started this letter many times and I still do not know how to begin. I recently heard a cassette tape of you playing. If the date is correct, you were still a student when you made it. The label is: Metamusic. I would recognize your playing anywhere. It has been a long time, Mahsa. It does not seem possible. If this early recording is a sign, you have surely done very well. I liked hearing your voice reciting poetry.

I will not bore you with the details of the life of a former Karachiite consultant which I am sure would interest you little. I have never forgotten you. When I heard your music, I heard sounds from our days in a Karachi that has disappeared. Perhaps you have not forgotten me. I am thinking of coming to Montreal. I will finish this letter now, as I do not know whether or not it will reach you.

Yours, Kamal

I read the letter all afternoon, smelled it, absorbed it. Was that a salt smell? The sea? His skin? The paper was alive and I memorized the words and burned the letter in the kitchen sink and did not write back.

One night Ali surprised me, said, Let's go to the 737 for dinner. Do you remember? He had completed a big deal and felt good. We dressed up and watched our city turning white with fresh snow. *Ma chanson ce n'est pas une chanson, c'est ma vie.* Our waiter glanced out at the wild and swirling flakes, said, A lovely evening, and Ali said, I will never get used to this cold, but I smiled, shrugged, smoothed, said, *C'est beau, vous avez raison.* Ali and I chatted as we had in earlier times. He told me about a new business acquaintance in Pakistan, received with pleasure my praise for his good year.

I had begun to feel our difference of twenty-two years. My children were almost grown, and he was nearing sixty with dark rings under his eyes. I sometimes felt a passing tenderness for the familiarity of him which turned to vapour in the heat of his first impatient word. But there was an ease between us that night as we sipped tea together, and he had a whisky. I said, Come to New York with us this year. Take a few days before you go to London. Asif and Lailuma would love it. You've never met Katherine.

Dry ice. He set down his glass and said, I hate New York. You know that. How can I drop things at work? People depend on me.

I was still irritating sand in his shoe.

I ignored the swift rupture, as I had ignored such moments for years. Ali paid the bill, and we made our way through the cold toward home. Inside the front door before I hung up our coats he said, After this trip, you won't take the children to New York anymore. They need to concentrate on their studies. I'll have a tea before bed.

Asif was standing at the doorway and I saw him register the command in Ali's voice. I remained silent, not to argue in front of him, and I was ashamed of my silence. My boy moved like Ali and I sometimes heard him ordering Lailuma.

I said to him, Treat your sister with respect.

He answered back hard and fast like Ali, I do.

Already he seemed to think this was how things had to be.

I gave Lailuma for her thirteenth birthday a pair of shoes with red heels from a New York boutique, remembering my own first pair of real silk stockings and going to the Metropole with Abbu and Mor. Lai's best friend was French and they shared clothes and still played with their dolls if they thought no one would see. They began to go to movies with friends from school, and were top students and busy with dance.

Ali said to me, I do not like her to wear makeup. Why did you give her heels?

I tried to persuade him, Ali, she's doing well and she studies Quran with me, and her friends are nice. Let her grow a little now. Children are different here.

She needs to be more modest. You encourage her.

He wanted us all to go to Pakistan. The city was much changed and violent and people moved with fear through the streets. Mohajir refugees lived in spreading slums. Islamists were closing down the nightclubs and theatres. Daily there were bombs and murders and my in-laws rarely left their neighbourhood. Teenaged boys with guns protected hotels and shopping malls. There were meant to be elections in December and Benazir Bhutto would run. She had promised to repeal the Hudood Ordinances and return to a parliamentary system. But the opposition of the generals was strong. I wanted the children to feel the sea air on the beaches, to visit the shrines, to hear the call to prayer. I wanted to show them my old school and Saint Patrick's cathedral and Zelin's. But not yet.

Ali said, They need to know where they are from.

They are from here.

Asif needs to begin to meet our business associates, he said.

He is fifteen, Ali.

His eyes were razors. I said, Why don't you take them for a short visit? They are grown up now and will be no trouble to Ammi-jaan. But you must bring them back well before the elections.

I want you to come.

Ali, I am not ready. Please.

Your uncle was good to you, he said. My mother wants to see you there. Someday she will not be able to travel.

I know, Ali. I have hard memories. The children are old enough to not be a burden. You take them.

Always you are stubborn.

I arrived an hour too early at the airport to pick them up. It had been a wonderful fifteen days on my own in Montreal. I went to the theatre with Monique, played at an open stage with Jean, took extra shifts at the Queen Elizabeth. I did not cook and I slept in after coming home late.

Monique said, Why aren't there any holidays in the wife-contract? Everyone else gets holidays.

We laughed as we used to and now I was longing to see Asif's bright eyes, to smell Lailuma's teenaged hair. I watched people walk out from behind the airport's thick glass doors, their greetings and cries of excitement and disappointment, each different as a fingerprint. I thought, Next time I will go, accept my destiny with Aunt and Uncle. It is a long time to stay angry. I would like to show my city to my children.

I waited and watched. The sliding glass doors opened. Asif, looking fearful and tired, walked through beside Ali. He seemed taller to me and muscled like a man not a boy and I experienced, as I often did, a fleeting surprise because my mind was crowded with the details of his childhood.

Where is Lailuma?

Asif's arms were around me and he whispered my name, Mor, as if it could protect him. Then he released me and stepped back. Over his shoulder I was looking into Ali's determined eyes.

I left her with my mother. She is staying in Karachi. You cannot control her.

III

Pursuance

KATHERINE

Midnight for me, nine P.M. for him. T got on someone else's phone in California and called me. He could not sleep. He was thinking of coming back to New York. A call I'd had a thousand times before.

He asked, Wanna hear something?

I lay in bed listening to his sax. I got up and put the phone by my keyboard and played him a new piece I was writing called "Soror Song," about a nun who wrote five letters from a convent to a French guy who deserted her.

That's real pretty, Katie. How're the kids?

Dexter got himself a job at the Jefferson Market Library. Did you know it used to be the Women's House of Detention? Bea got herself into LaGuardia Arts for dance. She's getting beautiful, T.

How 'bout Jimmie?

Dexter helped him find a double bass in a pawn shop and gave him the money for it. Dex hung a curtain around his part of the room. He says if he's getting into law school he's gotta study.

Jimmie playing?

He's into things, T. He disappears and I don't know where he goes. Igor caught him shoplifting and called me and said, I work eight days a week and I never own a house in this country, that boy not stealing here. I told Jimmie, How could you steal from anyone? And especially from our friend. I told him to go work for Igor to pay him back and he did for a couple of weeks and I can't make him do anything so he must have felt bad.

He going to school?

In the front door and out the back. You should come and help out, T. You've been away a long time.

You don' want me the way I am, KK. Put Jimmie on the phone.

He's not here. Come back, give things a chance.

You don't want me right now, babe.

Heroin sneaks up fast. At first it's warm bath bliss, your lover-god swinging with you in a sweet and mellow hammock. Then you crave that feather-soft first time again, but you can't get it and the more you try, the more it betrays you, gives you a taste, is over, and you can't get there so you try more. It sucked T down fast. He'd been handling all the other stuff for years but junk was killing him. He said, I'm standing in hell's door, babe, existence is fragile, violent, stunning. I answered, It's not romantic, T. I am hearing about you and you know what your friends are saying? They're saying, Hey, saw T, he's not doing well. And I keep telling them, Well, help him.

I sent him money when I had it but I knew it was getting poured down a rabbit hole. I never told the kids much, only, He'll be back soon, or He's on the road, or Take the cards you're dealt. My kids took me in through their skin and I wasn't going to let them take in bitterness. Parents carve pain into their children if they're not careful.

I said, There's programs here, T. There's one at the church I'm playing at. Remember Judson Memorial?

Not my style, Katie, I'll go in a room and do it. How come you playin' in a church again?

I met the pastor on Washington Square, Howard Moody. He was driving around in a van with cookies and coffee and a warm place for the hookers to have a break. A girl called over from the van that she'd seen me playing at the Gate. Howard came out and said, Want coffee? He's got a southern accent and short-cropped hair and big sticking-out ears and he looks like a marine. He's written a lot about civil rights. He calls the girls his invisible congregation.

He gave me the latest copy of his street magazine, *Hooker's Hookup*, and I asked the girl what show of mine she'd seen and it turned out her john was a big jazz fan so she'd seen me play a lot. Howard said, We have jazz at the church. You should come over and play. We can always use help.

I told him I worked late most Saturday nights, and the

prostitute laughed and said, Like me and even I make it to Moody's church sometimes.

I made the mistake of saying, I played a Baptist church in Canada for years.

Howard said, Our pianist called tonight to say he wouldn't be in for the service tomorrow. Any chance you could cover?

So I was stuck. A damn jazz-loving hooker is the reason I started playing for Jesus. For free no less.

I felt good making T laugh and then Bea woke up, and ran in full of sleep, Is that Daddy? They all knew the late-night calls, the tone in my voice. I handed her the receiver and her face opened, Daddy! When are you coming back? Listening to half of it, I heard all the things she wanted him to know about her dance and school and was he coming for Easter, and then, Okay Daddy, and she held out the receiver so we could all say together, Sweet dreams, Sweet Pea, tempus fugue-it, baby, fiddly doo diddly dee.

After she went back to bed he said, She sounds good. Why are you writing about that nun?

Mariana Alfcoforado loved her suffering because it made her feel alive. She wrote to her lover, Keep making me suffer cruel torment.

She only got five letters? That's it? Must have been some guy.

You all are, I said.

How's the story end, babe?

She lived the rest of her long life in the convent and

renounced her lover for God.

He laughed, said, It's midnight, babe.

I said, It's three in the morning here. And I gotta play soon.

He said, Katie, you made a pretty song there. Don't give me up for God.

We could be generous with each other three thousand miles apart. I liked floating in music and darkness on his voice, just T 'n me unspooling around dying stars and dawn.

I worked hard like any man. I kept moving on to the next new thing. I was a sideman for whoever paid. Raising our kids, everything was urgent and necessary, and it took twenty years of attentiveness. Then it was done. Like crumbs on a table. Wipe. Gone.

In the morning, Bea came out while I was making my instant coffee before I ran over to Judson. I asked her, Do you know where your brother is?

One's in bed.

The other one.

Not there.

Want coffee?

She had a comforter around her and she was wrapping her toes in it and shuffling along the floor. She said, I'm going to marry someone who sticks around.

She said what came into her head. There were moments when I felt like sliding down the wall and giving up. But I thought, I used to sneak out to play the bars.

I have to go, Bea. Come to church if you want.

I'm going back to bed. You and Daddy on the phone kept me up half the night.

She sounded like a satisfied old lady and looked like a messy teenager and I loved her. Jimmie came in with his bass on his back and he hadn't slept. I said, I'm going over to Judson. Why don't you bring your bass along. Let's swing that church. I'll split the fee with you.

I figured I could find some money somewhere. He surprised us both when he said yes. We played the service and Howard asked us to stay for coffee. He said to Jimmie, Would you come back again?

I came by accident today.

Then Jimmie drank his coffee down in one gulp and said, This scene's too white for me.

Howard said, You know, when I came here twenty years ago I had a talk that I've never forgotten with a man who pulled open his collar and showed me a six-inch lynching scar on his neck, put there by the Klan. He told me those Klan members met in a Baptist church and worshipped the God I worshipped. And he asked me, *What in the name of decency or reason, white boy, could persuade me to believe in the God you're trying to defend?* Well, that question silenced me then, and it has always stayed with me.

Jimmie asked, So, what you doing here?

Howard said, That old man's question feels like a door

without a doorknob. I keep working here because I figure that God might open it from the other side.

Jimmie let himself get pulled in by Howard. He started playing for Judson benefits and for the dance shows. He liked to call Howard *white boy* in front of me. I told him to be more respectful but Jimmie said, He knows I'm joking, as if Howard weren't there and Howard said, Sometimes people got to free themselves from *us*.

I said, I'm half Chinese, Howard. And he's only half black. Who the hell is the *us* you're talking about?

All southern charm Howard answered, Well, dad blame it, Katherine, I always knew there was something different about you.

I had to laugh. It was easier than being at my wits' end about Jimmie. With an angry teen you have to be willing to be tested, cold water relentlessly flicked against a hot griddle, someone checking out the temperature.

MAHSA

I pleaded. For weeks I cried, I screamed, I called Ali at work until he would not take my calls. I slept in Lailuma's room.

You do not listen, he told me. How can you be a good mother the way you are?

Behind his burning eyes was a new shine of rage. Fifteen years in the same bed but I was still discovering what he was capable of.

She talks back, he said. Like you. Ammi says she needs to be controlled.

Poisonous viper Ammi-jaan. I screamed at him, You can't do this to please your mother, and now he was shamed and he grabbed my wrist.

I will not tolerate Asif hearing you, he said. Control yourself!

The way you are.

I telephoned Ammi-jaan. Lailuma's voice was pleading behind, Ask when can I come home.

Ammi-jaan said, She is fine. I am taking good care of her. Try to please him more.

I hated myself. All those years of trying to create whatever it was that we called our family, waste, waste. There were no bruises. He hardly raised his voice. None of that was necessary to break us.

I lied to everyone, to Lailuma's school, to her friends. I told them her grandmother was sick, that she needed to spend some time with her. I said, It is our way. Family is important. I saw how people doubted but wanted to believe me. I took advantage of people's sympathy. I was Lailuma's betrayer.

When I called Katherine and told her the truth, she said, Go get her.

She understood nothing, how could she, but to hear her voice made me cry. I said, They will hide her passport. That's what they did to me. I can do nothing there.

Katherine said, Really? They took your passport? When?

To force me to marry Ali. Katherine, I have to get Lailuma back.

Let's hire a kidnapper.

Her wildness made me feel better.

What are you going to do?

Asif does not speak at home anymore.

You've got to get her back.

We talked about lawyers, about how Ali's family would

hide her, about trying to shame Ali at work. I was afraid of all Katherine's ideas.

I said, He might give in if I comply. His mother won't want her there forever.

What does he want you to do?

He thinks I should be home. He thinks Lai should be more modest. It's our culture.

Come *on*, Mahsa. That's not culture.

I wanted to hate her for the first time. We had always accepted everything about each other. What did she know of where I came from?

Finally she said quietly, My mother used to say, It's the way things are. But it isn't. Why should a person be anything but free.

I was afraid for Lai.

She asked, What does he want?

He wants me home.

Mahsa, leave.

I could turn my heart to stone and forget I had children or I could go back to him and comply.

I said, It is possible that I will not see her again.

Get another passport to her. And money. We will find a way.

They could make Lailuma disappear.

After a long silence Katherine asked, What are you going to do?

I've got to bring her home.

*

I cooked Ali's favourite dishes and dressed in a shalwar kameez that Ammi-jaan had given me. We sat together at the table and I said, Today I quit the hotel.

Why?

I don't need to work. You provide well for us, Ali.

With negotiating eyes he looked up and asked, Did you quit the university too?

It is the end of term already. I won't teach next term. I told Jean.

My heart was breaking.

He put a forkful of chicken in his mouth and said, What about playing with Katherine?

My heart sealed up in rage. I answered, I have no need to go to New York anymore. I want to be here for you and the children.

I loathed the sound of his chewing. When his plate was empty his eyes fixed on me and his neck arched back like a snake with an unstitched mouth. He said, I will have tea in the living room.

He was asleep when I went in so I left the tea beside him and went back to the kitchen to finish cleaning up. When I returned, his cup was empty and he was dozing again and I put my hand quietly on his knee and said, Ali, come to bed.

In the bedroom I unbuttoned his shirt and slipped it off and placed his familiar hands on my waist as I took off my top. I unbuttoned his pants as he was kissing my breasts and I pretended to be aroused. In bed I pulled him to me and waited for it to be over. I was dry and it hurt but I made no sign of pain and pretended pleasure.

KATHERINE

Ma wanted more. On the phone she said, Katie, I've got news.

I cancelled my gigs and took Dexter and Jimmie and Bea to visit right away, to see her still well. No one can know how it will go. How long from diagnosis to end.

She met us at the bus terminal and said, Put your stuff in a locker. We're going walking. We walked downtown past our old apartment and looked up at the window and Dexter said, It woulda been a different life here. And then she took us to the Connaught and they had prepared a meal for us and Ma stood with the kitchen staff joking and laughing while we ate and when we were leaving she said to them, I'm not coming back and I don't want you to visit me.

Out on the sidewalk I said, Ma, you've been working with them for years.

She said, And that's long enough. Then she opened her purse right there on the sidewalk and pulled out three American one-hundred-dollar bills and gave one to each of the kids. She said, I don't need money where I'm going. Now you won't forget me.

I said, Ma, stop it.

But Jimmie said, It's okay, I'll take it.

That evening we were sitting in her apartment and Ma and Bea were painting their nails red, and Ma was telling stories about the hotel and the musicians and the time they played a trick on Tommy Dorsey. Dexter was pretending to read but he was listening to her and Jimmie was barricaded in my old bedroom with his Walkman and headphones. Ma pulled out her Chinese teapot and gave it to Bea and she gave Dexter her *Bartlett's*. She said, I've got a soft spot for lawyers. They've done some good work for me. You keep going with that. Call your brother in.

She gave Jimmie her Les Paul album and she said to all of them together, I don't want you making a fuss over me, I've had a good life, and we're not going to waste money running back and forth. We're going to do this my way. You're not coming back. I don't want you to see me sick. Don't let time flap on the mast. Go and live your lives. Take care of your ma and each other. Tomorrow let's walk up the escarpment.

It was Jimmie who opened his arms and held her but she wouldn't let him hold her for long. She said, I'm not going to heaven because I wouldn't know anyone there.

The kids still shake their heads at that, and laugh.

*

It was a good week. We looked around the used record stores and walked back to the escarpment and one night I found the three of them playing around in my old schoolyard. Somehow they'd made themselves a team. I was always curious about brothers and sisters, having had none myself, and it seemed a great advantage to have someone who knows you in your blood when you were thinking about death. After that visit I went to Ma's alone. At first I wanted to be busy, to clear out her apartment, sort her papers, but she wasn't ready and there wasn't much to do and she did not want it all done too fast. No one wants to say, Well, that's that. My life cleaned up in a couple of hours.

So we sat around together and it annoyed both of us. She said, Go out and give me some peace. I went to a few of the old clubs, stood inside the Alexandra where I first laid eyes on T, went to the Downstairs Club. The steel business was faltering, bought up by new business interests that did not care about the workers on Ma's street and the city was depressed. The clubs were tired and the jazz scene was done. There was a bit of other music. There was a classical musician, Boris Brott, who brought the symphony to the steelworkers. The Connaught was half-empty. My god, I thought, what if I hadn't had the guts to leave?

Slowly Ma's bones began to poke upward in rounded mounds under her skin. Her eyes withdrew. She did not smoke as much. One low day she said, I had opportunities that I did not take. I couldn't.

I listened to her stories of digging out the unearthed papers from Belmont reformatory. She was proud of her years of work with lawyers and researchers, and getting brave enough to publicly admit who she had married. She said, Katie, you can't imagine how anyone would look down on you for marrying a Chinese. When I first wanted to clear my name I was frightened because I had papers in my name and in your father's name and I didn't know if they could arrest me all over again. The first lawyer I went to I pretended it was for a friend. I kept thinking that I did not deserve what happened to me. You know, Nan was the only person I told. You know what she said? Love is love.

Ma's hands got bonier and she had a little rubber thimble that she wore on her index finger to turn the pages and drugstore reading glasses and the way she set things up at the table I could see that she had spent many hours carefully deciphering the legal documents, slowly reading the transcripts of her court appearances, looking at photocopies of records from Belmont.

Here's the file for when I got you back, she said. I wasn't easy to work with. I couldn't remember dates the lawyers needed and when it was too much I would drop out of sight for a while. It's a flaw in my character. I always survived by hiding. The lawyers said, That's how you resisted.

She held out a thick file marked "Medical."

What's this one?

They thought all of us had VD, made it seem as if we carried some kind of blight. Where'd they think we got it? I didn't have it but they were treating me anyway. The prison doctor was experimenting on me, and the other girls too, burning and cauterizing us. She was a horror. For a long time I thought it was me, that I was bad or diseased or something, but I wasn't. It's in the files. She was a vice-president of a eugenics group. One of the girl lawyers helped me find her a few years ago but she was already dead. All I wanted was to tell her I knew what she was up to and that I'd turned out all right and I had raised my daughter and held down a good job and I wasn't a slut. The lawyers tried to be kind and they said, There's only so far we can go. But we are going to clear your name.

Ma was proud of her mealy government apology: Sorry we ruined your life. The letter said: *This Act had unfortunate and unjustified consequences for you and other women who were unjustifiably incarcerated under its provisions.* It wasn't well written, only carefully written. Ma said, It should have said *all* women incarcerated but I got tired of fighting. The day I received the letter, the lawyers took me out for a drink. Guess where we went?

The Connaught?

First time I ever walked in there feeling worthy. I called the Colonel to come and join us and he did. He bought us a bottle of champagne and I was on the served side and everyone made a fuss over me.

You phoned me that day, Ma.

I did this for you too, Katie.

She closed the file and put it back into the heavy cardboard box. She said, After a person's gone, there's still paper. What do you want to do with this box? I care about these papers.

At first when the pain was bad I did not recognize it. She said, Wouldn't it be nice to have a smoke and a glass of wine again?

She was standing in the bathroom looking at herself in the mirror. She turned around and held out her bony arms and said, Why didn't anyone tell me I'm wasting away? What's the big secret? You're all keeping secrets from me. I can feel it.

Her anger took me right back to my teenage feelings, when I was trapped in her frustration. I turned around and went into the kitchen.

She yelled, Why bother coming all this way to ignore me? Go back to your life. Lucky you've got one.

She was trying not to need me. I wanted to keep things light. I said, Hey, Ma, why didn't the skeleton cross the road?

Why?

Because it had no guts.

Like old times. The two of us alone, grating against each other, keeping each other company. We were always afraid not to love each other so we kept making space. Tried to get on with life. Except this time she was dying.

She was frail and brittle and small and as if she could hear me thinking, she said, Don't feel sorry for me. If you're going to be around here so much, I guess there's someone you better meet.

MAHSA

I got taken away from my mother, Katherine told me over the phone.

You're making that up.

I'm not.

Katherine liked to phone me from Hamilton late at night after her mother got sick.

She said, My mother wasn't married when she got pregnant and they put her in a reformatory for being incorrigible. When I was a baby they took me away.

How did she get you back?

She had to fight for me. Kids get taken away and survive. There's a jazz fan in New York everyone calls Baroness. Her real name's Nica Rothschild and she takes care of Monk, drives him around Harlem in her big limousine. She had to give up her five children to be a jazz fan. At least you got Lai back.

Lailuma was withdrawn, especially around Ali. Our lively daughter stayed in her room, used her little-girl-Abbu voice to please him. Her surfaces became reserved and she covered herself with large sweaters that I knew she took off at school. She no longer lingered in the kitchen to talk when she came home in the afternoons. She answered Ali's questions without looking at him and he moved struttingly. Living without forgiveness made me feel empty. Ali said to me, She is respectful now. You would never have taught her that.

I loved the smell of her hair and the feel of her firm arms and back and my cheek briefly on her soft face when she let me hug her. But mostly she avoided me, stepped away before I could touch her. Her eyes accused, You let him.

Katherine said, Thirteen was when I started to shake my fist at the universe. It is normal.

I remembered thirteen.

Then Katherine said, Mahsa, give her a way to escape if she needs it.

I was ashamed to talk about it. I asked, Want to hear what I'm playing?

She answered, Yes, I always do.

But the next day I went to my bank and I came home and gave Lailuma a thin envelope with a lot of money in it from my old student account, and Katherine's telephone number. I said, Hide this well. Keep it with you. In case. Memorize Katherine's number. You may never need it, but the children belong to the father.

Lailuma's eyes cracked like a china teacup. She asked, What would I do, Ma?

I pressed the envelope into her hand and said, It would depend on what happens. You will know what to do. I hope you do not have to.

Some women leave their husbands and children. In the dark, doubting hours I tried to imagine how it would be, the next morning, the next week, a decade later. I imagined pain waning in time. I imagined Lailuma and Asif's story: Our mother left us.

This could not be me. I could not live cut off from my children.

I put my troubles into a small box and forced myself to practise. My concentration became more and more pure. Month after month became a year, and then the next, my only precious life. I taught Lailuma verses of the Quran to please Ali and I said to her, Work hard, try for a scholarship, get your own money.

I watched the little frown-wrinkle like Ammi-jaan's deepen between her eyes.

Things were unalterably changed between us. I stayed home. I played. It was the only thing left to me. One day Lailuma came out of her room when I was practising and said, Mor, I can't concentrate with all that noise. I thought you wanted me to study.

Noise.

Finally I called Jean St. John, said, Jean, I'm dying.

Mahsa, you are coming to your senses. *De quoi tu meurs?*

Doing nothing.

You're lucky to have nothing to do but play. I hate administration. All I do is take care of broken contracts and students with broken fingers and pianos with broken strings.

I laughed.

He said, *Ne ris pas!* I have a Japanese student whose father has donated a great deal of money to us. He wants her to play jazz and not one of my instructors can do anything with her.

Let me give her a master class at my house in the mornings. I will pick up my pay in your office. Don't mail it.

Jean said, *Merde!* The mountain must come to Mahsa. Then he laughed and said, *Tu me manques.* I'll bring her tomorrow. Get yourself out, Mahsa, come play at Biddle's with me.

He never stopped believing in me.

To live, you must risk calamity. Abandon old ways to create something new. Love the life under the visible life. When Lailuma forgot that she was angry I saw in her grey eyes Mor's lively, laughing nature. I sometimes thought she smelled like Mor. I loved her firm, small breasts and her dark hair. I started to write music telling the story of Lailuma and Mor. I saw my mother's crumpled shot body on the floor. I saw the rigid body of a grieving child. Why is honour worth more than a child's love? All this I put in my piece and I called it "I Miss You, Mor."

With each day, the phrases and chords and ideas came from the thing in me that most needed to speak. After weeks and weeks, I sent it to Katherine and she called me back and played it to me over the telephone.

She said, Mahsa, this is beautiful. Do you want my real opinion? Try a major chord in the third line. Contrast the darkness.

Then she said, I love this piece.

I am a strange Karachiite to love winter as I do. Match came through the door, shaking snow from her boots and pulling off thick mitts and hat and unwinding her scarf. She wore her straight hair pulled back in a spiky ponytail. She had no ear for jazz. She loved Bach and she could not bring herself to improvise. She said, Who can improve on Bach? She wore short schoolgirl skirts and carried pink and black accessories and purses decorated with cartoons.

She said, My father is disappointed. He wants me to play like Toshiko Akiyoshi.

I said, I know all about people having dreams they inflict on others.

She said, You are the first genius I ever met.

Improvising is all about adding your own note, I told her, you can do it.

The next class she played a Bach fugue and when she came to the end she paused dramatically, added a single note, then lifted her hands from the keys and turned to look at me. She had her own wit. Jean called and said, I need tutors like you. Take some more students, but you need to come here.

So I found an easy solution. I went, every Wednesday. I told Ali I was volunteering at Lai's school. I wore a niqab on the street so I would not be recognized and stuffed it in my bag on campus.

I even played with Jean. He brought his double bass into my practice room and kicked my student out. He said, My turn.

He left the door open and students gathered in the hall to hear us and they gossiped about whether we were lovers. Sometimes I got up off the piano bench and went to the doorway and riffed on the poetry of Kabir, *Do not cut a goat's throat ... cut the throat of control* while Jean played ostinato. They told one another that we had played together when I was a student and Professor St. John was still a young professor. They heard, in our music, the technique of decades mixed with youth's eros. One day, Jean looked at his watch and said, I have to go. I've got a meeting. Mahsa, let's run away, ditch it all. He shouted to the students in the hall, Go make your own music.

What a sad waste, my family pretending to be happy. I did not know where Asif went with his friends, or where Lailuma wore the red-heeled shoes she hid in her backpack.

Ali became unwell and they found a prostate cancer. During the time of his sickness when I was driving him to treatments and appointments I had to give up teaching again. He directed the office by telephone. I took him in to work for a few hours, waiting, reading magazines, and saw how his staff loved him and were loyal to him. He was charming, talking about hockey and asking after their families. I was reminded of the young man I met in Pakistan. On our drives home he used to tell me with satisfaction how successful he was.

Soon Asif will take over, he said. I've built a good business. One day when he was tired and ill he said, Mahsa, we made a good life.

Jean said, I can pick up all your students, except Match. You've got to see her through. You owe me that.

I taught her a few standards with simple chord patterns she could perform for her father. I pulled out my old Minimoog and we played around. She learned to add few more notes. One spring day near the end of term, I asked her if she had a boyfriend.

He is in Japan, she said. I'm going to marry him in the summer and move to Vancouver. The Richmond Symphony has hired me part-time. My father is coming and I will introduce you and tell him you are my best friend in Montreal.

Does he like your boyfriend?

Oh yes. I am lucky.

Why lucky?

It is difficult for a Japanese girl when the parents do not approve.

I said, That is true everywhere.

Oh no, she said. Here is free.

I said, If you love him, be with him soon. Now, you improvise and I'll recite a poem:

Ask the lightning,
when it cracks through the nightcalm,
if it saw my love.
It makes me think of him.

Then Match said, You play and I will say a poem:

In dreams, on dream paths
with no rest for my legs
I go often, to you
all this is less than a glimpse
in the waking world.

Jean came for her official exam. He stood looking out the window, listening to Match play. I showed him her transcriptions.

Jean asked, What is that?

Match said, It is the Abhogi raga scale.

Jean asked, Jazz?

I said, Jazz is whatever you are. Who said that, Match?

Earl Hines.

What did Ellington say about Mary Lou Williams?

She was like soul on soul.

What did Mary Lou Williams say about men?

Working with men you get to think like a man. You become strong, but this does not mean you are not feminine.

Jean raised an eyebrow, asked me, Are you teaching music or politics?

I said, Match and I prepared an Arabic poem by Umm Ja'far bint Ali. She improvised the accompaniment. Ready? My mother taught it to me.

Match put her hands on the keys and played a few notes and I began to recite:

Leave me alone, you are not my equal.
You are not a man of the world
nor a man of faith
yet you want to own me,
you mindless twit.

Match riffed a little to end it, and we were all laughing and Jean said, Match, I see you learned to improvise. You pass, good work.

Then he put on his coat and said, Mahsa, come play at Biddle's tonight. You can recite that poem, I'll be the mindless twit who plays with you. *Ça fait des lunes qu'on s'est pas vu.*

I can't tonight, Jean. Ali's not well.

Merde, Mahsa, for a few hours? We are making the next *musique actuelle* festival in Victoriaville. Dig out your gold sari and find a way to get yourself there. I'll drive you if your worthless husband won't. Oh, this letter came from Australia for you, to the faculty. I forgot about it. Anyway, it is not my fault, *c'est toi qui as disparu dans la brume*. Get yourself out.

KATHERINE

Ma and Sean were lovers for twelve years. He was tall and thin, with sandy hair and a wistful smile. He had the hands of a man who has not laboured with his body. After the war he had gone back to school with the veterans' program and he became a lawyer, an unimaginable possibility for a boy who came from the neighbourhood he came from. He chose real estate law because he liked detail and predictable hours. He was a good man with a sense of humour who took care of other people's problems.

Ma said, Sean always makes people feel easier. He does that for me too. He can fix anything. Haven't you noticed how well everything works in here?

That was true. Taps did not drip and hinges did not squeak. The paint was fresh. He was a good cook. He said, My first day of high school I liked Jenny. She was pretty and funny and made all the boys laugh and a year ahead of me. I thought I'd never have a chance with her. She was miles out of my league but I kept watching her. When I finally got up the courage to talk to her five excruciating years later, she'd already quit school. I was hanging around a variety store trying to see her. She told me she was pregnant and I said, I'll marry you. We were both still teenagers. But there was war, and I knew I was joining up and I did not want to lose my chance with her. Anyway, she said she didn't think it would work out, she was still in love with your father. So I gave up and got married and went to war but I never stopped thinking about her.

Sean shook his head and asked, Why do we think getting married is getting on with life? I came home from the war to a toddler and we had another baby right away but then I stopped because I knew I wasn't in love and there I was already with two kids. I had my wife to thank for saving up my war earnings and not blowing them like a lot of the gals did. She didn't mind that I went back to school. My wife was loyal to me but my heart got taken long before I met her. That wasn't fair.

He reached over to take Ma's hand and she said, His wife has multiple sclerosis and he never could bring himself to leave her. I sent him packing when he told me he was still married. Later I decided, Life's short. And I thought, As far as I know I'm still married too.

She poked Sean and I knew it was an old joke between them. Sean took his hand from hers and put his arm around her shoulder. He said, Your mother's a saint. I am a lucky man.

Ma said, Katie, I should have told you. I did not want you to think badly of me.

I wouldn't have. I liked Sean. He was bright and tender and he put a shine on her days. She put a shine on his too. I thought, At least she found someone to love her.

If I had a favourite time in Ma's long year of dying, for me it was the spring. I liked the smell of the winter melt and the mills across the bay. I remembered waking up in my little basement bedroom, reading, listening to the first birds, knowing I was going to be outside all summer. My old bed still had the same mattress. I had hoped to make a bit of cash in Hamilton, but the scene was dead there. So I made myself learn how to sit still with her. Slow dying is quiet. A bit of sunshine is precious. A blade of grass looks like a work of art. Ma and Sean and I sat outside and we were grateful for more time after that long, long winter.

Ma said, I used to watch the kids from this porch on summer nights with Nan. Katie ran the street and bossed all the boys. She liked to play Mafia. There was a lot of talk about Johnny Papalia and the Black Hand Society when she was small. Down at the end of the street was a big sewer pipe she called My Office and no one else was allowed to go in. She liked to sit in there and read. She used to say to them, I'll break your kneecaps.

My old stories. When Ma was gone, they'd be gone.

Sean was always touching Ma, holding her hand, leaning sideways to have his arm around her chair. I'd never seen her let anyone touch her. He was interested in everything about her. It felt strange to see her with a man who loved her. I tried to imagine the years of their hidden life in her basement, the love that sustained them through his dogged sense of duty and her necessary secrets.

A scrap of 1942 newspaper, the year of Ma's marriage to my father, was wrapped around a souvenir spoon from Niagara Falls. The article was about a German submarine, a U-553, spotted in the Saint Lawrence River. I wondered if Ma and Henry had managed to go to Niagara Falls. When I showed her the spoon she said with great weariness, Katie, why are you going through all that stuff? Mind your own beeswax.

The dying live in a place which denies admission. I used to watch Ma stir, see her hand reach unconsciously to her bedside table as if for a cigarette. Then she'd look around and say, I'm still here.

Before she went to the hospital the last time, she asked me to get a shoebox from the top shelf of the wardrobe. Inside were envelopes of newspaper clippings and square photographs with fluted edges, my father's goodbye letter, a children's workbook where Ma practised writing her Chinese characters. I looked at the old photo of her and Henry Lau on their wedding day. She was so young, leaning her shoulder on his.

Ma traced her finger over his face and said, Henry felt pretty good, wearing his hat tipped down, rakish like that, trying to belong. He gambled away my ring money so he borrowed a ring and I had to give it back after the ceremony.

That's why I'm not wearing one in the picture. I wish I'd had it on.

She said, Katie, what happened with your father was more complicated than I've told you. I really did love him but it was beyond me to cope.

I said, Ma, you don't have to tell me. Let it go.

I want you to know, she said. It was disorganized. I had no one to help me. After I married him I found out he already had a wife in China. He said he thought it didn't count. Men are strange, aren't they?

I had buried the things from my childhood that I did not want to know. But now I was forced to look, and Ma's stories came out alive and screaming like a newborn baby. My father must have been desperate-poor to sail halfway around the world to a foreign country to find a job, and desperate-lonely to set up a tidy little home in a garage with slippers lined up at the door, pretending he was free, marrying twice. He must have been a bad-ass adventurer too.

Ma said, That's why I never let him move in with us. I was afraid someone would find out and take you away again. A girl who married a Chinese during the war had to take his citizenship. I didn't know until after I did it. But then I couldn't get a Chinese passport either. I had put us in a bad position and I regretted getting married. I did it to make you legitimate so they couldn't take you away again. I applied for a passport under my maiden name. It was illegal but I did it. I could have got five years. You thought I didn't want to come to

New York, you thought I couldn't be bothered travelling, but the truth is I've always been worried about crossing borders.

Our neighbours on Mountain Brow were salt-of-the-earth steelworkers with scrubbed forearms and red shoeshine boxes in their trim brick houses. They moved up there after the Stelco recognition strike when men defined themselves as in or out and made the USWA the biggest union in the country. They had middle-class aspirations and on summer evenings they put their families in Buicks and Fords and drove toward water: Cootes Paradise, the Beach Strip, LaSalle Park on the other side of the bay across from the mills. It was a time when mothers made their children eat what was on their plates and told them to think of all the starving children in India. No Chinese were hired at the steel mills. The well-paying jobs were for white men and some Italians, and later, for men coming back from the war. I finally saw what Ma was up against.

In those days the press could say an unmarried pregnant girl was *stained by shame and fear, a fallen-woman-child who has injured herself and disgraced her family*. There were neighbourhood groups that wouldn't let unmarried mothers move in. One woman said, I'd rather have a bunch of Negroes living next door than tramps like this. Growing up, I never knew the real reasons there was no restless man in our basement, because Ma always made us out to be something special like some prize-winning orchid. Kids don't like to be different. My kids were different too.

She said, I wrote to your father for twelve years after he

left. I sent him pictures of you. Then his wife found out and he wrote one last letter and said he couldn't write anymore and he didn't. One day to the next it was over. What gave him the right? I got so mad I burned all his.

Ma looked at me and said, I guess I shouldn't have. You might have liked them. This is the last address I have for him. In case you want it.

I received the folded paper with the address written in English and in carefully traced Chinese characters. I did not want to think about this. Ma was dying and I was out of money and I did not like leaving Bea in New York alone and I wanted to play and I had too many other things to worry about. Her story, not mine.

I said, Well, I didn't have any luck staying together with T either.

But I added, to please her, We both got good kids out of it.

Her brittle eyes lost their shame and she laughed and said, I guess I've always had a thing for married men.

We heard Sean pulling open the door upstairs and he called down, Hey, gorgeous girls. I'm home.

That was the moment we felt closest through those long months of her dying.

MAHSA

Yes, Abbu. I walked her home.

Asif hung up the telephone and I asked, What did Abbu make you promise?

Nothing, Mor.

Asif, you must tell me the truth. What did he say?

He looked away and his cheeks coloured at the tops of the cheekbones like Ali's and I felt his defiance and shame. He said, Mor, he asked me to watch Lai.

How?

My son looked down, said nothing.

Asif, answer me.

Mor, I am only doing what Abbu asked.

Asif, does your girlfriend's brother report on you?

He did not know that I knew about his girlfriend.

He said, I will tell when I'm ready.

I said, I know you have a girlfriend. Why have you not told Abbu? Or me? Shall I tell him? Why do you keep it a secret? Are you afraid he will not approve?

He said, Abbu wants me to take care of Lai.

I don't want you to.

He said, I know that you are teaching too.

It felt like a slap on the face. What was my son becoming?

But Asif did not have Ali's caged-in temper. He was charming like Ali, a Western boy who loved hockey and went to mosque with his father. Together they had started to do benevolent work and Asif was looking forward to his first business trip. He was a gentler version of Ali, not so angry. Always my son had seemed to me uncomplicated but I now felt a sharp twist in my stomach to see him divided inside himself in this alliance with his father.

I said, Asif, you are better than this. I will make you feel my anger.

Never had I spoken to him in a way that defied Ali. I saw him register a force in me which was unknown to him. My sweet-faced first child who I would have died for. Soon he would act alone in the world. Could he decide what was good? I knew his habit of trying to be water around stone. He wanted to satisfy me and Ali too. And this, of course, was impossible.

Lai came home one day, eyes bright again, and said, When you talk to Abbu tell him I've got my own money and I'm going to study in Vancouver and I'm seventeen and he can't make me do things forever.

That was how she told me she won the scholarship. Then she said, I'm going out.

I hugged her, took her hands and held her close again. I said, All right, no Quran today. Let's have tea to celebrate. I'll tell you a story before you go and you can memorize the last poem.

With a great sigh she sat down, showing me that she could indulge me even though she was now independent, but I knew she was happy. I told her the story of Iʿtimad who was washing clothes in a river in Seville when the Prince Muhammad ibn Abbad was visiting. He was walking with a friend and improvised the first line of a couplet:

The wind rippled a coat of mail in the water ...

He waited for his friend to complete the couplet but the friend could think of nothing. Iʿtimad, the girl by the river, spoke up with a second line:

What a shield it would make if it froze.

The prince was impressed, and he asked, Are you married?

She answered, I am Iʿtimad, and I am not married and my master is Arruamik ibn Hajjaj.

The prince bought her and married her. He was nineteen. She was eighteen. They loved each other deeply.

Lailuma asked, How do you know they loved each other? He bought her!

The story says they were in love, so they had to be. And he took a new title, Mu'tamid, which he made using her name. When I'timad said she would like to see snow, he planted almond trees on the hills over the town so she could look out on the white-as-snow blossoms. Years later, he was overthrown and imprisoned near Marrakesh. She stayed close to him and died a few days before he did. She sent a note, a famous poem, to him when he was travelling and far away:

I urge you, come faster than the wind to mount my
     breast
and firmly dig and plough my body
and don't let go until you've flushed me three times.

Lai memorized the Arabic lines and set down her cup and looked at her watch. Can I go now? I'll come back before dinner. When does Abbu get back from England?

I said, Another week. Meet me at Biddle's tonight instead. Jean phoned and asked me to play. We can get something to eat there. Don't you have a boy you'd like to bring?

Our eyes met and hers were bright. Perhaps she could begin to forgive me now that she could be free. Perhaps she could shed her anger. Family is an endless cycle of betrayal and forgiveness.

At the door she turned to say goodbye. Her hair was loose around her face and the little frown between her grey eyes was gone. She wore a bright blue scarf around her neck and tall leather boots. She ran back lightly and hugged me and said, I'm happy, Mor. Then softly she asked, Should I give you back the money?

I had often wondered where she had hidden it, if she had spent it. My sweet, frightened girl had learned to live a secret life. I said, Keep it with you, Lai. You never know. I have a student who moved to Vancouver. Here is her number. Don't tell the rest of the family where you're going. Why not keep that to yourself for a while?

Her silence spoiled our moment of celebration but before she closed the door she said, I won't tell anyone, Mor.

Lai arrived at the club during my second set, with Gaetan, a boy she'd known in middle school. I felt her studying me performing with Jean. After the set, we joined them at their small table and I invited everyone home and set out sweets and tea. Asif came out of his bedroom and Lailuma said, You should have heard Mor play, Asif. She's fantastic.

Asif stood in the door frame, staring at Gaetan. His lips tightened, as they have since he was a small boy trying to master a new skill. Gaetan dropped Lailuma's hand and they confronted each other, skin and smell and dominance. Gaetan said casually, Asif, *b'jour, ça va le ga?* Asif hesitated and, like the wolf assured of his place in the pack, he walked into the room and pulled out his chair and said, So, you're the mystery man. Then to Lailuma, About time you brought him home.

KATHERINE

Ma used to leave a cigarette burning in every room so she wouldn't have to walk over to the ashtray. That's the truth! That's how I learned to be efficient. When I want to get anything done I leave half of it in one room and half of it in another. I've got staff paper all over the place.

Sean and Ma were laughing. That's baloney, she said.

She was propped up and sliding down her pillows. She was difficult to move. Her last days at home haunt me like a dark, unfading bruise. When she could not stand there was bedbound toileting and washing and a painful bedsore to dress. When I had to move her, to roll her on her side, to trim her fingernails, she screamed at me, Go away. Don't touch me. You're hurting me. She made an awful, high-pitched scream. She tried to hit me and flailed out and sometimes I turned away, and when I came back, she still dreaded my touch. She said, Why are you doing this to me? Her finger and toenails were long and clipping them was painful. Even Sean's touch she sometimes flinched from.

The day before she went to hospital I was half-asleep in the living room, exhausted with the struggle. Sean was sitting beside her.

Are you in pain?

I can't seem to.

Sean's loving eyes reached for hers. She looked through constricted pupils, unfocused filmy eyes, worked hard to stay with us. Sean was not afraid, moistened her lips, kissed them. He said, Jenny, dear heart, we will do what you want. There is an easier. You know. People who know.

I know, she said. I will have to.

She did not want to go.

Sean and I pulled out the old records and tapes and set up her reel-to-reel to have something to do that last night home. When she drifted off, I played him "Dance of the Infidels" which he had never heard.

I looked at an old box of unlabelled tapes and wound one on. Ma stirred awake and we listened to me as a kid, playing those infernal scales, and trying to riff on "You Are My Sunshine."

She lifted her fingers off the blanket and said, I forgot about.

I threaded in another reel and turned the flipper and we heard the kids' young voices. We listened to the boys playing around with the recorder, taping themselves burping and squeezing their armpits and laughing, and then we heard Ma showing them how to rub the tops of glasses to make them vibrate. The boys liked the fun of recording and erasing. They did it a lot.

We listened to Ma's young voice telling them the story of the old woman who swallowed a fly and the little-boy voices joined her chanting, *Oh me, oh my! She swallowed a fly. Poor old woman, I think she'll die!* I played that tape to them a lot when I needed to get Bea to sleep. The night Ma made that recording I was nursing Bea and half listening to them, and worrying about where I was going to get the rent money. I was deciding I had to get back to work, to raise them on my own, the way Ma raised me. I needed to erase more, play, erase, record, erase. Let things go. Move things forward. Make a living. Let him go.

Sean laughed at the boys and said, Jenny, you were a good storyteller.

Her eyes shifted toward those old, old sounds. Opiates don't affect hearing as much as sight. I knew she could hear those tape recordings from a time when we both felt we could do anything.

A recording is a kind of grieving for something already gone. I like live music better. I like not knowing what's going to happen. Sean put on Ma's Sinatra record and squeezed in on the bed near her and he lay on his side and slipped his arms around her and she could tolerate his touch. I went to call Bea. I needed to hear her voice. I needed the living room.

I got a dog today, she said.

New York's no place for a dog. What does it do while you're gone all day?

She said, I thought of that. I got a jacket for him so he

passes as a guide dog and he can come with me. I tell everyone I'm training him. Reverend Moody saw us on the street and told me I was good to do service.

I liked her cheekiness but I said, I go away and what do you do?

Things changed between Bea and me when I was going back and forth to Hamilton. She got independent. That night she said, I miss you, Ma.

Bea, I have no choice.

She said, I know. You know what happened today? I was trying to get this boy to ask me out on a date. My friend went up to him when he was eating a pizza and told him he should go talk to me. He finally came up to me and I asked him, Do you know why I wanted to talk to you? You know what he said? Because you want some pizza?

We both laughed and I said, Sounds like Dexter, and she asked, Why don't boys think the same way girls do?

Oldest question in the world, Bea.

Isn't it lonely there with Gran?

It's okay. She's got other people around too.

I meant for you. Ma, why didn't you ever get married again?

I'm still married to your daddy, Bea.

You know what I mean.

I only ever loved him.

But so you wouldn't be alone.

Bea, it never worked that way for me.

Ma, how is it there?

It's life, Baby Bea. She loves you. We're taking her to the hospital tomorrow. Wanna talk to her if she's awake?

No, it's all right. Ma, remember tempus fugue-it, baby, fiddly doo diddly dee?

Of course I do. It's late. Sweet dreams.

Ma's eyes seemed caught behind a screen. She slept and woke and searched for us. I asked Sean where his wife thought he was.

He said, We've lived together but separate for a long time. She got used to it. We've had the same housekeeper for years. She stayed after the kids left. She loves my wife better than I did. Katherine, I've made a lot of mistakes but the mistake I did not make was to stop loving your mother. It took us a long time to admit it.

He was beside her, stroking her cheek, and she roused and was unusually aware that night. She said, I want to see the stars.

I looked at Sean and he nodded. We got her socks and slippers and a big robe and we pulled her up to sitting and wrapped it around her. She was bones now, awkward to move. We supported her up the stairs, one step at a time, pausing, resting, next. At the top we shuffled against each other in the small vestibule and finally we were outside in the night. She turned her small face upward toward the stars and said, Fresh air.

We got her far enough into the yard away from the street lights to see the brightest constellations, the tipped *W* of

Cassiopeia, and down below the glow of the steel mills over the bay. She said, Well, bye, moon, bye, stars.

Going back she tried to hold herself up, and to get her down the stairs Sean and I made a swing of our forearms for her to sit. She had pain as we lifted her back to bed and Sean was behind her, holding her, and her head rested back on his shoulder. I brought them a tray with tea and ice cubes and Sean organized her blankets and she held his hand. I said, I'm going over to Nan's. See you lovebirds in the morning.

I wanted them to have their last night in the apartment alone, and even though Ma was so sick, neither of them objected.

MAHSA

It began with a knock. Our house was always empty in the mornings. I opened the door and a man filled the frame. I knew his smell and I knew his eyes. I knew everything about him. It felt shocking to see him there, as if he were in flames, burning but not turning to ash, eyes bright, alive.

(So this is love, the pulsing in the head, the blood pitching, so this is love. Pain too and singing and music, so this is love, this trembling, you are in my head all the time, and now this aching, and these sweetly devotions, and you have come to me again, so this is love, the pulsing in my head, so this is love.)

Hello, Mahsa.

Kamal?

He lifted a hand toward me but I stepped back, then he did too.

What are you doing here?

(Twenty years? His eyes the same.)

I live here.

Here?

Could I come in?

How did you find me?

The music director at McGill.

You saw Jean?

Can we talk?

Kamal crossed the threshold and came into the place where I lived with Ali and Asif and Lailuma and his body felt strange inside these walls. He was looking with great curiosity, especially at me. He sat on the couch and I on a chair across from him and I offered him tea and rose to make it and he said, Mahsa, wait. Don't go.

I'm only going to the kitchen, I said.

Then we both laughed, and I sat down again. We began to slowly tell each other our stories like dutiful obituaries, whos and wheres and whats without the great swamp of why. He had been part of the Bengal war, a cataclysmic labour, three million dead, ten million escaping to India, a half-million women raped.

He said, I joined the air force and saw it from above like a corrupt god.

You never wrote about it.

After the war, he said, I went to Islamabad and worked in the civil service. I married and worked in Afghanistan in education for a while. After I divorced, I moved to Australia. What about you? What have you been doing for the last twenty years?

He asked this lightly, with a lift of his shoulders, in a way that made me laugh. We might have been any two old friends catching up on news. I was wearing jeans and bare feet and a camisole-style shirt with thin straps and my arms were bare. It was a humid August but I never put on air conditioning until Ali got home because I liked heat. I kept our blinds louvred downward, the light comfortably shadowed inside. It was too late to run to the bedroom to fetch a blouse and I felt almost naked sitting across from him with nothing on my shoulders and my hair down. Kamal sat, legs apart, leaning forward, elbows on his knees. He was still wiry and strong. His eyes, so familiar, looked at the rugs from Pakistan I had hung on the walls and my beautiful ceramic lamps and the photographs of the children and Ali, and a French-Canadian painting of snow. Though it was morning, in the warmth and darkness, I felt as if we were hiding, though I was doing nothing wrong at all, talking with an old friend from Karachi. I could not take my eyes from him. The corners of his lips deepened when he smiled. His hair was still thick but cropped shorter. He wore ordinary khaki pants and a plain, inexpensive short-sleeved shirt. He said, Mahsa, you are still very beautiful.

I turned from him and then he told me the age of his twin sons which was the same age as Asif and both of us were silently calculating what had happened and when. We must have married at about the same time, but we were not yet ready to speak of this.

He said, My sons are not good Pakistani boys. They have

lived too much abroad, and are lazy and like surfing and rock music.

He was pretending to be rueful, but I could hear his disguised love for them, and I was much charmed by how openly he expressed his affections, as if they were in the room and he were teasing them. His warmth soaked me like a monsoon.

He said, My wife left me for someone else when the boys were thirteen. He shrugged and I noticed how youthful his skin was and how smoothly and energetically he moved and he said, It was ill fated. We did not belong together. When she left, I decided to make a fresh start away from the gathering violence. I took the boys to Australia because I was offered good work there and they could study in a Western style but mostly they like to surf. They go to their mother during the holidays, she moved to Lahore. They are at Sydney University and they are in a band called Bebop Raga and they need me only for money.

I had forgotten how it feels when a man wants to win the attention of a woman. I knew his sons' Australian-Indian pop rock band.

I said, My daughter, Lailuma, likes their music.

Oh, Kamal said, pleased, you have heard of them, even that oxymoronic song, "Broken Energy Kundalini," with didgeridoo and tabla and rubab.

Our conversation stopped. To speak of our children was to speak of our love for them and to feel suddenly melancholy.

Even this we set aside in our curiosity about each other. We wanted to touch, and we did not know now what to do.

Kamal gestured to the piano. Would you play for me?

Always he had understood how to soothe me. It felt natural to walk across the room and to play for him. I wondered what to play and thought of "As Time Goes By" and decided not and I played him one of Katherine's pieces, complex and difficult. The sound in the room felt different. There was no resistance but a listening silence and I let myself be absorbed by the music and I played full and thick, and wound down to the last notes almost inaudible in their delicacy.

Mahsa, you play well, he said.

Then I asked again if he wanted tea and he said yes and in this way I could go into the kitchen and he could look around the living room and he called to me, Where was this picture taken? and You must be able to see the cross from this window at night? and Do you get back to Karachi ever? We talked through a doorway, stopping and starting like ordinary people talking, and the feelings did not subside. I was looking for something so I could say to myself, Oh, well, I was better off. But his energy was no longer devouring and I knew that I was not better off. We presented ourselves as if we had chosen the paths of our lives. I came to the doorway and leaned on it, waiting for the tea to steep, and he asked me about Ali's business and how I spent my days and I felt ashamed so I said, Well, I used to perform in New York, but

I wanted to be home for the children. It has worked very well. I teach a little. I have lots of time to practise. What about you?

Absolutely, he said. I can hear that when you play. I don't want to bore you with what I do. It is still education. I did get some schools going in Pakistan. It works well enough.

How long are you staying in Montreal?

I live here.

Then we fell silent.

I said, I have a student coming soon, though I did not and I had not yet brought him the tea. He stood and said, We should see each other again.

And then I understood the way in which he was changed. The young man I had grown up with had suffered and was ripe and self-assured. He was not the kind of man who would say, I am lonely, but I felt that too in him. We did not stray into the darkling territory of our shared past and how I did not resist being sent away, and how I stopped writing to him, and how we loved each other. It was impossible to speak of all this now.

I thought, We have never stopped seeing each other.

And though he left and I closed the door behind him, his presence was now burned into the air of my home.

From the window above the street, I watched him leave and the clouds were sharply outlined against the sky and the Montreal streets were alive with faqirs and Zelin's and donkey carts. Down below, Kamal Jamal turned back to look up at me in the window and he raised his hand when he saw me watching and I raised my hand to him. His opal eyes were so beautiful. The senses do not lie. The body does not lie.

KATHERINE

Ma opened her eyes and I sang her a bit of "All of Me." She preferred the Sinatra version, not Billie's. She said, I like a man's voice singing those words.

I'm the only man in the room, I said, till Sean gets here, and he can't sing.

She said in her raspy, drugged voice, You're killing me.

He shakes my ashes,
greases my griddle,
churns my butter,
strokes my fiddle.
My man, such a handy man!

She said, That was my mother's song. How do you know that?

I know all your songs.

I lay my hand over her cool fingers until she dozed. She woke and drifted off. Watching her die reminded me of my years with the babies when I counted time in moments not days or nights. I got her ice chips, moistened her lips, lifted her up on her pillow. I had to get some part-time work. The year had depleted me. I was broke.

Sean came in. Want to go out? Your family is here.

What?

They're at the apartment.

I pictured T walking down into that little basement, ducking through the low doorway. I wondered if the kids were taking him around the neighbourhood, if they'd introduced him to Nan. For the first time in all the months of waiting I cried. Why the hell hadn't he told me he was coming? Helping not helping. Doing it his way. But I was happy they were there. Damn him.

They came to the hospital and waited with me in the hall, in the hospice kitchen, with other people waiting for people to die, and we talked mostly as if no one was dying because what else do you do?

T said, I'm taking Jimmie on tour with my new band.

Just when I'm not there, you blow into town and think you can take over.

Jimmie wants to come, babe. He's good. You wanted me to help out.

I said, My mother's dying. Now all the hard work's done with Jimmie and he's a good young man, you're taking him on the road. T, you keep him straight.

He laughed but said a little quieter, Katie, I'm clean now.

He's lucky to play with this band. Don't you worry, babe, I'll take care of him. He's half mine too, you know.

That's what I'm afraid of.

But I heard that thing in his voice and I let him wrap his arms around me and it felt good, it always felt good, and he was trying to take care of us, too late, but I let my body tell me what to do and it was letting him hold me and it was soaking in his heat and resting after months of sitting and grieving and trying to keep things going for the kids and wondering what I was going to do. All those years of keeping everyone close, and now I had to let everyone go. I couldn't take care of them all anymore. They didn't want me to.

I went to the funeral home and made arrangements. I had to borrow money from Sean to pay for everything and he said, I want to do this, don't worry. By the next day Ma was in and out of consciousness and there was a terrifying force in her dying grip. She took my hand and held on so hard and her fingers were digging into the bones on the back of my hand, hurting me. It was a horrible clutching as if she were hanging from a cliff and I did not tell her it hurt and could not bear to try to ease my hand out of hers. T was outside the door, where I could see him, and Sean stroked her forehead and dabbed her lips with a little sponge of cool water. She was in and out of sleep and she opened her eyes and when I leaned in close to hear her raspy whisper she said, Ming, there are flying things fluttering over my forehead. Get them away, Ming, please.

MAHSA

When can I see you?

Let's talk on the telephone. It is difficult for me to get out. (I could lose Lailuma.)

Kamal said, After the war, I wanted to live. And teach. So much was lost. Half the country cannot read. Imagine not being able to read.

I watched the slant of the light through my window. As he described his sons as babies, I imagined the courageous woman who gives birth to twins but he said nothing about his wife. I watched the winter-afternoon light thin on the bare branches tapping on the glass.

The seasons changed again. Kamal's voice said on the telephone, I used to work with a man who lost his eyes in the war.

I listened and watched the sharp, bright summer light, and I lowered the blinds against the heat.

On a late-fall afternoon he said, I married in Islamabad and my father arranged it.

The street lights were making little haloes over dead, dried leaves on the sidewalk.

I told him about Katherine. He told me about his work and raising his boys so far from home, and one twilight as the room darkened he said, I never stopped thinking about you.

I learned how he grew into a man. He failed to move his ideas forward as our cities filled with shootings and bombs. I asked if his wife had any choice when he took his sons to Australia.

He said, She was with someone else. The boys spent all their holidays with her. But he did not answer what I asked.

Do you remember the last time we were together in Karachi? I asked. You said to me, We will never find this again.

He said, I do not remember saying that to you. I was smarter than I thought.

I laughed. My mother used to say in Pashto, Ask the fox, Who is your witness? And he will say, My tail.

The strangeness of Kamal and I when we were young was that we never said goodbye and we never made a plan for the future. Now, we understood everything about each other. There were things we could not talk about and there was neither impatience nor urgency because we were no longer young. Montreal was not supposed to be my life but a short season. Nothing was forgotten and nothing perfectly remembered either.

He said, After the war, I went to your house and your uncle was angry and he told me you were getting married.

I thought there was no more hope with you. I tried to stop thinking about you. When something is not working, I move on. I do not linger.

He was telling me what he remembered. But I had his letters and he did not stop writing to me that he loved me all through the war in Bangladesh and after.

I am building a school in Sind province, he said. I am raising the money and finding teachers. Perhaps my sons will teach music but also they have their own lives now.

He paused and said, I may be telling you more than you want to know.

I want to know everything about you.

Sometimes I felt a parchedness in him as if he had been too alone with his thoughts. I asked why he was so interested in talking over what happened to us, and he answered, You were the only other one who was there.

There was an industrial area down by the river where Kamal and I sometimes dared to walk together, among people without beds, among people who heard voices, who ate and drank and smoked things that numbed them. We shared their delicate company in that place where the river flows out to the sea. Sometimes a person gestured to Kamal for a cigarette, or saluted with a bottle, but no one ever spoke to us. People there wanted to be invisible and they made room for us with them. We still dared not touch.

I told him that I liked what we were doing.

Talking? he asked. We always talked a lot, even when we were young. I asked if I had been shy, said that we were together a short time, a few years. He said, I do not think that you were shy. Is a short time bad?

No, I said. Life can change in an instant.

Kamal said, Talking is not all that I want to do with you. We have to do something about making love. We already have, you know.

I was startled at this boldness and liked it and resisted it too. His mother had not been murdered for love and he had not been forced into marriage. I felt his coiled urgency and it filled me with pleasure. When I was young it felt like he would devour me. He wanted to devour everything back then. I did too. He had not stopped loving me, and he was not afraid to tell me. After all the years.

He said, When your uncle told me you were marrying, I believed you were afraid to say so in your letters. I gave up and decided to marry too.

I told him they had brought me home from school and taken my passport and forced me.

When did you marry? I asked.

August nineteenth, 1972.

I started to laugh and he smiled with me and asked, What are we laughing at?

We married on the same day.

Mahsa, he said. He put his arm around my shoulder and

I reached up and touched his hand and felt the shock of his flesh, again, familiar and natural, the first man's hand I touched that was not Abbu's.

When I heard your student tape, he said softly, I heard riffs only I would know. Even if you were not playing for me, you were playing for me. Were you?

I said to him, I cannot risk anything happening to Lailuma.

We walked by three men sitting in a circle passing around a bottle in a brown paper bag. One of them raised his fingers in greeting to Kamal who nodded back.

Kamal said, I have not asked you to.

Does this feel right?

To want to make love?

To do what we are doing.

Perhaps.

We have been talking for a long time now, haven't we? Has it been years? I shifted a little away from him and he dropped his arm from my shoulders and we continued to walk side by side, our shoulders brushing, but mostly separate again.

Kamal said, There is an Afghan expression that I am thinking of. God says, Start moving so that I may start blessing.

Heaven is dark yet from it streams clear water.

I had almost forgotten how feeling feels. I was often distracted by his skin's scent and the light in his eyes and often I had to ask him to repeat. There was a frequent tripping over each other's words, waiting, as we deprived each other of touch.

Did you ever go back to Afghanistan?

I did.

What happened?

I was working there, and I went to find my father. He left the city and academic life to fight. I found him deep in a mountain. He sat on a worn carpet of red and blue and green. His beard was long and he was sinewy and thin. His face had been burned. Before I could see him in the darkness of the cave, I heard his voice, Son, you have endured a difficult journey.

He was blinded by a mine hidden in a thermos but he recognized my smell. He was a teacher, not made for fighting. It was after the Soviets, the beginning of the Taliban, and he joined men who knew nothing but war.

That is how humans are. They do something. Even if it is the wrong thing.

Kamal said, My father had to give up his rubab. All music was forbidden and in the great stadium they executed the instruments, smashed and burned them. But Plaar buried his, wrapped it and hid it underground. He said to me, A bird only flies as high as his wings take him. There are many things to do in life. I must stay here. You go and teach.

I told him, I got my wings from you.

So I left him there. I walked back out of the mountains and got across the border and I knew I would not see him again and I did not. Have you ever been?

No. I was always afraid of what my relatives might do.

Blood will have blood. But I met a man from Helmand in Karachi. He lost his legs in the war. He used to sit outside a store near my school. He'd say to people passing by, Did you send for my legs yet? I'm waiting for my legs. That is all I need to go back and be a shepherd again.

Kamal said, We Afghans have relentless hope. I travelled in the mountains, guided by a young boy whose skin was already weathered, who wore a neat and threadbare coat over layers of sweaters. I walked behind him and looked down into a valley and saw the empty space of sky. Below, a woman wrapped head to foot in a red burqa stood in the doorway, alone. She was the only colour on the grey mountain.

I said, I have not thought of these things for many years. I feel at home with you. In Karachi I saw little Pashto girls still wearing short skirts in the marketplaces, practising the dignified, straight-backed movements of their mothers. Those children shed awkwardness early, copy the dignity of the adults. I saw little girls doing all the things women did, carrying babies and shopping bags, and soon they would do these things covered by a veil or a burqa. They would eat ice cream under the veil. These are the images I have of my mother's people though I never went there.

We did not talk about your parents when we were young. Why?

There were many things we did not talk about. We could not.

Why?

I was ashamed.

And I was impatient about what I could not change, he said. Patience is not a quality a young man thinks about. Now I can admit my mistakes. When I was a young man, I could not show weakness. Tell me about your parents.

I told him about their dancing and Abbu's movies. I told him that Abbu took me to hear Dizzy Gillespie play at the Palace Cinema when I was six years old, and that we heard Jack Teagarden and Artie Shaw at the Rex Cinema Hall. I told him about the day I was called from class to learn that Mor and Abbu were dead.

Mor was her father's favourite, the only child of his third and youngest wife who was his pretty second cousin and did not read or write. Her father was impressed by the Americans he met in the Helmand Valley and he had sacrificed for Mor to be educated and to learn English, but he had never dreamed that she might run away with one of them. How fearless she must have been to leave everyone she knew for an American stranger. When her half-brothers from Helmand found out that Abbu and Mor had not gone to America but were still in Karachi, they said, *karo, kari*, black man, black woman. In Pashto they said, Kill them for their transgression.

Here, in Montreal, this story seemed from another world. I said to Kamal, As the sun's shadow shifts, so there is no permanence on earth.

Forgive me, Mahsa, he said. I should have asked you about them. I did not know how when I was young.

There is nothing to forgive. I could not speak about it. I loved them so much. Lailuma and Asif still do not know how they died. I do not want this to be their family story.

Perhaps someday, he said. He asked me many questions then, where my father was from, how they eloped. I asked, Do you remember me playing for you "Kansas City"?

Kamal said, Of course, I remember all your music. *Zan, zar, zamin*. Much blood has been spilled. Your parents are the legendary lovers of Karachi.

I asked him, Are you and I legendary lovers?

Of course, he said, except we did not stay together.

When I told you I was leaving, you were angry.

I do not remember that.

Did we find love again?

Our questions were a way to be close. Love thrives in perfect freedom. When we were young we learned together the burdenlessness of love. People always want the next thing. People are tempted away from the exquisiteness of the waiting-moment.

I was curious about his letters and I went to read them at Monique's. In his last letter he said that he hoped I liked life in Montreal, that what we shared in Karachi was a different life.

I remembered this as the end of us. But he had continued on the second page: I know what we were and I have not stopped loving you, but I do not know what we are now.

Kamal said, I kept your letters too.

Did you read them?

I was afraid to. Did I think the paper would burn my fingers? I thought maybe I had got it all wrong.

I misremembered your last one. It was after the war in East Pakistan.

What did I write?

Mostly that you loved me. I remembered that you said it was over but you did not say that.

Kamal shook his head. He said, I learned in the war that when something was going to hurt, powerful men did not flinch. Either a swift flight or a swift blow. I threw myself into everything, but especially things that hurt. When pain was coming at me, I took it and got in close and learned how to inflict. I hope in my letters I was not unkind.

As he talked I watched the sunlight through a cloud.

But you were afraid to read my letters.

Yes.

When we were young, you had other girls. Why?

In those days, there were girls who were friends and girls for the rest. You were young. I always wanted to spend time with you. Later I knew that I wanted to be with you. It felt strange, like a leap, trying to bring these things together.

What made you take the leap?

You did.

KATHERINE

The living are in a hurry. The dying can wait. Death does not come fast enough at the end and the moment of death is too quick. I was pacing, thinking she was asleep, and she opened her eyes and startled me when she spoke. She said, Katie, you always were impatient.

The nurse was cleaning her up and remaking the bed, and I drummed softly on the bed railing, chanted as much for the nurse as for her,

What you gonna do when the bed breaks down?
Tried it on the sofa.
Tried it on the chair.
Tried it on the window.
Didn't get nowhere.
What you gonna do when the bed breaks down?

I wished I had loved her more. Why hadn't she told me about Sean? I tried to let go of the things that Ma and I never worked out. Her life. My life. When she went into the coma Sean said, She knows we are here.

I asked the doctor, Does she?

The doctor said, There are many kinds of knowing. Be with her.

And then, a night and another day and a night. I was sure she squeezed my hand. People have twitches. I talked to her, sang to her. You cannot leave alone the breathing, still-warm body but the outside flesh becomes cool. A person grunts and rasps toward death, listen to the ragged breath, stop, start, unplayable rhythm, wait wait wait, suck in again, wait wait, rasp out, and wait, wait and wait and then.

(I wondered if my father in China was still alive. I would have told him that she was strong to the end. I would have told him that he should have tried harder with her. I would have wanted to hear about his life. I would have wanted him to know that she found someone, that she was not alone, but that she did not stop loving him, she still said he was handsome when she showed me the wedding photo. I would have told him that I wished I could have met him, once.)

MAHSA

Now, I said to Kamal.

He answered, Are you sure?

We walked hand in hand to his place. I called it the tree house because it was high above Montreal and looked down over the river. It was austere. A table and a wide bed and windows that opened to the stars and moon, and we were wrapped in darkness, and breathed light. After all the many years, we made love again, and we remembered a few things, yes many and beautiful things, and observed some new things, our senses open and excited. Our bodies were different graves now, shallower, filling quickly, two lifetimes of high-hatted and passing joys that made lighter the years of duty and displacement and earning livings and raising children. We were two people who had tended our hope. He took and gave what was his, listening to me. I opened the door for him and I took and gave what was mine. And we touched and kept listening to each other after the years of waiting, our love a great failed love, fleeting as spring ice. Love has many expressions and cannot be forced or judged. Its quickened breath cannot be quieted and it cannot be made a tyranny. All forms of love are right.

He asked, Do you believe in fate?

Destiny is a donkey. It goes wherever you lead it.

Yes, he said. I think that is right. And then he sang for me. I love his voice singing. One note is a sound, two notes a song.

KATHERINE

The divine is alive. It needs room to split your skull. In other places people cut their bodies in mourning and dress in rags and sit in the dust, but there were things I had to do. I had to sign papers and empty our old apartment and take her clothes to the Sally Ann. Sean said to me, I cannot do this. I told him I'd do it, I had T and the kids to help, and it took less than a day to wipe her traces away. Sean went home and I went to the Connaught to say goodbye to the people in the kitchen and I saw the Colonel and he said, Well, Mrs. Goodnow? I answered, I'm not Mrs. Goodnow, that was my mother. I went to visit Lily upstairs. She said, I don't think I'll rent it again. It's going to be strange to be alone in the house after all these years. Do I owe you the first month's rent? I said no and thank you and keep in touch and I asked her if she still played hearts and she said, It would be nice to play again but it's not much good with two and I said, Well we were the four dames, weren't we? After that I was in a hurry to go back to New York because here I was like a swallow on a window ledge separate from the life inside the room, so I handed Lily the keys and walked away for the last time from Mountain Brow and I felt a weight like a bucket of heavy ashes blow off me. You can mourn and still be released.

Back home, I slept. Everyone came in and out and T and Jimmie left to play in Boston. One morning I woke up and I hardly knew how many days had gone by but the light was crisp. I could taste the bitterness of my coffee. It was a slow-creeping feeling of still being alive after being gone for a long long time, receiving and ready. As a child I used to look at grass and sky and wish I had *made* all this. I put my fingers on the keys and made a sound and another and another and I heard the opening vamp of "New Thing at the Surf Maid." It was already in me. Marian McPartland called and said she was getting her agent to book a tour to Asia for me. She said, Cecil can go too. Jazz is hot there, and you're free now to go.

Ma, things came together for me after you died. It felt like an Art Tatum two-finger run, it was fast and light and fully formed. Ma, I hope there is love for you wherever you are. You would have liked this piece, but mostly I think you would have wished to be still alive. There should have been more time for you. I got up early in the morning and wrote and in the afternoons if there were no paying gigs, I walked in Central Park until twilight. It was a simple routine and calmer than I have ever lived and I was happy though I have never cared about being happy.

I wrote "New Thing" quickly in three parts. It begins with love and ends with death. In the middle is struggle. The gods want to fill you. All you have to do is keep making room for them.

I sent the charts to Mahsa and she phoned, laid the receiver on her piano and played it back to me. She said, It is good, Katherine.

I said, It's not done.

She said, I know.

It is love we do not talk about enough. People talk about sex all the time, never stop talking about it. Ideas were pouring out of me. You have to keep doing it all. You have to keep chasing your favourite things. Don't stop. Don't wait. Keep going.

Mahsa mailed me a clipping from the *Gazette* with a photograph of a wedding ceremony, a young man and woman facing each other, holding hands. The love in their eyes shone through the newsprint. They were delighted with each other. He wore a casual checkered short-sleeved shirt and she wore her hair down. The girl's name was Jassi and her family owned blueberry fields on the West Coast. She had been offered in marriage to one of her father's business associates, forty years older than she was. Jassi had other ideas. She fell in love on a family trip to India with Mitthu, a rickshaw driver, and she ran away and married him. One night driving on his motorbike along a dark road, they were stopped and her throat was slit and her body left in shallow water. Mitthu too was left for dead but he survived. Telephone records and bank statements and family business connections pointed to Jassi's family hiring out the murder in India. But nothing was done.

Mahsa wrote on the scrap of newspaper: *Katherine, write this.*

My piece started with the old couple in the Brooklyn deli and turned into something else. It was Lucia di Lammermoor. It was Jenny Goodnow. I wrote it for two pianos and I put in Mahsa's "I Miss You, Mor" and I phoned her every morning to play the next new bit. I put in power and law. I put in sex. And longing. And love and grief. I put in everything I had ever thought. I took it to Harvey Lichtenstein at the Brooklyn Academy of Music and told him, Here is a story to tell. Bea's going to choreograph it. Let's find some dancers to perform it. I've got the other pianist.

I called to tell Mahsa.

She said, Ali's parents will be here.

I said, Four years, Mahsa. I haven't seen you for four years. It is time. The charts are in the mail. The performance is only three nights. Your kids are fine now. We record opening night. Get yourself down here. I'm going on tour to Asia after but next time I want you to tour with me. The most radical thing a woman can do is live.

Harvey brought in dancers from one of his high school programs and when I met them I asked, So you are the high-risk kids? I stage-whispered, What they don't know is that we take high risks.

They danced till their feet ached. We did blind casting and everyone had a chance to perform. The lovers were Hispanic, black, Asian, white. Bea asked me where I got the idea and I said that it came from Mahsa.

Bea said, I think you're writing about Gran.

If it was her story, we wouldn't be here.

I thought, It is time she knows about her grandmother, and so I told Bea how Ma was arrested for being incorrigible, about a morality so cold that fathers imprisoned their own daughters. I said, Baby Bea, Gran was in a reformatory and I was taken away and she had to fight to get me back. She was still a teenager. When she got out she was frightened to be married to a Chinese man so they never lived together. The last blow was years later when she found out he had another wife.

Bea was quiet for a long time. She said, You could have told us.

That was that. The last shreds gone. Ma, I kept your secret from my kids until I did not have to anymore. They heard the story as sad and unjust, but also as quaintly from another time, a time when girls wore white gloves and filled up hope chests to get ready to marry. Ma, your grandkids grew up half black when people marched and protested and burned cities and died so we could all go to school together and sit on the bus together and live in the same neighbourhoods. Ma, your grandkids loved you with your silly rhymes and old songs and handing them hundred-dollar bills on the street and telling them you didn't want to go to heaven. They loved you, and found it a curiosity that a woman could be arrested for following her own desire. We were all fine. Blemished, imperfect, but fine.

MAHSA

Katherine and I played parts of "New Thing" on the telephone to each other every day. She described the choreography and practices and said, You should see how well they move to your "I Miss You, Mor," it is very emotional.

After the months caring for her mother, I felt her intense energy. I so wanted to see her again. In the mirror I saw a woman losing her freshness, and when I looked down on the keyboard the veins pushed up from under my skin in little rivers and mountains. My breasts were less taut, a thing I noticed with Kamal in the strangeness of us remembering our bodies in youth. What had I done in all the years? I had tried to make a marriage work, raised two children. I had lived in a clay shell that was now cracked and falling away. I wanted so much to play this concert. And so, I begged Ali, Let us take your parents to New York this summer. You have been sick and it is a chance for us all to be together. I felt my stomach clench, waiting for his impatient *No*, and I had planned that whatever he said I would go and take

Lailuma with me. The perversity of who I had become was that I continued to try to please him. I was placating and I sickened myself. But he surprised me, said, Perhaps you are right.

Soon Ammi-jaan was phoning to ask how long was my concert and how many days to rehearse and how long would I be backstage and where would we stay. I wanted to scream, How would I know? I have hardly been out since you kidnapped my daughter. She asked what hotel would we use and would I take her shopping and were there some restaurants where Daadi could find plain rice, and preferably rice porridge in the mornings. I reassured her that I would have lots of time to show her New York and she sent me a lovely shalwar kameez richly embroidered in greens and yellows, made of fine silk, expensive and exquisite, and wrote on the note, This is for your show.

What a fool I was.

She phoned and said, I have found a husband for Lai. He is educated and has already worked with Ali. He might be pleasing to Lailuma, I think quite handsome. He has worked in London, but Ali could find him a place in the business in Canada. Would we not be happy to see her settled? We can introduce them, we must not wait too long. I worry so much about Ali's health.

Nothing they were afraid to use to have their way.

He was fifteen years older than Lai. Ali said, It is decided. It is my greatest desire to see this for Lailuma.

I said, Ali, let her take her scholarship, finish her education. She is too young and will be difficult.

Even when I have been sick, you resist me, he said. She can go to school after she is married. She herself has not seen him to decide. I agreed to you playing the concert. Always you want more.

She does not want to marry. She wants to study.

It is time for her, he said. What is wrong with getting married?

KATHERINE

It was so good to see Mahsa. I pulled her close to me. She was thinner and in each other's eyes we saw the recent years of struggle. I said, Let's play. You start, I'm going upstairs to listen. I watched her settle in and touch the keys of one of the Bösendorfers and I leaned over a front balcony above to hear how the sound resonated up there. An open grand looks like a harp tipped on its side from above. I love the acoustics at BAM. Mahsa was nervous like a little racehorse ready to burst out. I called down to her, You sound great, wait, I'm coming to play with you. On the way down I listened to her still feeling for the sound she wanted. I love empty concert halls. It was so damn good to be with her. I sat down and we looked at each other across the spruce cabinets and sound-boards, and we were young and playing together side by side at the Surf Maid again and we listened to the rims begin to vibrate, piano wire resonating under our fingers and we were swinging together in one string hammock, the shining wood reflecting our faces.

We warmed up with "Two to Love," and then I said, Let's play it straight through, and she nodded and waited for my opening bars. Her head and shoulders were bent forward over the keyboard and she had taken off her jacket and was wearing a light shirt and she closed her eyes. She knew the music perfectly and when I stopped to work at our dynamics, she could pick up anywhere. We played as if we had never been parted. The score was on the floor beside her. I love playing with Mahsa. At the end of the third movement we stopped on the same breath, a single hand smoothing the sheets.

There was a hell-bent feel to her touch that I had not heard before and I said, You're playing strong, and she said, It's your music, and I said, And yours too.

Ali came in to watch the end of the rehearsal, stood arms crossed, leaning against the wall inside the back doors. He wore his expensive suit casually, and though Mahsa had told me he was sick, I saw a man accustomed to taking up space. He strode down the long aisle, introduced himself charmingly and said, Mahsa has spoken of you so often. Can I bring you anything? I said, We should relax before the performance. I wondered, fleetingly, if Mahsa had been afraid of nothing all these years. He was urbane, worldly. When he left, Mahsa sat down again and played for fun a blues bit that she often played when we were young. She always called it "Karachi Baby" but I think it was an old Beatles tune. I watched her shoulders start to move, her body get loose, and when she finished she looked around happily and said, I feel as if I am on my own brink again. That always happens to me with you.

Me too.

Then she dropped her hands to her sides and swung around on the bench and said, Katherine, I've got this bad feeling.

It's jitters, I said. You haven't performed for a long time. Let's get something to eat.

A few hours later the auditorium was full and the dancers were behind us and she was performing like her hair was on fire.

MAHSA

On stage, dressed in black, Katherine looked like a tall, elegant man wearing a woman's hat, and the fine silk of my shalwar kameez shimmered against her suit. The opening twelve bars of "New Thing" were hers and then the second piano came in as the lights came up on the dancers. We got to work. No intermission. Straight through. One moment. One story.

The lovers wore bodysuits under their wedding clothes and during the violent slow-motion attack scene in the second movement, the young woman's fancy silks were torn off as she was pulled away by her brothers. Her lover was left holding a scrap of her torn dress, his own clothes also in tatters. That movement ends with the chorus, faces covered by veils, dancing to "I Miss You, Mor." Before the allegretto, Katherine looked across the piano at me ready to complete the long unbroken piece.

The final tableau is my favourite part of the dance. The first piano answers the second. On the bare stage the ghosts of the lovers dance a passionate pas de deux of lost love. They move in and out of unmoving pools of blue light. I had been preparing to play this moment with Katherine from the time I first sat beside Abbu on the piano bench as a small child.

When it was over, in the dark, on stage, Katherine hugged me, said, We played well.

I knew we had.

I'm going to check with the recording engineers to see if they got it, she said. Go and enjoy the party, I'll be there in a minute.

I was not aware that he had come until I was off stage and saw him standing half-hidden near the door in the hallway to the green room. Kamal. In New York. A group of young dancers jostled by the door, running with great excitement in and out of their change rooms, and a student who was amiably drunk, a dancer's boyfriend, stumbled between us. He looked from Kamal to me and asked, Sorry. Is this your guy?

No.

The drunk looked at me in surprise, as if I had tried to tell him that the earth is flat, said, Then do you wish he was your guy?

I laughed as I used to with drunks in the hotel bars and said, I'm just getting my sweater.

The drunken young man moved along and I whispered to Kamal, I have to go. Even a drunk can feel us.

Kamal said, Not yet.

I have to get my things.

In the dressing room were empty water bottles, dancers' bags, coats in a pile on a couch. When I turned, Kamal was standing inside the door and we were alone.

Mahsa, you played beautifully.

Kamal, thank you for coming.

We heard people in the hall and I moved away from him and he slipped into a side room as a stage manager showed Ali in.

Ali said, Mahsa, you know I am waiting. What are you doing? Who was that?

One of the theatre staff, I said.

Come, I have someone waiting to meet you.

At the reception, I felt the unpleasant confusion I used to feel with people after performing. Ali guided a French-Canadian businessman I had met several times in Montreal through the crowd to me and he said, Mahsa, it was magnificent. Then to Ali he said, Where have you been hiding her? He pulled in a young man and said, This is my son Sebastien. He wants you to play at his *boîte*, Nuage bleu, when you get back to Montreal.

Ali said, Of course she will play for you.

Where were Asif and Lailuma?

A mandala of light bulbs was strung over the tall windows of the Lepercq Space. Along the walls of the cavernous room were risers and scaffolding and the centre was set with round tables and a long bar and candles and big trays of food that the dancers wheeled around like small flocks of starlings. Some were wrapped in scarves and heavy leg warmers and others wore light silk camisoles and their parents approached, to tell me they'd never heard two pianos, that their children had been inspired by the work. Katherine brought Harvey, who wore a plaid jacket and a black fedora, to see me. He wanted me to meet people from the school board. I had not imagined how many people Katherine knew, or what this production meant. Finally I made my way back to Ali and asked, Where are the children?

They went to the hotel with my parents to make a late-night celebration for you. We will meet them there.

I wanted them at the reception with me. I wanted to stay here all night with everyone else, to enjoy this moment.

Ali said, It is late.

I made my way round the party one more time and saw Bea who was excited about her first choreography and she asked, Where're Lai and Asif? I haven't seen them.

I found Katherine who said, Mahsa, this is the fun part. She turned to Ali and said, Stay a bit longer. Everyone wants her at the opening-night party.

He answered her charmingly, You'll understand, my parents leave in the morning, early. Tomorrow night I hope you'll allow me to invite you and your family to a post-performance dinner.

When I nodded Katherine shrugged and said, All right. Meet me here tomorrow at five thirty.

In the cab Ali said, I hate that kind of theatre.

I looked out the window at the Carnegie Hall tower with its glazed bricks. I thought, I won't let him spoil my night.

Almost naked dancers, said Ali. This is the sort of theatre you choose. Hell is full of women.

Inside our hotel, under the chandeliers, walking over the thick carpet, past heavy wooden desks with fresh flowers, I still did not know. I was looking forward to celebrating with my children. I still did not know, walking down the long hotel hall, thinking about performing again tomorrow.

But I knew when I stepped inside the door and we switched on the lights, when Ali closed it behind us and swung the brass security bar across. I knew this kind of emptiness.

She'd never made it to the concert. No one had. Not Asif. Not Ali's parents. While I was settling behind the piano on the darkened stage, while we played the first notes as the dancers appeared, they slipped away. They forced her. They forced her into a cab. The door to the cab closed. The car pulled away to the airport.

That is how fast a life can change.

KATHERINE

I was living with a new silence inside. After the party, I went
home alone and played the whole performance through in
my head. There was a fresh passion in Mahsa that I hadn't
felt before. I wished she could have come home and sat up
late and talked like the old days. I thought I might change
the timing of the opening of the second movement. I couldn't
sleep and I wished T had come. Ma was inside me in a
different way now. Ma, I want to turn from you as from the
cold ashes of a dead fire. But you burn like hidden embers.
You would have liked that Baby Bea choreographed. I'm glad
that I saw you with Sean. You were a woman who was loved.
I am going on the road again because I have wanted to sleep
in strange beds and to play for new audiences every night ever
since I first got pregnant and gave all that up. I have new ideas
for two pianos. One piece will be called "Bye, Stars." I am
hearing new sounds that begin with your Ma-filled silences.
The longer you are gone, the deeper I feel you. Am I just
beginning again? A woman becomes mustard seed light when

her old and her young are gone. Is this how you felt when I left?

I heard my grown-up kids come in and sit at our kitchen table as I lay in bed. Now I had what I always thought I wanted, empty space and time to write real and true things. I was thinking about new sounds when I heard the telephone ring, and Bea answered and she listened for a long time. Finally she came into the bedroom and asked, Are you awake? Lailuma's on the phone.

MAHSA

I passed ahead of Ali into the silent room.

Do not try to stop this, he said. I will divorce you. I will say the three talaqs and be done with you.

His eyes were black beads in his flushed, old skin. He seemed to me suddenly deformed, and a stranger.

Ali, he's too old for her. Please.

They marry tomorrow. You and I leave for Montreal in the morning. We are all tired of your resisting.

I should have stayed in New York, should have played the last two nights with Katherine. All I could think about was getting Lailuma back, and so I left with him thinking I could do more from home than here. They count on that.

I saw the unlit cross against the late-morning light and I looked down at the great, wide river cradling the city. Though I have lived here longer than anywhere else, the sight of forest from the air still seems exotic to me. Ali shifted in his seat and touched my arm and I felt revulsion. I pulled away and put my forehead against the small window. I would call Katherine, and then I would call Aunt, who I had not spoken to for years, to ask her to take Lai shopping and hide her. I would have to get out of the house to call. I could go to Jean's, or Monique's. I had to act quickly. We moved through the lines for baggage and customs and Ali showed our passports and when the immigration officer asked, What was the purpose of your trip? Ali said, Just pleasure. He looked at me and I nodded. He put our passports in his jacket pocket and then we took the airport express bus downtown and I was thinking, Where is Lailuma now?

Ali lifted his large suitcase up the steps to our door, and I had only my purse with no money inside. Ali unlocked the door and stepped ahead of me into the hall. He put the suitcase down and was removing his coat. Then he stopped and shouted at me, Lock the door. I was startled by this new rage until I saw what he had seen in the living room.

He yelled, What are you doing here? Where is she?

Asif stood up, pale, with black rings under his eyes. He hadn't been to bed. A bedroom throw was lying in a heap on the floor beside the couch, and an empty plate. He said, She refused, Abbu. I could not make her. She made a terrible scene at the airport. As soon as she walked through the metal detector, she started shouting, They're taking me, and she ripped up her boarding pass and dropped it on the floor. All the people in line were staring at us. Daadi could not get to her and I was still behind in the lineup and they blocked all of us. Security officers took her away. Abbu, we never saw her again. They took her into a closed room.

Ali shouted, You could not get her on a plane? You helped her!

No, Abbu, she wouldn't stop shouting. She was crazy. It was terrible. The whole place was silent. When the Americans and then a Canadian questioned us I told them she was going home to help Ammi, like you said, we all said that. Daadi started to argue with them, saying it is our family matter and they had no right to interfere, he'd sue and all kinds of threats. When he started talking like that the official got angry. He said, Your granddaughter has told us you are taking her against her will. This is an offence. She is of age. I will release you only to take your flight. I recommend you do not miss your plane, sir. It will be preferable to dealing with the authorities here. He told me to go home too. Abbu, he was very angry. There was nothing we could do. I slept in the airport and took the first flight back. After security we never saw her again.

Ali shouted, *Gaddha!* If I had been there.

He grabbed a ceramic lamp and smashed it against the fireplace. Sparks scarred the air. He spat at me, *Kutti!*

Our family became a snarling, weeping many-headed creature in the time it takes to turn a shirt inside out. Ali shouted at me, Does a father not have a right? Tell me where she is.

I do not know.

Mera laan choop!

Ali! Stop!

Ali said, Call that woman.

Slowly I dialed Katherine, looking at Asif's eyes to see what he knew, but our son was terrified. I misdialed, put down the receiver, said, Wrong number.

Ali grabbed the phone and said, Tell me her number.

You can't call now.

He said to Asif, You know the number. Dial it.

Asif took the phone, saying, Stop, Abbu, stop, and he dialed and I heard Katherine's sleepy voice say hello.

Ali grabbed the phone. Where is she?

Who the hell is this?

Ali held the receiver to my mouth between us and said, Tell her.

I said, Katherine, Lai's disappeared. Did you hear from her?

Ali shouted, Where is my daughter?

I don't know what Katherine said.

KATHERINE

It was a damned mess. Lai had already made up her mind to go west to study. I told her to come to my apartment for the night but she was afraid that Ali would find her. Bea and I went out to the airport and helped her organize her flight to Los Angeles and to Vancouver from there. She said, I'll sleep here. Bea stayed with her. I needed to get home and get some sleep and call the understudy and rehearse with him to perform the last two nights. It was a damned soap opera.

I was done. I wanted to get on the road again. I wanted to know what silence is, how the dead live inside it. I don't know why the hell she stayed with him. I wouldn't have stayed.

The tour got off to a rough start. Cecil booked us into the Trout Forest Music Festival in Red Lake without telling me.

I said, Cecil, I know this is about a girl. You go and see her and meet me later. There's nothing but mosquitoes up there.

He said, Kat, I've never been above 109th Street alone,

and that girl invited me. Come and play one night with me. I want her family to know I can play. It's all set.

Who paid the air tickets?

I did.

Cecil, we're going on a big tour and you're pulling stunts before we even start.

Just this one thing.

How'd you meet her?

She was at the Blue Note. You don't know about love, he said.

We ended up on a float plane flying over a thousand miles of bush and lake, his double bass laid across our knees. We checked ourselves into the red-roofed Norseman Inn and I picked up a telegram from Sean, Good luck on your tour. No word from Mahsa, but I didn't expect any. We were a sight in that tiny place, big powerful Cecil hauling his double bass around, and me in my hat and veil.

The young woman in question appeared in a four-wheeler with her boyfriend who had Paul Bunyan–sized scarred arms. The boyfriend said, I told her no New York souvenirs but there's no plane till morning.

The festival organizers found me an electric keyboard and Cecil and I joined the opening night with a group called Big Boogaloo that played rock and roll and Latin. Red Lake had never heard the likes of us and most of them dug it. At the end of the night I said to the settled-in crowd, This last piece is dedicated to my ma who died this year.

Big Boogaloo stepped back and Cecil's low, low tones felt like old spirits moving on the face of the Shield rock in the crisp northern night. The audience was with us, and then the music disappeared into forest and sky like a last breath. Ma, I was picturing you sitting in the doorway in the basement of the Connaught, smoking and bouncing your foot, listening to a girl playing scales on an untuned piano.

At the end of the night, the young musicians asked us, Wanna go out? We're heading to Howey Bay Lounge beside your motel.

Cecil was eager to be anywhere but his room so I said, I'm crashing. You go if you want but I do not want a beat-up bass player down on that dock in the morning no matter how much you drink. I need your hands and ugly mug in one piece for my tour.

They all laughed and moved on and a man with destroyed-looking eyes and red drinker's flesh on the heels of his hands stepped out of the darkness.

I liked your last piece, he said. You leaving on the morning plane?

Yes.

Do you want to see our art gallery?

It was two in the morning but I let him take me to Red Lake's main drag and he opened the gallery with a key on a strip of leather and flipped on the lights. The walls were hung with four enormous canvases of great-eyed creatures connected to each other by black lines, animals and earth and water and sky and the round-eyed ones he called fish-people. He offered me a cigarette and I turned in the room slowly and studied the paintings.

Yours?

Yup.

Is this about the spirit world?

Some people say that.

Where my mother went.

Or where she's from.

His lips twitched back and he flicked ashes on the floor. The skin of his face was heavy with pockmarks and a scar up his left cheek. He looked like one of his own creatures. We sat together on the floor in the middle of the room and smoked another cigarette.

I asked, Does that door lock? and he nodded and locked it and turned off the lights. He was tender and laid out his flannel shirt on the floor for us. Near dawn, he drove me back to the motel, and Venus was a single bright point in the northern sky. I never saw him again but I saw his art. Back in New York, I saw a new canvas with a tall, black-haired woman connected by those strange lines to something bright at the top of the frame. I like the people and the chance things that happen on the road. I like the pursuing.

MAHSA

I should have felt complicated, full of turmoil. But I did not. I felt whole. Who I most am. Some water fills locks, emptying with the sluice gates. Some water rises from springs and flows freely in clean, open streams. If the love is true, it is not wrong. Love has many forms.

For days Ali would not look at me. Then, one night, he came into the kitchen, sat on the edge of a chair. He said, Ammi is disappointed. My father does not speak to me. I have been sick, Mahsa. You will help me fix this. I know you know where she is.

With Lailuma gone, my days were even longer. I sometimes met Kamal in the mornings. As soon as I crossed his threshold I pulled off my niqab and before my coat was gone, his arms were around me. We made love, and we were easier together, not sleeping, but quiet.

He asked, Why do you wear it?

I shrugged.

Why?

If I am discovered, I will be like the amputee outside the grocery store, not a leg to stand on.

Jokes like ice, meant to soothe. The world shifting forever begins in small ways with little words. I finally said *now* to Kamal. All my life I have said *for now* to survive. I left Pakistan for now, kept making my marriage work for now, kept my daughter safe for now, put off playing with Katherine for now. I loved better Kamal's word—*always*. He said, I have always loved you. He said, I always think about you. He said, We always did this first.

Lai finally telephoned and asked, Mor, why? I never did anything. I was good.

There was no answer. Sometimes a fox is in trouble because of its own pelt.

She said, What did I do, Mor?

You did nothing wrong, Lailuma. We knew this might happen. Where are you?

I promised Katherine not to tell. She said it's the only way to be safe. We don't know what Abbu might do.

So, I was to remain invisible.

I talked with her for a long time, did not want to hang up. I imagined her across the continent in a place of dark trees and totem spirits and free jazz.

I was so afraid at the airport, Mor. I did not know if they made me go what Daadi would do to me. He would never let me go out alone. I don't know where anything is in Karachi.

320

Daadi tried to push past the security people at the airport when they were taking me away. You should have seen Asif's face.

Her voice became lighter. She said, Mor, it was sort of great. When the officials told me I was of age and free to go I couldn't believe it. I didn't know that I was of age. Why did you not tell me?

I had not known it either. Why had I not found out these things and talked to her?

She asked, What if they had forced me to go?

She described flying west alone and she said, Mor, the money you gave me was enough for the tickets. I always thought you were crazy giving me so much money. What if I had not had it?

She told me how she had carried it in a waist belt she made herself and that in high school she was always afraid of losing it. She told me how much she missed home and she asked, Will Abbu hate me forever? In the background I heard someone playing Bach. I recognized that touch. Match. I said, Lai, a broken hand can work but a broken heart cannot.

She said, Mor, I don't want Abbu to hate me.

Your Abbu loves you.

She said, Well I better go. And then she said, Nice way for Abbu to show it.

I watched leaves twist in funnels outside the window and listened to the winds. The djinn who imprisoned a woman in a glass coffin held fast by four steel locks kept her under the sea because he loved her, but still she managed to escape. Back in the world, she took a ring from each man she seduced and when she met two wandering princes, her ninety-ninth and hundredth men, she took their rings as trophies. She said, Men should not lock their wives in glass coffins because it only teaches them cunning.

Who condemned me to live with honour but without meaning? To keep peace in my family? I could have left, but Ali was having treatments again. How could I leave him with no one to care for him? Where love and duty wrestle there is no joy in the victory of duty. In my dark and lonely moments, desire pulled at me with a pulse eternal as the night sky full of dead and living stars.

When I could finally talk with Match again, she said, Do not worry, I am helping her.

How's married life? I asked her.

I like it very much, she said. I will soon have a baby. And I am teaching piano. Classical.

Across the wires I felt the hope and energy of young women and I wished I were there with them.

One night Lai dared to call the house when she knew Ali would be home. She said, Happy Thanksgiving, Mor. Ali heard me talking and he asked, Is that her? I turned from him but he took the phone and said, You're dead to me.

Ali grew thin. He forgave Asif and trained him to take over the business. He said, Family is a torment to be endured. Ammi-jaan called, How is Asif? How is Lailuma? as if nothing had happened. The holidays were lonely, Christmas, Eid and the sad, sad Easter spring. My home was still and empty. I drove Ali to his appointments. We spoke of the weather. Somewhere in London there was a woman who had loved him longer than he had known me. I taught again. Then came the moment when he began to truly die.

He pretended things were all right. One evening, he asked, Is Lailuma not almost finished her studies? She should come home for the summer.

I do not think she will, Ali.

She is still promised.

I know.

You must persuade her.

I stayed with him because I could not bear to be the last blow that would finally break our cracked family apart. It was not love. In the place where I was born it might be called honour, and here it might be called loyalty, but these words do not describe the flesh feelings of a woman who has taken care of a man and borne his children whether she wanted to or not. Perhaps I should have been more ruthless. I could have gone to New York. I could have gone west. I had spent my marriage veiling my heart, and the price I paid was a life imprisoned.

KATHERINE

That tour with Cecil was a blossoming time. He rocked his bass. We were playing very free, and teasing each other on the stand, and bringing each other out, and soon we were making love after the shows. I liked the feeling of those big bass-player hands on my back. The lover-bed felt good after all the years of making it on my own, and my god, what a good time we had. Sweet sex. Happy sex. Blowing-off-steam sex. Tired-and-fall-asleep-almost-in-the-middle sex. All of it was fine with me. Fine with him too.

He joked, Since I do not have a girlfriend in Red Lake anymore.

I felt like a kid. My mother was dead and my kids were grown and I was fetterless. I improvised like crazy, played night after night through Japan and Indonesia and India. Our last stop was Pakistan. We were exotic in most places we went, and our music swung. My brain was fully lit on all sides. Home was wherever I was. What a good time we had.

I asked to be booked at the Beach Luxury Hotel for our last

stop to see where Mahsa came from. In the closets were prayer mats and Qurans. On the desk was a metal arrow pointing to Mecca. But it was not Mahsa's city anymore. It was a place of slow-motion violence, months before Operation Blue Fox. The leaders were already talking openly about cleansing anyone in the Mohajir Qaumi Movement. I hired a car to take me around the city, to see the Jinnah Tomb, the camels on the beach, the snakes in the markets. There were guns and army and food carts and wandering musicians. There was a transvestite begging in traffic. Veiled women walked in small groups, while others with uncovered heads wore Western heels. Shipping containers blocked roads to slow the traffic. Hotels and shops were swaddled in barbed wire.

We played in a little club called the 007 at the Beach Luxury and a guitarist called Norman D'Souza showed up with some Goan musicians and jammed with us. They knew old rock and roll songs, and we ended with "Love Is All Around" which Cecil did not know but was easy for him to follow. I wrote Mahsa a postcard from the hotel in the morning: Look where I ended up!

Cecil sat up in bed and handed me his coffee cup.

I said, One of the waiters thought I was playing a rhythm from a folksong in his home town. How do you think it got there?

I picked up *Dawn* and looked at the newspaper's daily city map of the previous day's shootings and bombs, like New York in the seventies.

Through your skin, Kat, said Cecil.

I thought how little I knew about Mahsa.

Cecil lay naked under the sheet, loose, relaxed in the heat. We'd worked hard. He said, Last day. I don't wanna go back.

I knew what he meant. I could have gone on forever. I said, When I was a kid I went to the corner store for smokes for my mother. I saw two hitchhikers from South America. They were carrying backpacks and wore red and yellow and orange scarves around their necks. As soon as I saw them, I felt I belonged with them. I've wanted to be on the road ever since.

I drank Cecil's coffee and nudged him over and said, In wandering cultures they shared their wives.

Right.

The Inuit. If a woman offered sex to a visitor it was all right with her husband.

Think if I went down the hall and knocked on a door and said I was a visiting man?

I laughed, Go try.

They get jealous?

I don't know. The husband called the visiting man an *aipak,* his other-me.

Cecil took my hand and pulled me to him. That solves a whole lotta problems, he said. Tonight's the last night, Kat. Day after tomorrow we're back in Manhattan. You gonna go back to your other-me?

MAHSA

Always Ali had strong hands. When he was well he raised his arms to make himself bigger, and when he judged me his hands were fisted and hard. He would open his right hand and point to the front door with a thumb raised and the index finger straight to tell me he would be late. These gestures he was not aware of. I felt his decline in his weakening grip. Now I needed him to hold me so I could shift him in bed. He was less and less able to move himself, to slide his buttocks and legs so that I could raise him. They say in English, dead weight. This is accurate. Are you in pain? I asked. As long as I don't move, he answered. And so, to change the bed, to keep him clean, to raise him for a sip of water was ordeal for him. The body does unnerving things. Does not give up easily. After he was catheterized there was little movement. That is a final turning point. A marriage like ours is a constant denial of something missing. The easiest way to live with such absence is to never, ever acknowledge it. The months of caring for him felt long in the same way that a dream can feel long even when you are dreaming it. I left the room when the palliative nurse came each afternoon or when Asif sat with him in the evenings. I moved a cot to the foot of his bed and slept, listening for any change in his breath as I used to listen through sleep for the changing sounds of my newborn babies. His body shrank and aged and he looked uncannily like his father. When Ammi-jaan and Daadi came for their last visit with him, we moved through the rooms quietly, and Ali took solace in the hours with his mother who wept each time she left the room. Ammi-jaan sat at the kitchen table with her tea and said, He wants Lailuma. You must bring her home.

Ammi-jaan, I do not know where she is.

The crease deepened between her eyebrows and her gaze penetrated me with the purpose of having what she wanted. By force or by wheedling. Always I was to be a servant in a doorway.

She said, It is his last wish. I will tell Asif if you will do nothing. You cannot stand in the way.

But I could.

I cooked, chopping soundlessly, arranging the pans so that there was no clatter when I took them from the cupboards, and on that visit I cleaned every window. If I pressed lightly enough not to squeak it was a quiet task. I could better keep peace with Ammi-jaan if I worked. I meditated on the molecules of light outside passing through the perfectly cleaned glass. I rose hours before the old people who were suffering with their own grief because no son should die before his parent. At dawn if Ali was sleeping I sat under the window and watched the dust motes in the air. I imagined myself spinning with them as I prepared myself for the day. Though his needs were different now, I knew what made him comfortable and what he desired of me. In his dying, he commanded the world with less authority, but still he tried. I wanted for him his dignity and he sometimes thanked me which, after all his years of indifference, felt cloying. One day he said, You don't fight this. It happens to you. And I nodded because I knew that it was true.

Then began the eyes' cloistered look. I brought him, one morning, photos of our early years together, when the children were young, when he was a handsome and vibrant man born in Karachi, educated in London, starting his family in Montreal, when I was still hopeful and trying to please. We were at our best in the first year raising Asif together. I sat on the bed beside him to share them but he only glanced and pushed them aside. I had hoped for a word from him for me. But he could not bring himself to give me this. He said, What time is it? Asif is coming. You need to go do the shopping.

I returned early that day because he had been so weak and when I stepped inside the door, a woman was in the hallway putting on her coat to leave. She flushed when she saw me, said in a British accent, Asif let me in. I'm an old business associate. Pleased to meet you.

I shrugged. It did not matter anymore. Part of me wanted to ask her to share a cup of tea, but it was curiosity, not real interest, and so I let that go too. Difficult to nurse the dying, but good to do it well. Mor used to say, Give even an onion graciously.

Lailuma came home. When she saw him, emaciated and so sick, she stepped backwards, then stopped herself and approached him with her arms open. He was stiff and patted her back and she said, Abbu, I am so sorry. He answered, You are promised.

She tried not to be alone with him, and in their chaotic sorrow she and Asif put aside our family's turmoil to try to show their love. Watching the three of them I saw—finally without shame—the closed throat of our family's lies. Soon I would be a widow and free, not with youth's heedlessness but with a battered liberty. The children came and went from Ali's room, their faces still with apprehension, and Lailuma has never told me what she did or did not promise her father. Neither has Asif. It was their first dying. They could not know that they would not feel better when it was finally over. I massaged his cold feet. Once, when we were alone, he looked at me and said, I think I have done well.

Yes, Ali, you have done well.

I wanted to dissolve any last hardness between us. But this is something that cannot be willed. There are veils between man and God, between man and himself, seven heavens, seven gates to hell. Ali and I could not find a way to say to each other, Things that do not belong to us ordained our lives. The last time he was able to speak coherent words I said to him, We tried, and he shrugged and answered, It was a life.

When Ali died, at three thirty-seven in the morning, Asif disappeared to their office downtown. He came home after sunrise, said that he had telephoned the family and business associates abroad, including Ali's oldest friend in Pakistan, the family to whom Ali had promised Lailuma. Asif called Lailuma into his bedroom, and when they came out again, her face was clear as it had not been since she was thirteen. Whatever the obligation around the marriage was, Asif had managed to free Lailuma. Money must have passed hands. I do not know. Money solves many problems and it is a bitter and shallow way to solve them. Better to use the eyes and soft speech. But not always possible.

According to tradition, a woman is not to mourn for the dead for more than three days, except for a husband, for whom the mourning is four months and ten days. A widow is to wear simple dress, no kohl or perfume, except a little qust or izfaar when she cleans herself after her period. But I am finished with tradition. My children are grown. I stand naked and unperfumed. Let the lions come. I release myself.

Asif washed and wrapped Ali's body in the kafan for burial. I bathed his familiar skin, now wasted and cold, and I smoothed the crease between his eyebrows one last time for his passage to paradise. They carried him to the Islamic cemetery in Laval.

My son went into one door of the mosque, Lailuma and I into another. We heard the Salat al-Janazah, prayers for the dead.

> O God, forgive him and have mercy on him,
> keep him safe and sound and forgive him,
> honour his rest and ease his entrance;
> wash him with water and snow and hail,
> and cleanse him of sin as a white garment is cleansed of
>   dirt.
> O God, give him a home better than his home
> and a family better than his family.

I prayed with the women the final taslim, *Assalamu Alaikum Warahmatullah,* Peace and blessings of God be unto you. By my own will I could not extinguish my fury, not in another day or a thousand. No woman is allowed by the graveside when men are there, and so, from a car, Lailuma and I watched Asif and the other men guide Ali's body into the earth, and when the men were gone, Lailuma and I were permitted to be by the closed grave.

That night, we were finally alone. Lailuma and Asif sat together talking and looking at photos of their father, and I wondered what memories they would settle on. Children sometimes blame the parent who lives on. I left them, a widow now. I walked through the darkness down to the river. I pulled my niqab out of my pocket, dark cloth that Ali had never seen. I tied it into a tight bundle around a stone. I stood on the bank and tossed it far away and watched it disappear under the black fast-running waters that flowed with neither joy nor remorse toward the sea.

KATHERINE

I have a full album of material written for two pianos that I will record with Mahsa. We have moved on since "New Thing." I have to do the gig at the Women in Jazz Festival in Ohio and the tour to Brazil. Mahsa sent word that Ali died when I was in the Black Forest heading over to Berlin, and I wrote her a card. I had to say something so I wrote, Dear heart, you are in mine.

Nature does not care for music or children or lovers or the length of anyone's time. Nature relentlessly pursues life. When I got home I phoned Montreal on the way to Ohio and I told Mahsa my agent was booking our tour, to get practising.

She said, Come back soon. I am ready.

MAHSA

The first time I saw Kamal after, I did not want to make love. I wanted to sit and cry and he sat near but not touching. We had not seen each other for a long time. He put the kettle on to boil and I said, I feel like walking into the river and floating out to the ocean.

He answered, I'll come with you.

I was not used to a man wanting to be with me in this way. I had forgotten his warmth. I answered, Well, not yet. Let's do a few things first. I still want to play.

And I let him put his arms around me. We always did this first.

MAHSA

She's gone, T said on the telephone. No warning. Nothing.

T said, People like Katie don't die. (My arms, though stretched out, remained empty.)

T said, She was just back from Brazil and we were sitting around with the kids. She was on my knee and I was rocking on the chair which always annoyed her because I broke a few like that. Bea was squeezed in on Dexter's chair complaining about someone not taking her seriously and Jimmie said to her, You got the creds to say whatever you want. You don' need anyone's go-ahead.

Katie leaned into me and half whispered, See what we did, and Jimmie asked, What'd you do? and everyone was laughing and having a good time. She liked it when we were all together. I didn't do it enough for her. No one thought there was anything special about her going to bed. She was jet-lagged. She called me from the bedroom and I didn't pay much attention because I was enjoying myself, but the second time she called I went.

It was an aneurysm.

The road's hard, T said. She was always running around. I know she thought she was making up for lost time. She never wanted to be still except when she played, and that was not stillness, that was just being in one place. I heard that thing in her voice and I knew what she wanted so I went to her because I always went to her when I heard that. We always went to each other when we heard it.

Then, silence.

I wanted so much to hear Katherine's voice. I imagined narrow basement stairs to underground rooms in the little clapboard house on Mountain Brow and the smell of stale smoke and her mother putting to bed a little girl whose father was in China saying sometimes in the winter and sometimes in the fall and I thought of Katherine watching her own baby daughter break a dozen eggs so she could listen to Coltrane and I remember inviting her up to play with me at the Surf Maid when we were both new in New York, the night we became friends, and the years of playing over the phone to each other. I was so free when I first met her, before I got married, travelling back and forth on the bus.

What about our tour? How selfish the living are. I imagined T coming into the bedroom that last night, her tall man, walking through the doorway, not so pretty anymore, and how she must have looked at his eyes, were they tender or desiring, or was she feeling already any weakness, any pain, and did he embrace her that last night? Other people's loves are mysteries, what they accept and what they do not. T and Katherine were supposed to have plenty of time. She must have watched him close the door shut and pull his T-shirt over his head, and climb in beside her. I imagined them falling asleep wrapped in each other's arms that last night on earth. Sleep is most perfect beside the beloved. Who can explain the miracle of love that lasts a lifetime?

Lailuma came from the West Coast carrying a small backpack. Asif flew down and stood with Dexter and Jimmie. The memorial was at the Promenade Theatre. Jazz artists played and students read tributes and I saw lots of young people who had been at the BAM. Bea danced. T played, the sound she loved best in the world, except her own playing, or, maybe, playing with me.

Bea spoke from the podium they covered with baby's breath and black tulips, everything dramatic like Katherine. They had three of her biggest hats hanging from a hall tree and a picture of her on an easel and of course they played her music. Bea said, The most important thing in my mother's life was her piano. We moved here in a red convertible from Hamilton so she could play. When she wasn't playing and teaching she loved walking in New York and she loved reading. You could walk with her for hours. When I was a little girl, she played for my ballet lessons and after we'd hurry home because my brothers were waiting. She took me to my first ballet in Hamilton and we got in standing room but someone who knew her gave her a couple of seats right up front. I think she was always a bit lucky but when I said that she'd always say, The harder you work, the luckier you are.

Dexter said, She had complete self-confidence. We came here with nothing but we never knew that. We'd walk through the markets and she found bruised tomatoes that people threw away and she held them up and said, Look at that, nothing wrong with it. I'm going to make you a ratatatata-touille tonight. She could survive on nothing, and she did, for music. I do not know when she slept. When we first came here, she'd more or less put us to bed then go downstairs to play and she was up in the morning to get us to school. She was so happy about her first solo recording. She put us on the cover.

Jimmie said, I'm not much good at words. She was too young, that's what I keep thinking. And she had terrible taste in clothes.

Everyone laughed thinking of her second-hand cocktail dresses. Jimmie said, What can I say? Ma stuck by me. I look out at all of you and I see people she played with and people she taught and I think she stuck by most of us in this room, one way or another. Now her friend Mahsa Weaver's going to play.

All my favourite pieces with Katherine were for two pianos and it was too difficult to choose something to play alone so I made a new arrangement of "Two to Love." I could not play both our parts but I did what I could.

The reception in the lobby overflowed into the aisles of the theatre and T came to me through the crowd. I said to him, She is the best friend I ever had.

T held me with god-abandoned grief and after a long time he released me and said, Her body was cold when I woke up and I put my finger on her blue lips, and there was nothing. I tried to shake her out of it, how could my best girl die like that beside me?

Lailuma and Bea and I walked in Central Park. Bea told us what she knew of Katherine's Chinese father, and how they had finally talked about her grandmother's arrest when Katherine was writing "New Thing."

What do you know about it, Mahsa?

I knew grief's dark maw. I said to her, When we first met, we were two young women who loved jazz. We talked about music and we always talked about our children. Katherine liked best to look forward, not back.

Lai sat with us on the bench in Central Park, her skin clear, her hair loose, red-coloured fingernails and red boots. The day was cool, damp. Clouds covered the sun and the air turned chill. Bea said, I'm going to meet my brothers now. Come over later.

We watched her run lightly across the park, graceful even in her raw and ferocious and untouchable mourning. Lailuma asked, How could they have done that to Katherine's mother?

There is a moment when you understand your children

are not yours anymore and it feels right and melancholy. I could not yet bear to tell Lailuma more. I could not yet bear to tell her about her Afghan great-uncles, of losing my beloved Abbu and Mor. Aunt used to talk about the fury of the dead. Finally I cried and Lailuma put her hand on my arm and said simply, Mor.

My baby daughter had become a strong woman who could comfort another. I wanted to tell Katherine.

I made my first solo recording, *Live at Nuage Bleu*, and I dedicated it to Katherine. Kamal joked, Not me? Lailuma and Asif asked, Not us? I wanted to include a piece that Katherine had been writing called "Violet." When she played bits of it on the phone I had found it obscure and haunting. But she never sent the score and Bea said she could not find it in her papers. Maybe it stayed in Katherine's head.

Bea and Jimmie and Dexter came to my launch party and we celebrated. I included the recording of Katherine and me playing "Two to Love," and I recorded a poem by Hafsa for Jean.

After the party as we undressed for bed I said to Kamal, What my heart desired did not happen.

He completed the second part of the proverb, What Allah wanted was done.

He asked, Do you believe that?

We sat together, looking into the darkness beyond the window. He had put on my recording and we were listening to it. I said, Katherine would have been happy for me. I can hear her voice saying, Don't out-cut me.

Love reaches beyond death. When we are all gone, the music will still be here.

Kamal and I are plants with a second flowering. I feel free, as I did in those two brief years before marriage. I asked him, How are you?

And he answered, I found what I was looking for.

What would that be?

Life, and a lover.

We had not been capable of the miracle of a life together, working and raising children. But he had risked finding me again.

I spend most of the day practising now, and writing and walking and being with him. Heed the troubadour, burn the dinner, Kamal says. He calls me to come and eat with him. At the table he says, Do you want to hear a joke? Priority is good in all things but death. Is that not good?

I laugh and answer, Do not die until death comes to you.

We no longer have a lifetime ahead. And so we live as if we have all the time in the world. With Karachi generosity we excuse each other, say, We were young.

Years ago, near the Arabian Sea, how good his hands felt on my skin. How good they always feel.

He has this lovely thing he does with his hips, like he's playing a soft slow beat on a drum, and he goes far away and takes me with him. Some love does not die. Now Kamal waits for me and I wait for him.

Our dead are in us and we will be with them soon enough. I live with the living and when I look at Kamal I see the young man I was charmed by as a girl, the bull-of-heaven I loved and left. I see the life-battered man who found me again, time-shaped and wise, still laughing at the absurdity of it all. And when I turn to him—this is the miracle and mystery—his arms are still open to me.

Sometimes I think, All that struggle? Is that what life is? An excuse to keep riffing until you get back to the first notes?

Patience is bitter but it has a sweet fruit.

I want our life-lovingness to go on forever. Love is not ended by that which fills the graveyards and separates mother from child, lover from lover, friend from friend. Katherine died too young. Now I have to play both parts. I still hear her voice and see her fingers on the keys. I have toured with others and Kamal travels with me when I ask him to come which I always do. I play the music she wrote for us. I think of what Jenny Goodnow said: I had opportunities I did not take. I think of what Mor said: On earth it is hard and heaven is far away.

This morning I asked Kamal to tell me his favourite people and places and he said, You. Your arms, and I said, Oh, that's only love-talk, and he said, No it isn't, and I said, Well, I like it.

I do not think death will come for either of us today. I

343

have so much more to do. There is vastness of eye and hope for another season, a summer and a fall. We are teetering on our own brink. But there is still time. Time to slip between the sheets, with nothing on at all.

you will remember
for we in our youth
did these things
yes many and beautiful things

–SAPPHO, *FRAGMENT 24A* (TRANS. ANNE CARSON)

ACKNOWLEDGMENTS

I am grateful to Julia Ghani for consulting on culture, Shalini Konanur, legal counsel at South Asian Legal Clinic of Ontario, for consulting on law and culture, Jamil Ahmad (*The Wandering Falcon*) for advice on Afghan custom, Mohsin Hamid (*The Reluctant Fundamentalist*) for a discussion of culture, literature and psychology, Zarmina Rafi for literary and cultural discussion, Dinshaw and Dinaz Avari at the Beach Luxury Hotel for ongoing Karachi historical consults, Menin Rodrigues and Norman D'Souza for music and historical culture in Karachi, Sister Mary and Sister Berchmanns at Jesus and Mary Convent School, Karachi, for reflections on education in Karachi. I am grateful to Ameena Saiyid and Asif Farrukhi at the Karachi Literature Festival for the opportunity to share in vibrant literary discussion. I am grateful to Alan and Leslie Nickell for introductions to new communities, for discussion about jazz, writing and relationship. Louie Fleck was most generous with historical research from the Brooklyn Academy of Music, and Marieke Meyer with jazz research. For help with translations, thank you to Nie Zhixiong, Dr. Lihua Gui and Haneen Tamari. Thank you to Dr. Janice Williamson for probing cultural discussions and for discussing the work of Sherene Razak, Yasmin Jiwani and Sunera Thobani, and to Ann Simpson for reading and discussion. A special thank you to Sandra Campbell for our years of discussion of all things literary and cultural.

The team at Hamish Hamilton are without parallel. Thank you to David Ross, Shaun Oakey, Karen Alliston, Brittany Lavery, Ashley Audrain, Stephen Myers and Deborah Sun de la Cruz.

Nicole Winstanley, president and publisher, is the energy and inspiration at the centre of this talented team. She loves literature and is a risk-taker, an editor par excellence and friend. A special thank you, Nicole.

To friends and family, a special thank you to Adam and Ann Winterton, Mark and Joanne Echlin, Ann Echlin and the late Randy Echlin, Barb Clark and Ken Foreacre and to Paul Echlin for your endless support. My mother, Madeleine Echlin, believed in my writing when the page was still blank. There are three very special people who live with the dailiness of writing, supporting it with the intellectual curiosity, humour and pleasure in language that I love. Thank you to my husband, Ross Upshur, and to my daughters, Olivia Upshur and Sara Upshur, for all that you do.

Under the Visible Life

About the Book 352

An Interview with Kim Echlin 353

Discussion Questions 360

A Penguin Readers Guide

ABOUT THE BOOK

Under the Visible Life, Kim Echlin's fourth novel, is a story of extraordinary breadth and a beautiful rumination on love. It travels from Karachi to various cities in North America to tell the stories of Katherine and Mahsa, two seemingly different women whose lives connect through music. Daughters of courageous mothers, Mahsa and Katherine both experience gender and racial inequality at an early age, and both find freedom and purpose in practising their art.

Mahsa's story begins in Karachi, Pakistan, the Bride of Cities, where we learn of her parents' great love for each other. One day she is abruptly pulled from class and told that her parents have been killed by her mother's brothers. "No prayers. No goodbye. Nothing." Though her parents embraced the cosmopolitan and liberal Karachi of the 1960s, her mother was never forgiven for marrying a westerner. After Mahsa is left orphaned, she is adopted by conservative family members, and she plays the piano in her uncle's workplace, the Beach Luxury Hotel. Here she finds freedom in music and meets Kamal, her first great love.

Music provides an awakening for Katherine, who listens to a Bud Powell jazz album and says "the first day of my real life was when I heard 'Dance of the Infidels.'" In Hamilton, Ontario, in 1940, she is born to a mother who is incarcerated for being "incorrigible"— she has married a Chinese man and had a daughter with him. As a child, Katherine suffers discrimination from her peers. She develops a deep love for jazz and at a young age becomes a celebrated part of the Ontario jazz community. She meets T, a black saxophone player with "a blade of rage in him." She falls in love and they have three children together. But T's life on the road outweighs his ability to be a full-time father and husband. Katherine makes the difficult decision to raise her children alone and to leave Hamilton to pursue her music in New York City, as the Civil Rights movement continues to dominate American politics.

Mahsa, meanwhile, is sent to Montreal as protection from the uncles who killed her parents, and to further the family's business interests. She falls in love with the city and the freedom it offers her. "Our dead are in us but in Montreal I could forget mine for a while." She plays piano at the Ritz and studies at McGill University, where she learns about jazz and improvisation, and the world of music opens up to her. When she hears a recording of a female jazz pianist named Katherine Goodnow and then meets her on a trip to New York City, their deep friendship is born. But when Mahsa marries a man chosen by her family in Pakistan, the independence she once enjoyed is impossible to maintain.

Within a complex setting of racial and gender inequality, Echlin portrays two strong female characters who pulse with passion. In prose as musical as the jazz she describes, Echlin tells a poignant story about memory, devotion, courage, and love. As readers have said of her previous novels, *Under the Visible Life* is remarkable, electrifying, and powerfully moving.

AN INTERVIEW WITH KIM ECHLIN

Q: You once stated, "It is the job of fiction to give meaning to facts, and the job of language to shape the world." Is this book drawn from a "real life" truth?

I discovered that Ontario's legal system used to include the "Female Refuges Act" (1913–1964), under which women could be arrested for "incorrigibility."

The law was used to criminalize women who had sex outside of marriage and interracial relationships, even for card-playing or entering a bar through the wrong door. Do you remember when taverns had "Ladies and Escorts" signs? Husbands used this law to get their wives out of the way for a time; fathers used it to control recalcitrant daughters. The "real life" truth of this law felt very close when I considered that my grandmother and mother were subject to it. It was arbitrary and part of the fabric of social pressures they experienced but didn't have a name for.

At the same time, I was discussing with a poet born in Lahore the social restrictions women face in Pakistan. The Hudood Ordinances (1979–2006) were laws on rape, adultery, and fornication, and were part of a larger systemic oppression of women. I saw parallels and differences with our Canadian history. I wanted to explore in fiction how such laws are part of our individual consciousness, no matter where we are in the world. ∎

Q: Why were both Mahsa and Katherine's stories important to you?

I am interested in women's friendships. Mahsa and Katherine find in each other constancy. Under their surface lives of family and their daily struggles, they have a relationship with each other that embraces obstacles and accepts change. When they can't be together, they continue to encourage each other. They use the telephone and play their music and listen to each other. I wanted to show what it means to keep believing in someone without judgment. No matter what happens with their husbands and children and work, they say to each other, Keep going. And they have fun together. I have had this kind of friendship. It is a profound expression of love. ■

Q: Music is freedom to Mahsa and Katherine, and although Mahsa, at times, struggles to find a place for music in her life, both women are steadfast in their love of playing piano. At times, their love of playing seems to outweigh the risks of alienating family and lovers, yet they both continue to play. Why was this fact important to you?

Both Katherine and Mahsa have a passion for music that is undeniable and gives their lives meaning and pleasure. Each young woman understands that her ability to play is most truly who she is. Each young woman knows that to stop would be to slice away a piece of her soul.

Developing their passions is good, and should not alienate their families and lovers, but you're right, at times it does. Those who want to control them create conditions meant to limit or extinguish their passions. This kind of resistance is common, and intolerable, and both women keep pursuing their music. Mahsa's and Katherine's children eventually understand and respect their mothers' music. Why should we be anything but free? ■

Q: There are a number of different languages in the novel, music being one of the most important. Why did you choose jazz as the music both Mahsa and Katherine came to love?

I love jazz and its restlessness. I was fascinated by the popularity of jazz and rock and roll in 1960s Karachi. Jazz is international, a music of improvisation and creativity. Great jazz composers know their tradition and work from it. Jazz is associated with a powerful social history. I also like its oral idiom. Jazz has, historically, been difficult for women performers to penetrate. This was a more subtle aspect of its part in my novel. ■

Q: Your descriptions of Mahsa's early life in Afghanistan and Pakistan are evocative and compelling. How did you conduct your research of Pakistan and Afghanistan while writing the book?

I do my research by reading and listening to people. In this case, I had a wonderful Pakistani poet who read for me, and several Afghan and Pakistani writers who discussed culture and literature with me. I did have the chance to visit Karachi, where I met musicians from several religious groups, Irish nuns, and Goan businessmen who were part of the scene in the 1960s. It was fascinating to hear their stories about Karachi a half century ago when it was a peaceful, cosmopolitan port city. We were meeting in the context of contemporary Karachi, where a young soldier with a rifle was stationed outside my hotel door, where, as a single (foreign) woman, I certainly faced lots of challenges when I wanted to go out alone in the city. But I managed to visit the places I had read about, the seashore where there are still camel rides, sacred shrines, a museum with a superb collection holy Qurans. All the old dance clubs were closed.

I experienced strange synchronicities doing this research. I had already written several drafts of the novel and I had chosen the Beach Luxury Hotel as one of the settings. I wanted to go to Karachi but I needed an "official" reason in order to get a visa. I was looking around and discovered the Karachi Literature Festival. Then I saw that it was being held at the Beach Luxury Hotel. So now, of course, it was impossible not to go. My hosts there were marvelous because it was not straightforward for me to attend. Everywhere I went I experienced courtesy and resilience and a deep respect for the arts. Beyond the surfaces of violence and upheaval and barbed wire, the people I met in Karachi wanted to talk ideas and art. And meeting musicians in their seventies whose music had been forced underground was very moving. Imagine if all the music of Yorkville or Woodstock had been pushed underground and then someone from across an ocean came fifty years later and wanted to hear what it was like. We had very warm discussions. ■

Q: Kamal becomes a part of Mahsa's life again many years after they first meet. What were you exploring by reintroducing their love back into the story?

Mahsa was forced into marriage. She was young, and she could not find a way to resist when her family removed her passport and confined her. She had already lost both her parents to violence, she was living as a foreign student cut off from home, and she had no deep ties in Montreal, though she found friends and was successful in her studies and work. After she marries to get back to Canada, she quickly becomes pregnant and decides to make her marriage work. The psychological demands of cutting oneself off from one's family are complex and very difficult. Mahsa hopes to make a relationship with her new husband, to be able to keep an attachment to her home culture while creating her life in Canada. She is also afraid of losing her children.

Mahsa knew what love feels like. She had fallen in love with Kamal but her family opposed the relationship. When he comes to Montreal, she recognizes that her feelings are unchanged. Their love has survived familial and cultural opposition, emigration, marriages with others, children, and twenty years of separation. Their passionate love is now patient, and waits for Mahsa to fulfill her obligations to her children. ■

Q: In this and your previous three novels, you handle the complexities of love experienced by your characters skillfully and movingly. Do you feel that your ability to write about love has changed at all since you wrote your first novel, *Elephant Winter*?

I hope it has. I would say that the more time passes, the more important love is. ■

Q: Balancing the roles of mother and artist are challenging for both Katherine and Mahsa. How do you, and other women you know, strike a balance in this regard?

I understand what you mean, but I don't think there is a balance. This may sound a little too simple but I think that we just do our best, all the time, in both realms. There are times when the responsibilities of being a mother will take precedence. That said, I need to work every day and I usually get up early in the morning to write. More than the idea of individuals striking a balance between work and family and our creativity, I think we need more social awareness and action on the role of care-giving in our culture, beginning with a national daycare system and continuing forward to include much, much better elder care. ■

Q: Do you think you look for similar things in music and in writing?

Writing is verbal and linear, and music is non-verbal and we can hear many voices or lines (harmonies) at the same time. I like what is allusive in both forms, and I like their patterns, or styles. I appreciate the artistry unique to both forms. Art expresses what has not yet been expressed. This is transformative. ■

Q: The structure of the book (short chapters, alternating the stories and voices of Katherine and Mahsa) seems almost like a conversation, or two musicians riffing off of each other. Did the structure of this book come naturally?

One of the novel's greatest capacities as an art form is to explore the inwardness of characters. We are able to hear their thoughts, their contradictions, their changing self-knowledge. Katherine and Mahsa, and their mothers before them, live with challenges and secrets that at certain points they cannot, or refuse to, articulate. Many people live with stories they cannot tell. Sometimes it takes a lifetime to tell our stories. I wanted to give voice to the invisible lives of my characters, including things about where they come from that they may feel, but may not be very aware of. In the structure of alternating first person voices, the reader feels the common rhythms of very different lives.

Doris Lessing said, "Have you still got your space? Your soul, your own and necessary place where your own voices may speak to you, you alone..." In this book, I have been interested in discovering what that place was for both Mahsa and Katherine, and what their voices needed to say to them. ∎

DISCUSSION QUESTIONS

1. Jazz music is, in many ways, the heartbeat of Echlin's novel, and both Mahsa and Katherine learn about life through their experience of playing music. Why do you think Echlin chose to begin the book with the quote by John Coltrane: "I start in the middle of a sentence and move in both directions at once"? What kinds of freedom did jazz music offer Katherine and Mahsa?

2. Katherine and Mahsa lose their mothers in very different ways, at very different stages in their lives, yet both mothers are constantly present in their minds. How do these memories affect the two main characters and the decisions they make throughout their lives?

3. What do you think Echlin means by "To live, you must risk calamity. Abandon old ways to create something new. Love the life under the visible life." How did Katherine and Mahsa risk calamity and love the life under the visible life?

4. Examples of gender inequality and accepted anti-feminist behaviours appear frequently in Echlin's novel, yet near the end of the book Lailuma refuses to return to Pakistan to be married. Did her courage at the airport give you hope? Why do you think the author chose to demonstrate female empowerment in this way? Can you think of other examples of female empowerment in the novel?

5. Katherine and her mother have a sometimes fraught relationship, and at one point Katherine states: "I was not going to let her pain be mine." How does Katherine attempt to cauterize the pain, and how does she try to do things differently with her own children?

6. Right after Mahsa's parents are murdered by her uncles, Mahsa states: "This is the unsayableness of my life." Do you think that "unsayableness" changed for Mahsa as she aged? Do her silences affect her relationships with the people she loved?

7. Almost all of the characters in the book are of mixed race and are from different countries and cultural backgrounds, yet there is much overlap in their experiences. What do you think Echlin is saying about shared human experience? How does music fit into this?

8. Echlin's prose often seems inspired by the jazz she writes about; it is musical and improvisational. How did this affect your reading of the novel?

9. Katherine grows up without a father, and her three children also grow up without the constant presence of their dad. Katherine doesn't fall into the trap of hating T while he is absent, and she finds a way to make him a part of their family when he is capable. How did you respond to the complexities of Katherine and T's relationship?